MATTIE'S STORY

To the memory of Marilyn Russell, my first writing teacher.

*Ewen and Sara Lamont in their old age. The story
of their marriage proposal, as told to the author's
grandmother, is the germ of this novel.*

MATTIE'S STORY

MARGARET A. WESTLIE

Selkirk
STORIES

Cover design by Fresh Media

Chapter One

Mattie Cameron finished her long division and sat up straight at her desk. Her brown braid felt heavy between her shoulder blades, and she pulled it forward before copying the next problem from the board. She stretched, then bent again to her task.

Golden light filled the schoolroom. It illuminated the motes of chalk dust floating in the air, and gleamed off the round stove sitting cold in the corner. A fly buzzed and thumped against a window pane seeking exit to the red clay fields beyond the rippled glass. Thirty children scratched away at their slates.

Mr. MacDonald peered over shoulders, offering advice and correction. The dry smell of chalk dust went with him. Twenty-three years of teaching had begun to tell on his face, although this was a labour of love more than an obligation. His first duty was to his church and its congregation of Scottish settlers.

"Two minutes," he said in English. He clicked open his watch to check the time.

A sigh went up from some of the slower students.

Eight-year-old Callum MacLeod licked his finger and rubbed at his work.Mattie looked up from her problem. Callum's freckled face was red with the effort of learning to add three columns of numbers. Mattie tore her slate rag in half and handed it across the aisle. There'll not be much left of this rag soon. This is the second time this week, she thought.

She gazed out the window at the red fields already shadowed with the green of new oats. The grove of maple trees at the back of the schoolyard, bright with young leaves, had not yet darkened into the mature green of summer. From a branch a swing swayed in the breeze from the Northumberland Strait.

I hope there's more blueberries this year, she thought. There weren't many last year and they were kind of small. Momma said she'd teach me to make jam this summer. Maybe she'll show me how to make jelly, too.

In the autumn, jars of jam lined the shelves in the cool, clay cellar at Mattie's house. There were always purple blueberry, scarlet raspberry, with its little flecks of yellow seed and rich strawberry, thick with fruit. A barrel of apples stood in one corner of the cellar and a keg of molasses opposite. In the darkness of the farthest corner potatoes, carrots, turnips and parsnips were heaped.

Mattie thought of the apple juice dripping

pinkly clear through the jelly cloth, the smell of boiling sugar, the first taste of new jelly hot off the wooden spoon. Her mouth watered. She licked her lips.

A sense of being watched took her attention. Mr. MacDonald stared at her from his desk. His great brown moustache, streaked with grey, hid most of the expression around his mouth. A queer shiver went down Mattie's spine, and she bent her head over her slate, even though she had already finished her problem.

Mr. MacDonald cleared his throat. "Pass your work forward, please." The clatter of slates passing from hand to hand filled the room.

"Class dismissed. Mattie. I want to see you."

Mattie jumped at the sound of her name. "Yes, Mr. MacDonald?" The soft sibilants of her 's' were more in evidence with her unease. She rose from her seat and went forward to stand in front of his desk, her hands folded in front of her.

"How old are you, Mattie?"

"Fourteen, sir." Her voice was no more than a whisper. "Fifteen this month," she said more loudly. He knows that already, she thought, he baptized me.

"You'll be finished school in a few weeks?" It was more a statement of fact than a question.

"Yes, sir."

"What will you do then?"

Mattie looked at him blankly. "Help Momma." What else is there to do, and why is he asking me these questions?

Mr. MacDonald stared at Mattie. A trickle of sweat ran down her back. She hunched her shoulders. The classroom seemed too hot for May. It seemed much smaller, and Mr. MacDonald much larger than he had a few moments ago.

He sat for several minutes stroking his side whiskers.

Mattie found it difficult to hold his gaze. I wish he wouldn't stare so. Her eyes would not stay focused on his face. She gave up and began gazing at her bare toes peeping out from beneath her homespun skirt. The silence deepened. "May I go now, sir?" she quavered at last.

He nodded, then rose from his chair. "Tell your father and mother that David Matheson will be calling on them soon."

Mattie picked up her shawl and hurried from the classroom.

"What'd he want?" asked Cora, waiting for her in the shade of the maple tree by the gate. Although Cora was a year behind Mattie in school, having started a year later, they were the same age. It seemed as if they had been friends since the beginning of time.

"I don't know," replied Mattie, lapsing into Gaelic. "He just asked me how old I was, and what was I going to do when I finished *sgoil*."

"Maybe he wants to give you job." Cora spoke in Gaelic as well. "I heard him say to Poppa the other day that he really needed help with the little ones; there're so many of them."

"No, I don't think so. He said to tell Momma and Poppa that David Matheson would be coming to call soon."

Cora's dark blue eyes brightened. "Maybe he wants to come courting," she teased. She danced along the narrow track beside Mattie. "Oh, wouldn't that be exciting."

"Indeed, it would not. I don't even know the man."

"Well, you know who he is."

Mattie shook her head.

"Yes, you do. He was in church at the last sacrament. He was the one who came and sat with Rachel's father. Remember?"

"The one you said was so handsome?"

"That's him. His father's from here, but his mother's from England. She was staying with family in Charlottetown for a year, and they came out here to visit and he married her, but she couldn't stand to live away from town. So after Mr. Matheson was born they moved to Charlottetown, and now he has his teaching certificate and he was given the school in Orwell Cove two years ago."

"How do you know so much?"

"I listen. I heard Momma tell Isabella MacQueen all about him when he was here last summer. Don't you think he's handsome?"

Mattie only vaguely remembered him. She had seen him just once. "He's all eyes and beard," she replied.

Cora tossed her head. "Well, I think he's handsome, and I'd be that pleased to have him come courting me, and so should you be."

"Och, he's far too old for me, and besides …" Her voice trailed away. She scuffed her bare feet through the sand of the roadside sending up little puffs of pink dust.

"He's only twenty-three, and besides what?"

"I don't want to talk about it anymore." Mattie quickened her pace.

"C'mon, besides what?"

"Besides, that's all." Mattie walked faster.

"If the wind changes, your face'll stay that way."

Mattie tried to smooth out her features.

"So, besides, you're afraid, aren't you," said Cora.

"Yes, I am, so now you know." Mattie slung her shawl over her shoulder and stomped toward home, her bonnet bouncing between her shoulders.

Cora hurried after her. "What's there to be afraid of, for heaven's sake?"

"Nothing. Everything." Mattie stomped on,

passing Cora's gate in a small cloud of dust.

"Will you slow down!" Cora panted. Her short, legs had all they could do to keep up with Mattie's stride. Her cheeks were red with the effort, her dark hair escaped from her braid and clouded around her face.

Mattie came to a halt, and Cora bumped into her.

"So what's there to be afraid of?" Cora licked her fingers and brushed the hair from her eyes.

Mattie wrapped her arms around herself. "He's too old for me, that's all."

"Well, you'll be fifteen in a few more weeks, and that'll be plenty old." She propped her hands on her hips. "My sister had her first baby when she was fifteen, and she'd already been married for almost a year."

"She was nearly sixteen when she had James." Mattie fell silent thinking of the mysterious business of having babies.

"She had a hard time, too, so Momma said."

"What kind of a hard time?"

"Oh, you know." Cora brushed at the *streels* of hair in her eyes. "The baby was a long time coming because my sister was small inside. Momma said she was like all the women in our family, too narrow in the hips for having babies."

"Oh," said Mattie. The May sun on her bare head made her dizzy. She shook her head to clear it, her braid swung behind, making her head ache with its weight. I should have put my bonnet on, she thought.

"You have lots of brothers and sisters. Don't you know about having babies and how hard it is sometimes?" Cora watched Mattie's face. Her cheeks twitched in an effort to hide a smile of triumph.

Mattie pulled her shawl tightly over her small bosom and watched the progress of an ant carrying dirt to his anthill at the edge of the track. "Momma always sent us over to Mrs. MacNeil's, and when we came home the next day, there was the new baby."

"And she never told you about having babies?"

"No, but I suppose you're going to."

Cora stuck her lower lip out in a sulk. "Only if you want to know."

"Maybe I don't want to know." Mattie stood in the narrow roadway with her fists on her slender hips.

"You'll be sorry," said Cora in a sing-song voice. "You won't know what's happening to you when you start being sick in the morning; and when the pains come, all you'll be able to do is scream in agony." She turned to go.

Mattie thought back to the day when Johnnie had been born. I don't remember Momma screaming in agony. She just hustled us out the door and told us to go to Mrs. MacNeil's until Poppa came for us. She grunted once and she looked so angry I thought maybe I'd been a bad girl again. She closed the door behind us, and put the lock on. When Poppa came to get us the next day he told us we had a new baby brother.

Mattie's stance in the middle of the track lost its aggressiveness. "Wait then. What do you know about having babies?" She watched Cora suppress a smile of satisfaction.

"Momma told me that it hurts, and that if you're too small the baby gets stuck inside and it can't come out and you die. She says the pain goes on for hours, and that it's awful, and there's nothing you can do about it. It feels like you're ripping apart inside."

Mattie looked at Cora in horror. "I don't believe you. I don't believe you! You're a liar, Cora Smith! Don't you ever speak to me again!"

She turned and began to run down the road, oblivious to the pebbles beneath her feet. The two miles of red track fell away in minutes. She climbed over the rail fence, leaving a tuft of her only shawl decorating the top rail like a tiny brown flag. Mr. West's bull held no terror for her. She passed her younger brothers as they chased minnows in the brook in the shadows of the over-hanging trees, their hands and feet white with the cold of the water.

"Come and play, Mattie," called William, but

Mattie didn't hear him. Her feet were driven. Momma! Babies! Ripping apart?! She could feel her own flesh giving way to the grasping, pushing hands and feet of her imaginary infant. Her bones seemed to crack in the effort to deliver this child. She continued her race toward home.

She ran through the spruce woods and across the hay field, the stubble of last year's hay sharp among the soft growth of new grass. In their own small cow pasture she startled the cows into a lumbering run. From long acquaintance with the pasture path, her feet avoided the worst of the thistles.

I suppose I've spoiled their milk for today. Momma'll be cross again. Opening the pasture gate a crack, she squeezed through, stopping just long enough to close it behind herself. She was gasping for breath as she entered the kitchen, allowing the door to bang behind her. "I don't believe her!" she exploded, then lapsed into silence at the sight of their next door neighbour.

"Matilda Cameron! Have some manners!" Her mother spoke with more than her customary sharpness. "Excuse yourself to Mrs. MacNeil."

Mattie blushed and focused her attention on her mother's friend. "I beg your pardon, Mrs. MacNeil."

"Pardon granted," replied Mrs. MacNeil. "I can see you have a lot on your mind, dearie, so I must be going. It's nearly time to start supper for Himself anyway." She heaved herself out of the rocking chair, and put on her bonnet. "I'll look out that recipe for you this evening, Mary. You can pick it up the next time you're over."

The porch door shut behind Mrs. MacNeil. Mattie's mother bustled back into the kitchen, her long skirts swishing. "What do you mean by bursting into the house like a *hoyden*?"

"I'm sorry Momma," she whispered.

Her mother began preparations for supper. "Set the table." She swung the stew pot away from the fire and lifted the lid. "A fine thing it is when I can't even have a cup of tea in peace in my own kitchen. What was so important anyway?" She gave the stew a vigorous stir sending droplets of it flying into the fire where they hissed on the logs.

"Nothing, Momma." Mattie picked up the cutlery basket and kept her eyes on her task.

"Nothing? It must have been something to bring you charging in here like a bull in a china shop. And get that hair out of your face or the next thing you know we'll be having hair in our supper."

"I'm sorry, Momma." Mattie swung her braid back over her shoulder and brushed the loose strands away from her face.

"Well? I'm waiting."

"It was Cora." Mattie's voice was barely a whisper.

"That lass has about twice too much to say for herself. If she were one of mine …" Mrs. Cameron returned the lid to the stew pot with a clang. "Well, what did she do that has you so upset?"

"She said that it hurts to have babies and that I might die. It's not true, is it, Momma?"

Mrs. Cameron looked away. "Just because them Smiths can't bear children without making a big to-do about it, they think no one else can either."

"But does it hurt?" asked Mattie. "Can you really die?"

Mrs. Cameron looked at her oldest daughter, and she remembered the birth of each of her children. Her voice gentled. "It hurts some, and some women die from it, but it's our lot in life. The Bible says that in sorrow ye shall bring forth children. It's our payment for having been the ones to have brought sin into the world."

"Does it feel like you're ripping apart inside?" Mattie was almost crying.

"What in the world did that young imp tell you? Of course it doesn't. I suppose that's what her mother told her."

"She said that her sister had a hard time having James, and that's what it felt like."

"Them Smiths always did like to be dramatic." Mrs. Cameron pursed her lips in disapproval. "I won't tell you it doesn't hurt, because it does some, and it's hard work. Probably the hardest work you'll ever do. As for dying, some women do, but they're like that skinny sister of Cora's, too small in the hips to carry properly, and sickly besides. You have to be strong to have babies."

"Are my hips big enough, Momma?"

"You're a Cameron, aren't you? Cameron women never had trouble having babies."

Chapter Two

The schoolroom was quiet except for the screech of a slate pencil. The younger pupils had been dismissed. The sound of their voices carried faintly on the soft May breeze as they dawdled their last few minutes away before returning to their homes and the inevitable chores. Mattie's thoughts wandered.

It's only three miles from home, but it seemed like another country the first few times I came to school, and now it's almost over. I'm glad Tommy was with me.

She propped her chin on her hand and gazed out the window. Tommy and I always stuck together against Momma and the rest of the world. Ellie's never much fun. She never wants to do anything. Most of the time she's sort of just there.

An awareness of being watched brought her back to herself. Her soft blue eyes met Mr. MacDonald's penetrating gaze. She ducked her head and tried to concentrate on the sentence she was parsing. Concentration wouldn't come. She peeked upward through her soft brown lashes. Mr. MacDonald was staring down at his hands and frowning. At least he's not staring at me, she thought.

Mr. MacDonald rose from his seat behind the desk. "Pass your work forward." He opened his pocket watch, looked at the time then clicked it shut.

Mattie squirmed in her seat. Oh, dear, I haven't finished, and I haven't any excuse. I'll just hold back my slate. Maybe he won't notice. She took the stack of slates from the pupil behind her and passed them to the next child up the row.

"Mattie. Your slate is not here. Bring it forward, please."

Mattie's heart dropped. She picked up her slate and carried it forward.

"Your work isn't finished?"

Mattie looked at the floor. "No, sir. I'm sorry, sir."

"Did I not give you enough time?"

"No, sir. I mean yes, sir."

Mr. MacDonald returned her slate. "Finish it now. It will only take you a minute."

Mattie hurried back to her seat. The sentence seemed to jump all over the slate. She forced herself to settle down and concentrate. The silence that followed was oppressive. Her slate pencil screeched. She cringed at the sound.

"Class dismissed."

Oblivious to the noise of the others leaving, Mattie worked on. She pinned down the agile sentence and reduced it to its various parts. She looked up, surprised to find the classroom empty. She cleared her throat. "I've finished, sir."

"Fine. Bring it here and then you may go." Mr. MacDonald held out his hand for her slate. "Has Mr. Matheson called at your house yet?"

"No, sir, not that I know about."

"Hm. Well." He regarded her in silence for a few moments. "You may go, then."

Mattie picked up her shawl and fled. Cora was waiting for her by the schoolyard gate.

"You really are the teacher's pet, aren't you. How'd you manage that all of a sudden?"

"I don't know." Mattie came to herself again. "I am not!"

"Are too."

"Am not!"

"Are too! Look what he did to poor James last week when he did the very same thing. He gave him a good scolding and five more sentences to work on at home. Poor James had to do all that and extra chores. And besides that, his father switched him."

"Well, I wish I wasn't." Mattie slammed through the narrow white gate, almost taking it off its hinges.

"He's probably just being kind because you'll be finished school in a few weeks."

"And I'll be glad, too." But I'm not really glad,

she thought. I love being at home minding the little ones, but I like being in school too. I like to work arithmetic problems, and read stories from the advanced readers. Mattie walked on in silence, her bare feet scuffing up little puffs of pink dust as she went. Cora trailed behind her.

"What'll you do this summer?" asked Cora.

Mattie shrugged. "Look after the children and tend the house so Momma can help Poppa with the farm, I suppose." She trudged on in silence for a few more minutes. "What're you going to do?"

"Momma's taking me into Charlottetown to visit Sarah for a week. John's just old enough now to be fun to play with. He's past that slobbery stage that babies go through. It should be fun."

"When're you going?"

"In July. Momma said that Sarah and Ian are going to take us to the shore for a picnic."

"Lucky thing. I wish I could go. I've only ever been to the shore once in my life."

We tried to have a picnic on the shore once, she thought. It was just before Johnny was born. I looked forward to it for days but it was a disaster. I wished we had just stayed home.

It was Poppa's idea. Momma agreed to it and packed up a lunch for us after chores on Saturday. We spread our blanket in the shade of the sandstone. The sand was lovely and warm. It felt so good. I felt so free and the air was so fresh

with that sea-weedy smell. Then Tommy had to
fall and graze his knees. He didn't say anything,
but I know he almost cried. I could see the tears.
Then William kicked sand into the butter. He got
smacked for that. He set up a howl that could be
heard all the way to Wood Islands, so Momma
said. She skimmed the sand off the butter and we
ate it anyway. It kind of gritted. Later we all went
wading. Except Momma, of course. I remember
stepping on an open clam shell under the water.
That hurt when it closed. It was all I could do to
keep from crying. It clouded over by mid-afternoon and we had to scramble to get home before
the rain came. That was the end of our picnics.
She brushed the memory away with a small sigh.

"I've never been to Charlottetown either," she
said.

Cora's eyes brightened. "Maybe you can come
with us. I'll ask Momma."

"Don't bother. My Momma'd never let me go."

"I'll ask anyway."

"If you want to, but I know it won't do any
good." They reached Cora's gate. "I'll see you
tomorrow." Mattie trudged on towards home.

Cora's so lucky, she gets to do everything. If
I even thought about doing half the things she
does, Momma'd smack me. Mattie's face drooped
into a scowl and a lip. Momma says she's just
spoiled. Her lip retreated a little as she thought

of some of Cora's escapades. Maybe she's right. Maybe Cora is just spoiled. Her mother lets her do whatever she wants. Not that she could stop her. Mattie scuffed her feet through a patch of warm red sand on the track.

"Give that lass an inch and she'll take a mile." Mattie's mother's pronouncement on Cora's behaviour echoed in Mattie's memory. Her bare toe struck a stone and she hopped a few steps to ease the pain.

Imagine her saying that Mr. Matheson was going to come courting me. Mattie's lip came out again as she hobbled along. What would he want with me? Where would we live? What would I do? A picture of herself in a placeless kitchen somewhere on the Island blossomed in her mind. It was the same featureless kitchen she had imagined all her life whenever she thought about being married. She imagined peeling potatoes for dinner. The damp red earth still clung to them in places as the thin layer of peeling ran away from beneath her knife to expose the white flesh. Its starchy juice wet her fingers.

She came to a halt with her left hand on the fence around Mr. West's pasture as her mind concentrated on the picture in her head. It seemed more real than the bright day around her. She set the pot of potatoes over the imaginary fire to boil and began setting the imaginary table and cutting the imaginary bread. Soon her imaginary husband came in and sat in the rocker to take off his boots. The face that had always been feature-less in the past now resembled Mr. Matheson as she remembered him. The memory was mostly black beard and blue eyes. The enormity of all it implied startled her into awareness just as Mr. West's red bull came to investigate her presence at his pasture fence. He snuffled the air to get her scent, then shook his great horned head and snorted. He came closer.

Oh, no! Mattie backed away from the fence. That's what I get for daydreaming. Now I'll have to walk around. I'll be late getting home and Mom-ma'll be cross. Serves me right for wasting time thinking silly thoughts. I shouldn't have listened to Cora at all. Mattie trudged around the outside of the fence. The bull followed her, snorting every now and then.

He's never been cross before, she thought. Mattie stepped on a thistle and winced at the pain. She kept a respectful distance from the fence. We always take the short cut if the bull isn't in sight. She stopped and looked at the bull, then looked at the path across the field. She looked at the bull again and decided. I'd better not. You never know about bulls. She plodded on, picking her way around the patches of thistles as she went. Her thoughts returned to Cora and their mothers and other women she knew.

Cora's mother always looks kind of vague and worried. It's as if she's never quite there, and she's always suffering from her condition, whatever that is. Momma always looks cross. She's always scolding about something, and she'll be scolding me yet if I don't hurry. Mattie walked a little faster. I'm liable to get smacked for being so late. She thought of the sting her mother's work worn hands could deliver. She looked down at her own little hands that hadn't yet grown into their adult strength. I suppose my hands'll look like that someday too. It's one thing for sure, I'll never smack my children, no matter what they do. She thought of some of Cora's escapades. Well, at least only if they deserve it.

The bull snuffled at her from just over the fence, his warm saliva spattered her face. She jumped in fright and began to run. The bull thundered close beside her all the way around the field to where the short cut ended and she was able to rejoin the path toward home. She ran a few steps further then slowed again to a walk. The bull snorted and pawed the ground, and swung his huge horned head.

Mattie turned and stuck her tongue out at him then hurried away. Her thoughts returned to their previous topic. Mrs. MacNeil seems happy enough. She always calls her husband "Himself."

It always sounds capitalized, as if he were God. All the old ladies do. I suppose it's only polite, although Momma doesn't do that with Poppa. At least, I don't think she does. She always says "your father" in that certain tone of voice. Mattie made a face. I don't think she likes him very well sometimes. She skipped a few paces past the brook. But Poppa's nice. He always has time for me even though I am a girl and can't help him much.

She thought of her father's tanned face with its broad cheek bones, bright blue eyes, and square chin. He always shaves. His father never did. Pa always looked like that picture of Moses in Mr. MacDonald's Bible. She chuckled out loud, then sobered. I wonder why Momma doesn't like Poppa? I wonder how many other women don't like their husbands? Her musing was interrupted by her arrival at their own pasture fence.

She climbed over the gate and walked slowly across the field. The cows lifted their heads from their grazing and gazed at her with their liquid brown eyes. Their jaws worked rhythmically. The children were nowhere to be seen.

That's strange, they always come to meet me. Mattie hastened her steps. I hope they didn't do anything wrong. Momma can be just fierce when she's angry.

She opened the gate to the barnyard a crack and

squeezed through, closing it behind herself. The barnyard was unusually still, even the chickens were not in sight. A black horse was tied to the fence. A sense of foreboding crept over Mattie.

I wonder whose horse that is? It was just two nights ago that I saw that falling star, and last night I saw a light over the barn. Apprehension grew in her and she quickened her steps toward the house. The porch door squealed a little on its hinges, a reassuring and homey sound. Muted conversation came from the kitchen. Mattie hung her bonnet and shawl on the hook behind the door. That sounds like Dr. Moore. I wonder what he's doing here?

Apprehension turned to fear as she stepped into the kitchen. The fire had been allowed to die down to embers, the hearth had gone unswept. The dinner dishes were still stacked in the pantry beside the dishpan filled with soapy water which had been left to grow cold. Johnny and William were sitting silently side by side on the lounge, their small faces looking strained, their eyes watchful. Ellie sat in the corner beside the fire-place, the tracks of former tears were white and salty on her cheeks. Tommy came and stood beside Mattie. Dr. Moore was just closing his black bag. Mrs. MacNeil stood beside Mattie's mother holding her around the waist.

Something's wrong, thought Mattie. Momma

never leaves her work undone for the neighbours to see, and why's Mrs. MacNeil here? Momma looks so small and helpless. I've never seen her like this.

"Try to keep him quiet for the next few days, Mrs. Cameron," Dr. Moore was saying. "Keep the wound clean and change the bandage when you need to. I'll leave this medicine to help with the pain. Don't give it to him any more often than a teaspoon every four hours. I'll be back on Thursday to see him. If you need me sooner than that, send Tommy for me. John will have a difficult night this night. It's a nasty cut, but he should feel a little better in the morning." He closed his bag with a snap.

The nugget of fear that had planted itself in Mattie's middle exploded with the closing of the doctor's bag. "What's happened? Where's Poppa?"

"Hush child," soothed Mrs. MacNeil. "He's just resting for awhile."

A little of the fear seeped away from Mattie's chest. At least he's not dead. "Poppa never rests in the afternoon. Why's he resting today?"

"Your father's had an accident." Mrs. MacNeil tried to break the news gently. "He's lost some of his fingers on the scythe."

"Never! Poppa's always careful." The fear came back inside her. Poppa without his fingers. How will he care for us all?

Mrs. MacNeil shook her head. "I'm afraid so, child. You're going to have to be a big girl and help your Momma. She needs you more than ever now, and so does your Poppa."

Mattie's slender shoulders drooped. "I'll put supper on," she said in a small voice.

Mattie washed the dishes and made supper. "William and Johnny, clean up your plates." Mattie's tone was sharp. "Momma, you have to eat more than that, Poppa needs us to be strong right now." Her mother pushed her food around on the plate.

"At least have a cup of tea."

A restless murmur began in the bedroom. Her mother jumped up and hurried away. The lump of fear that had migrated from somewhere in the region of Mattie's stomach since supper, expanded into her throat. She swallowed hard and blinked back the tears that were threatening to overflow. She began clearing the table, bustling and clattering to cover the stillness in the kitchen.

"I'll be out to help you with the milking in a few minutes, Tommy. I'll do the dishes first. You children go and feed the chickens, then fill the wood box, and draw some water. Run now." She shooed the others out the door. "Ellie, go and see if Momma needs anything."

"I'm afraid to," whimpered Ellie. "What if he's dead?" The restless murmur from the bedroom had ceased, and the ensuing silence was worse than the sounds of distress.

"He's not dead, or Momma would've told us," replied Mattie. "And even if he were, he's still our father, and he won't hurt us dead, anymore than he did when he was alive. Now go!"

Ellie jumped up and scurried toward the bedroom. She returned in a few minutes and climbed onto the lounge, drawing her legs up underneath her skirt.

"Well?" prompted Mattie, "does Momma need anything?"

"She says not."

"How's Poppa?"

"Awful. He didn't know me, and he's terrible restless. Can I go out and play?"

"In a minute. Dry these dishes first."

"I don't want to," whined Ellie.

"Well, you have to." Mattie picked up the tea towel. "As long as Poppa's sick, I have to do Momma's work and my own work too, and I can't do it all by myself. You're old enough to help, so get drying." Mattie flung the tea towel at her sister.

"You're not my mother. You can't make me." Ellie threw the tea towel on the floor, jumped off the lounge and ran toward the door.

Mattie grabbed her by her long auburn braid bringing her to a halt with a howl of rage and pain. "Listen to me, Ellie Cameron! You will too!

Momma needs us all to help now, and if you don't, I'll tell her who let the pig out last week."

"It was an accident." Ellie was crying for real now. "You know how that old sow always crowds the door when we go to feed her. Please don't tell Momma, I'll get the switch."

"You'll dry the dishes?"

"Yes, yes, I'll dry the dishes, only please don't tell Momma about the pig."

Mattie released her hold on Ellie's braid and handed her the tea towel.

The evening passed slowly. Her father's restlessness increased as infection set in and his temperature soared. Mattie scrubbed faces, and washed hands and feet, and generally oversaw the bedtime rituals of the two little ones. She settled Johnny on her left hip and shooed William up the stairs ahead of her to the boys' bedroom under the eaves.

"Tell us a story, Mattie," pleaded Johnny, snuggling down under the covers.

"If you promise to be good and go to sleep, I will," Mattie bargained, tucking them into the three-quarter bed.

"We promise," they chorused.

"Once upon a time ..." She sat down on the edge of their bed and propped her bare feet on the single cot that was Tommy's bed.

Johnny tugged at Mattie's sleeve. "Is Poppa going to die?" Fear was in his little face.

"I hope not."

"What if he does?" asked William.

"Oh, Willie, I don't know. We'll just have to look after each other and Momma, I guess."

"Will they send us to the poor house?" asked Johnny.

"What do you know about the poor house?"

"I heard Momma say that we'd all be going to the poor house if Poppa couldn't make the crops grow, and now he can't make the crops grow 'cause he doesn't have any fingers."

"Momma won't let that happen."

"But what if Momma dies too?"

"She can't die," said Mattie. "Anyway there's still Tommy and me. We'll look after you. Now, do you want this story, or not?"

All evening after the children went to sleep, Mattie helped her mother tend her father. She tore old shirts into bandages, and carried pans of cool water to the tiny candle-lit bedroom off the kitchen where her father lay alternately shivering and burning in the shadowy light. The cooling baths administered by her mother barely slowed his climbing temperature. Indeed, the heat from his body raised the temperature of the water so that Mattie had to make several trips to the well to get the coldest water possible. His restlessness turned to dreams and then hallucinations. Mattie heard words from him that night that she barely knew existed, and had never heard from her father's lips before.

"Mattie, dear, you shouldn't be hearing such things," mourned Mrs. Cameron. "It's the fever speaking. Your father's a good man. Go and sit in the kitchen until I need you."

Mattie did as she was told, grateful for the opportunity to sit down. She stirred up the fire and added another log. Sparks flew up the chimney and the room brightened. Tommy slept on the lounge. The mutterings and cries from the bedroom grew louder. A long wail from the other room brought Tommy awake.

"Was that Poppa?" Tommy rubbed his eyes and yawned.

Mattie nodded. "He's been getting worse all evening. Momma sent me out here because he's been saying bad things in his sleep."

"Mattie!" Her mother's call was high-pitched with anxiety.

Mattie hurried to the bedroom. "What is it, Momma?"

"He's started bleeding again. Get me some clean rags."

"There aren't any, we've used them all."

"Tear up that new sheet I got from Mrs. J.D. last month. It's a shame that I'll have to use it for this. I traded that nice piece of homespun I had left over from Tommy's new coat for it." Mrs. Cameron began peeling away the old bandages. "Oh, no." The words were barely a whisper.

"What, Momma?" asked Mattie returning with the sheet. "What are those red streaks on his arm?"

Her mother didn't reply. "Where's Tommy?"

"In the kitchen."

"Send him for Dr. Moore."

Dr. Moore came and stayed for awhile, and then left. "There's nothing more I can do for him right now. You continue with the poultices and I'll be back in the morning. If he's no better then, I may have to amputate."

Mattie's mother stifled a cry of alarm and Mattie's heart contracted painfully in her chest. Tommy came and stood beside her.

"Surely it won't come to that," he said.

CHAPTER THREE

Mattie's father lived through the next three days and nights. Mattie and her mother took turns caring for him. Neighbours came bearing food and comfort.

Mary-Angus brought a chicken and some new leaf lettuce. "I started it in trays and transplanted it a few weeks ago," she said. "I read somewhere that it would come along faster than waiting for the frost to leave."

Aunt Rachael Cameron brought a *bonnach* and a cake. "There's nothing like a raisin cake to lift the spirits. It's gotten me through some very heavy weather before this."

Eliza MacMillan brought a pie and advice. "You tell your mother to keep a good bread poultice on that hand. It'll cure most anything."

Mattie took the pie and ignored the advice. If Dr. Moore can't cure him, I don't think a bread poultice will do much good, she thought. "Thank you, Mrs. MacMillan. I'll tell Momma."

Robert West helped Tommy with the milking and other chores in the morning, and Norman Martin came by every evening.

Mrs. MacNeil showed Mattie how to set bread. "Now, dearie, you have your water hot but not too hot. You don't want to kill the yeast. Put in a good handful of sugar and a spoonful of butter and let that all melt and stir it together while you proof the yeast." Her plump hands worked swiftly. Mattie concentrated trying not to miss anything.

"Put a little sugar in some warm milk and then a tablespoon or so of yeast and set it aside to grow for about fifteen minutes. When the fat and the sugar are all dissolved, cool the water a little. By that time the yeast should be ready. Put it in with some flour and a little salt and stir it up. Then keep adding flour until you can't stir in any more." She clapped her hands together to rid them of flour dust.

"I'm going down to talk to your Momma while you do that. When you're finished come and get me."

Mattie did as she was instructed. Soon the warm dough was too heavy and she had no more strength for stirring in flour. She crept to the bedroom door and stood silently listening to her mother and her friend talk.

"I don't know if he's going to get over this," said Mary. "I can't get the fever down except for a short time. This is the first he's been cool since last night." Mattie heard the fear in her mother's voice and shivered.

"Hush, now, Mary. It's no good thinking those kinds of things. They'll only take your strength, and you need to be strong now for the children."

Mary wiped her eyes on the tail of her apron. She drew a deep quivering breath. "You're right. I can't let go. There's only me now."

Mattie felt as if the fear was choking her. She coughed to clear the lump. If Momma can be that strong, then I need to be, too. Mattie stepped into the bedroom. Oh, thank you, God, Poppa's still breathing. Mattie raised her head and stood as tall as her lack of height would allow. "Mrs. MacNeil, I need you."

Mrs. MacNeil followed Mattie back to the kitchen. "Flour your board and dump all the dough on top of the flour. Then you knead it as you work in more flour."

"Knead it?"

"Yes, like this. You've seen your mother do it." Mrs. MacNeil began the rhythmic pulling and rolling of the dough, adding flour as it began to stick to the board. "Here, you try now."

Mattie floured her hands and the great lump of dough, and began a weak imitation of Mrs. MacNeil's movements.

"You have to put your back into it, child." Mrs. MacNeil put her hands over Mattie's and began the process all over again. Mattie's body soon took over the rocking rhythm of Mrs. MacNeil's. Her hands pulled the far edge of the mound of dough toward her and folded and pushed it in upon itself. It feels good and soothing, she thought. It feels as if I own it. Gradually the dough came alive under her hands. "How long do I have to knead it?"

Mrs. MacNeil tried the dough. "You know by the feel of it when it's ready. It feels stretchy and resilient. I think it's ready now." She put it back into the bowl. "Now you cover it and set it by the fire to rise. Poke it down and let it rise once more, then grease your pans and fill each pan about half way. When it rises again you can bake it."

Mattie's bread was as good as her mother's. They had warm bread and butter, and molasses for supper.

Mattie spent her days caring for the children, cooking for the men, and cleaning. At night she washed small faces and heard their bedtime prayers, kept the fire burning, and went to the well for cold water which was soon warmed by her father's fever. She napped, when she could, in the rocker.

I don't think I've ever felt so tired, she thought on the evening of the third day. I can't believe I ever wanted to stay up all night just to see what it was like. She dropped into the rocker and leaned her head back. She did not begin rocking.

I wonder if this is what it's like to feel old?

The porch door squeaked on its hinges and she opened her eyes again. Someone tiptoed to the kitchen door and scratched on it. Mattie winced as she got to her feet, then smoothed her hair and went to the door. It was Cora.

Mattie stood looking at her friend as if she didn't know her. It seemed years since she had last seen her.

"Can I come in, Mattie?"

Mattie continued to stare at Cora.

"Mattie? May I come in?"

"Oh! Oh, of course, you can." Mattie stood aside to let Cora pass. "I'm just surprised to see you, that's all. I wasn't expecting you."

Cora shrugged. "Well, I didn't want to come, but Momma sent me. Her condition, you know."

"Oh, yes, her condition What is it this time? Another disagreement with her sister?" Mrs. Smith's condition seems so far away now, she thought.

"It's the same one as last month." Cora giggled, then stopped and cleared her throat. "He's not dead yet, is he?"

"No, and he's not going to be."

"That's not what Poppa was saying. He heard at the store that he was on his last legs, and they're already discussing who your Momma's likely to get an offer from once he's gone. After all, there's all you children to take on, too."

Mattie's eyes widened. "Well, they can save their breaths, he's not dead and he's not going to be." What will we do if Poppa doesn't recover? she wondered, then swallowed hard against the ever-present knot of fear in her throat.

"Well, you have to be prepared," continued Cora.

"Prepared for what?" asked Tommy, just in from the barn.

Cora blinked at his sudden appearance. "W-why, prepared for the future."

Tommy went and stood beside Mattie. "We are prepared." He stared down at Cora for a moment, then turned to Mattie. "I'll just go in and see my father now."

"My, he has grown into quite a man." Cora smiled and admired Tommy through the bedroom doorway.

Mattie shrugged. "He's been working with the men for the past two years, so I suppose it has its influence." Tommy has grown into a man, she thought. And almost overnight. What's happening to us all?

"Handsome, too," observed Cora.

"Handsome is as handsome does." Mattie sniffed. "Shall I make us some tea?"

"No, thanks, I was just going. Momma said not to stay too long. She just wanted to know how you were getting along and how your father was doing." Cora rose from her seat on the lounge. "Don't bother to see me out, I know the way." She disappeared in a flurry of skirts, not quite slamming the door behind herself.

Mattie slumped back into the rocker. "If she weren't my best friend I could hate her sometimes," she muttered and closed her eyes for a moment.

At least it seemed like only a moment before Tommy was shaking her awake. "Mattie! Mattie! Wake up. Poppa's worse, and Momma needs you."

The raving had begun again. Mattie jumped to her feet and hurried to the bedroom door. "What do you need, Momma?"

"Have you washed out those bandages? I need more well water, he's burning up again."

Outdoors the sky was pricked with stars and the breeze held the sweet smell of grass mixed with the salt air from the Northumberland Strait. Mattie hastened to the well. She took a deep breath, braced her feet against the well curb and began winding up yet another bucketful of cold water.

It's a beautiful night to die on, she thought. When she realized the portent of her thought she gave a hard turn to the windlass nearly upsetting the bucket

"Drat!" That's all I need to do is spill it and have to wind it all over again. Cora's got me thinking this way. I'd better not say 'drat' in front of

Momma. She trudged into the house with the bucket of water, stopping to take the clean bandages off the clothesline as she went.

"Is that all the bandages there are?" Mrs. Cameron eyed the stack of folded linen in Mattie's hands.

"That's all," replied Mattie. "I couldn't get the others clean enough."

Her mother sighed.

"Is that all you need, Momma?"

"That's all. Get some sleep and you can spell me in a few hours."

The night passed slowly and silently except for the feverish cries of Mr. Cameron. In one brief period of lucidity, when the fever had cooled a little, he opened his eyes and looked at his wife. He patted her rough hands.

"Mary, you've been a good wife. You'll need help running the farm. Tommy's good, but not quite up to a man's job yet. I want you to marry again as soon as you decently can. Robert West or Norman Martin. They're both good men, hard workers, and not fond of the drink. Presbyterian, too. I owe Norman two shillings for that seed I brought home the other day."

His gaze wandered away from his wife's face and he pointed to the darkest corner behind the wash stand. "Here's Pa and Poppa. Momma's with them, too. They're looking well and happy." His arm dropped and his voice faded to a whisper. He stared into the corner and held muttered conversation until his eyes closed and he began to cry out and whimper again. His temperature rose once more and he grew restless, plucking at the sheets and picking imaginary things out of the air.

Mrs. Cameron continued bathing him with cool water. It did little to alleviate his fever. At four o'clock in the morning she rose stiffly from her seat beside the bed and went into the kitchen to find Mattie wrapped in a quilt in front of the cold hearth, and Tommy asleep on the lounge.

"I need you, Mattie. Your father's dead."

The fear that had taken up residence in Mattie's throat suddenly shifted its position and fell into the pit of her stomach. She struggled to her feet.

"What do you need, Momma?"

"Build up the fire and boil the kettle. Brush his suit and be sure he has a clean collar. Tommy can help me wash him and dress him." Mrs. Cameron's voice was dull with fatigue and suppressed grief. "In a little while you can run across to Mrs. MacNeil's and let her know. She'll know what to do."

Mattie nodded. "Yes, Momma."

"You're a good girl, Mattie."

§

The day brightened slowly. At six o'clock Mattie ran over the red fields to Mrs. MacNeil's. The grass was cold and wet on her bare feet. The air was filled with the twitter of barn swallows and the bubbling call of bob-o-links. The breeze blew fresh and salty off the Strait. Mattie shivered a little in the morning air. Mrs. MacNeil answered the door on her first knock.

"Your father's gone, has he?"

Mattie nodded. "Momma needs you."

"I'll be right there. I'll just go to the barn and tell Mr. MacNeil where I've gone. He'll tell the others." She hurried across the yard and disappeared into the shadowy darkness of the barn. Presently she returned and she and Mattie set out across the fields toward home.

"You're a good girl, Mattie," said Mrs. MacNeil. "You've been a wonderful help to your Momma these last few days."

"Thank you, Mrs. MacNeil," replied Mattie. Why would she say such a thing when I have been only doing what's been there to do. It's just like Momma says, a woman does what she has to do. The realization of what the thought implied struck her so forcefully that she stumbled. Does this mean that I'm a woman now? She hurried on after Mrs. MacNeil's round bustling figure. I can't think of this now.

The house soon filled with people. Neighbours brought more food than they could ever hope to eat: round crusty loaves of bread still warm from the oven, strawberry jam, sweet butter, curds, pies and a roast ready for the oven. Robert West came and measured Mr. Cameron for his coffin. Norman Martin helped Tommy with chores.

"You'll be needing help with the harvest," he said.

"Yes, sir, I will," replied Tommy.

Cora's mother, her condition forgotten for the moment, brought black dresses for Mattie and Ellie, leftovers of Cora and Sarah from when their brother had died two winters ago. Mrs. MacNeil had brought one for Mrs. Cameron. It was wool and smelled of camphor.

"I've had it put away since my first husband died. I was much smaller then, so it should fit you fine now," she said.

William and Johnny sat side by side on the lounge like little statues, their eyes round and frightened. Ellie sobbed and wailed from her chair in the corner beside the hearth until Mattie couldn't stand it any longer.

"Ellie, will you stop that racket and make yourself useful," whispered Mattie. "I can't do it all."

Mattie had been keeping the kitchen somewhat organized, although whenever she appeared to be doing any real work, someone took it from her and made her sit down. Her mother sat in the rocker most of the day, grey-faced and grim. Tommy escaped to the barn. Mattie wished that she could too.

The next day every seat in the church was taken. Mattie sat in the front seat on one side of her mother, and Tommy sat on the other. William and Johnny sat beside Mattie, their feet dangling a foot off the floor.

They're wearing the shoes that Poppa made for them, thought Mattie. She remembered her father's hands at work on the little shoes as he sat beside the hearth of a winter evening. Who'll make shoes for them now?

The church windows were open, for the day was warm. The air was sweet with summer flowers, fresh earth, and new grass. A soft breeze lifted a wisp of Mattie's hair that had escaped from under her bonnet and tickled her cheek. She sat staring at the nail holes in the coffin during the singing of the Psalm trying not to cry.

That's not really Poppa in there, she thought, looking at the waxen, slack-faced remains of her father in his casket. His mouth was slightly agape and his hands were folded stiffly across his stomach. She closed her eyes to shut out the sight and allowed her mind to wander to happier times. She remembered her father sitting before the fire carving her a new face for her doll when the old one had dried and split. She remembered how he used to pull them on the sled all around the farmyard after a snowstorm.

Once he even took us across to Mrs. MacNeil's and back, she thought. I can still hear the squeak of the snow on the wooden runners. The sled shifted underneath us, just so. She squirmed a little in her seat, adjusting for the unevenness of the remembered sleigh ride. There was just me and Tommy then. She smiled, earning herself a fierce glance from her mother. She forced her face into a more serious expression but continued to let her thoughts drift.

She thought of the time that she had pestered him into letting her plant a garden. "You're too little for all that work," he'd said. "Aw, Poppa, let me try," she'd pleaded. In the end he had agreed to give her ten of his precious peas, four sets of potatoes, and a few tiny carrot seeds. The garden had grown more weeds than food, although she had managed to salvage one dinner's worth of vegetables. Poppa said it was the best meal he'd ever eaten, thought Mattie. She suppressed another smile.

The service plodded on. Johnny slid to the edge of his seat and began stamping his foot on the floor.

"My foot ritches," he complained in a loud whisper.

"Ssh," Mattie whispered. "It's gone to sleep. Just rub it."

The funeral sermon seemed to last forever. Mattie's back itched from the heat and the wool dress, and she wanted to squirm too. There's just the viewing left to get through, she thought. She carefully shifted her weight. The seat creaked and she caught another look from her mother.

The congregation rose. Mattie and her family remained seated. Neighbours and friends filed past the open casket to say their last farewells. Robert West, who had measured him for his casket, ran his right hand along its edge and silently admired his handiwork. Norman Martin, who had helped Tommy farm for so many days, stopped for a moment, cleared his throat, then moved onward. The Smiths followed. Cora's father looked grim, her mother sobbed into a sodden handkerchief, and Cora stared into the casket. Big Callum MacLeod did not look at all, and Little Callum stared and began reaching out toward the corpse until Mrs. Callum grabbed his hand and pushed him onward.

Neighbour after neighbour passed. They stopped to greet Mattie's mother, then hurried outdoors. Their faces were serious with the solemnity of the moment, each sensitive to the fleetness of time, and the uncertainty of the future. Tomorrow it might be one of them gone to meet his creator to be held accountable for all his sins. It was, indeed, a somber moment.

The pall bearers closed the lid. The sound of their hammers echoed from the high ceiling of the church. Then they shouldered their burden to carry it to the church yard where the red earth from the grave had been piled by the grave digger. The mourners gathered and the graveside service began. I'm glad it's not raining, thought Mattie wiggling her toes inside the unaccustomed confines of her shoes and shifting surreptitiously to ease the ache in her back. Her mother's hand fell firmly on her own and Mattie stood still again. Mr. MacDonald's voice flowed on and on, the softness of the Gaelic intonation in contrast to the harsh reality of his message and the day.

At last the service was nearly over and the coffin was lowered into the earth. The requisite handful of soil thumped hollowly off the lid, tossed in by her mother, as silent and grim as ever she had been since her husband's passing.

No tears for Momma, she thought. Mattie had gone to the barn yesterday evening after everyone had gone home. She had buried herself in the prickly hay left over from last year, and cried herself into exhaustion.

Tommy's handful of dirt followed. It was her turn next, then Ellie's, then William's and Johnny's.

The sombreness of the ceremony was in sharp contrast to the sunny June day. A trickle of perspiration ran down Mattie's back, and the wool dress, borrowed from Sarah, itched her skin. Sarah was a much taller, plumper girl, and the dress was too long and too big for Mattie. I suppose this is what it'll feel like to always wear a long dress, I won't be able to run and climb with the children anymore.

In the hay field across the fence a bee buzzed from clover to clover. Mattie looked up after the final prayer to find Mr. MacDonald gazing at her. She ducked her head and turned away.

The days following the funeral slowly brightened. Mattie had more responsibility now, but she had expected that since she would no longer be going to school. Ellie, as irresponsible as she had been in the past, was finally learning to be counted on for some of the smaller tasks without baulking too much. Her mother helped Tommy with the farm work, her face grimmer than ever, her hands becoming ever more calloused and red. William and Johnny did their chores, mostly without being told. "I help you, Mattie," was Johnny's frequent offer.

Mattie took over the running of the household. Her own hands reddened and dried and cracked until they bled at the corners of her nails. She tended the garden, and minded the children as best she could. Churning the rich cream to make butter held no mysteries for her, she had been delegated that task when she was eleven. She could tell by the feel of the paddle when the butter had formed and knew how to wash it and save the buttermilk for baking.

Her housewifely skills increased rapidly. Cheese-making was a new skill. Her mother hung the milk in a large kettle over the remains of the evening fire. Mattie added the rennet, washed the curds when they formed and made them into rounds. She then packed them into the barrel with the heavy stone on top to solidify and age. The completed rounds of creamy cheese were all that Mattie could have hoped for.

Her only respite from her labours was the few days that she took William and Johnny and Ellie picking the ripe blueberries, the ruby red raspberries, and the wild strawberries, that grew along the fences and in the clearings.

"Mattie, d'you suppose Poppa's watching us pick berries?" William's freckled face was solemn.

"Maybe," said Mattie. "If he can, he will be." I don't think he's smiled since Poppa got hurt, she thought.

"D'you think if I waved at him up in heaven he'd see me and wave back?"

Mattie's throat spasmed with a rush of tears. She swallowed, then swallowed again. "Oh, Willie,

I don't know. Knowing Poppa, if he's anywhere around, he's waving like everything and making silly faces to make us laugh, but we can't see him."

"Why can't we see him?"

"Because we can't, that's all. He's gone to heaven."

"I want to show him how I can turn cartwheels. D'you suppose he'll be able to see me?"

"Why don't you turn some, and if Poppa can see you, he'll know that you can turn them."

"Yes, but how will I know if he's seen them?"

Mattie thought hard. "I don't know, William. We can't know about things like that. You heard Reverend MacDonald in church the other day, first we see through a glass darkly, then face to face."

"What's a 'glassdarkly'?"

"A looking glass in a dim room. Now go and turn your cartwheels, and then pick some more berries or there won't be any jam for this winter."

They had fresh berries and *bannoch* with butter for supper that night, and the next morning her mother left instructions for making the jam. Mattie followed them to the letter, and her jams were as pretty as her mother's when she had arranged them on the shelves in the cool dimness of the cellar.

The hay had ripened, and the oats were ripening, and suddenly Tommy was faced with the monumental task of harvesting them.

"Mr. Martin said he would help me, Momma. I'm going to go and see him today." Tommy put on his boots and left the kitchen.

Mrs. Cameron sighed. "He's grown up so much these last few weeks. He's not a boy any longer."

"We all have to grow up sometime." Mattie began clearing the breakfast table. I feel like I'm a hundred and one, she thought. She filled the dishpan with hot water from the kettle. "I'm going to weed what's left of the garden again today." She dropped a little soap into the water. "I've been trying to keep ahead of it, but sometimes I think the weeds grow faster than the carrots."

"I've been meaning to do it," replied Mrs. Cameron, "but with all the other work, I can't seem to get at it. It's hard to decide what's what after the mess that old pig made of it."

"The carrots did kind of get pushed into the onions," chuckled Mattie and then stopped, startled by the sound. Laughter feels strange, she thought. I haven't laughed since before that last day at school. Am I being disrespectful? She straightened her face into more serious lines. "That new seed we planted in June is growing good, but it'll be a month or so before it's ready. I hope we don't have an early frost."

Mattie finished her chores in the house and went out to survey the garden. It's gotten out of hand already. It's going to take me all week to get it weeded. I'll have to be cooking for extra this week too, what with Mr. Martin and his brothers helping Tommy and Momma. Her thoughts ran on as she began weeding.

It seems natural to put Tommy with the men now, he's changed so these last few weeks. Harder or something. He used to be so unformed. She tugged at a particularly stubborn piece of lady's thumb. Even Ellie's changed. She's not nearly so hard to get along with these days. Nor so lazy either. I hope it lasts.

By the end of the week, Mattie had the garden trim and neat again. She put away the hoe and stood for a moment surveying her work. The end rows were still crooked after the depredations of the pig, but the vegetables were growing strong and lush.

There now, tomorrow Ellie and I and the boys can go picking apples. That wild apple tree in the hollow's early this year, and I see there are quite a few ripe already. It'll be a few weeks yet before our own are ready to pick. I'll have to get Momma to show me how to make jelly. I'll wash the jars this evening.

She turned and trotted into the house, stopping in the porch to wash her hands and face. A low murmur of voices rose and fell in the kitchen. That sounds like Mr. Martin, she thought. A curious sense of having lived this before came to her. I wonder what he's doing here so early. They can't be finished this soon. She stopped splashing in the basin and listened. He sounds anxious. I hope nothing's happened.

"I know this is very soon, Mrs. Cameron, but I think you need to be considering what I have to say. Tommy's a good boy, and a good worker, but he's too young to run a farm of this size by himself. In a few years this land'll have all gone back to wilderness if it's not taken care of properly. It won't be long before he'll be wanting to get married and start a home of his own, and then where'll you be with Mattie and Ellie and the boys?"

Mattie could not hear her mother's response.

"Now, I know I have the reputation of being a confirmed bachelor, but I've always wanted a wife and family. I'm not rich, but I am comfortably off and I can provide for all of you. We can save this farm for Tommy so he'll have a place to bring a wife in a few years."

Again, her mother's response was inaudible.

"Mrs. Cameron, I'm not very good with fancy words, but will you have me?"

"Yes, Mr. Martin," she replied. "It'll be a good bargain."

Out in the porch Mattie stifled a gasp. Momma's going to marry Mr. Martin. Another thought followed right on the heels of the first one. He'll be my father. She tiptoed outside, careful not to let the porch door slam, then ran to the far end of the apple orchard. Her thoughts tumbled one on top of the other. A swing hung from the branches of the one chestnut tree. It swayed a little in the late afternoon breeze. Mattie climbed into the seat and began pumping her feet to send it higher and higher.

It'll seem strange calling him anything except Mr. Martin. I wonder what he'll want to be called? How will Tommy take having Mr. Martin for a father? she thought. Good, I suppose. They get along well enough now.

She swung harder, trying to out-distance her anxious thoughts. Where will I fit in the house? Maybe there won't be room for me. A stabbing sensation in her chest came with the thought. She pumped her legs harder to get away from it. Perhaps Tommy and I can stay living here in this house, and Momma and Ellie and the little ones can move over there. I wonder if he'll want me to call him Poppa? The lump that had been gone for the last few days was back in her throat and choking her. "Oh, Poppa," she whispered.

"Mattie! Mattie!" her mother's voice called. "Where are you? It's time to start supper."

Mattie sighed and gave one last hard kick to the swing. I suppose I have to go, she thought. Momma'd think it strange if I didn't appear, though I don't know how I'll face the two of them knowing what I know. She dragged her bare feet on the cool red clay to slow herself down.

In the kitchen, Mattie went about her tasks without looking at anyone. Soon supper was on the table. She was horrified when Mr. Martin sat in her father's place. Tommy looked over at her, a question in his eyes. She shrugged her shoulders and ducked her head.

"Children," said Mrs. Cameron, "Mr. Martin has asked me to marry him, and I have accepted."

The silence stretched almost to discomfort, then Tommy said, "I'm pleased to welcome you to this family, Mr. Martin." He rose from his seat and offered his hand to Mr. Martin.

So that's how it's to be, thought Mattie. What's to become of me? She swallowed hard against the persistent lump in her throat, and said, "I'm happy for you, Momma."

CHAPTER FOUR

The Camerons had prospered since Mattie's grandfather had arrived with his parents from Scotland on one of the Earl of Selkirk's vessels almost a half century before. They had left the Isle of Skye to come to a new island in a new world.

I remember Pa, thought Mattie. He always seemed to be old. I used to sit on his lap in the rocking chair and he rocked and told me stories about how he had come to the Island with his Momma and Poppa when he was thirteen. He told about how the Island had been divided into lots by the British Colonial Office and each was offered at auction to wealthy people in England for a price and the payment of the quit-rent.

Suddenly Mattie was a small child again and her grandfather's voice took up the story. "The Earl of Selkirk was one of the few buyers who took an interest in his purchase and settled three shiploads of Scottish immigrants, mainly from the Isle of Skye, on his land. He came himself to oversee the distribution of land and the initial settling of the people.

"The *Oughten* was the last of the three ships of

Lord Selkirk that landed here. The *Polly* came first, and then the *Dykes*, bearing the Earl of Selkirk, followed soon after."

The story, told in her grandfather's soft Gaelic, sent shivers of excitement over Mattie's skin. She could see, almost as plainly as if she had been aboard the *Oughten*, the line of tents along the shore, each with its campfire, and the belongings of the families stacked in untidy heaps around the dwellings. "Every household could be identified by its tartan," her grandfather said. "They were bright against the darkness of the forest that grew down to the shore. 'Tis a shame we don't wear them anymore." He sighed and fell silent.

Mattie tugged at his beard. "Tell me some more, Pa."

Her grandfather took up the story again. "The *Oughten* was almost three weeks later arriving than the others. We had already started cutting trees and building houses, for it was nearly fall and the nights were getting cool. Every day we walked through the wilderness to where we were building, men and women both. Everyone worked, even the new mothers. The older children minded the younger children. Even Aunt Cassie showed her mettle by cutting down some trees with old Jock's broad axe. She was always such a lady, don't you know.

"There were two houses almost finished, and

when the men from the *Oughten* arrived the work advanced more quickly, and we soon all had at least a roof over our heads and a fireplace. We built our houses in groups so we wouldn't be lonely and we'd never be more than a mile from help if we needed it. It was foresightful of the Earl to settle us that way for it has helped us preserve the old ways and prosper. We were well off, indeed, after the first winter. Even the first winter wasn't all that bad, for there was game in the forest and we'd each brought enough oatmeal and flour to last us until spring. We ate a lot of hare that year, and once Lochie killed a bear."

"What about the cows and the pigs and the chickens, Pa? Did they have enough to eat?"

"Och, the poor beasts, they had to fend for themselves. They all ran free in the forest and became half wild and hard to catch. In the spring when the hens started to lay again the women and children would have to go to the woods and search for their nests. And those hens were mean. They would peck you when you tried to take their eggs, some would even fly up and beat you with their wings."

"Not like now?"

"No, not like now."

They rocked in silence for some minutes. "Pa? How'd this house get built?"

"My Poppa built it for my Momma. It was made

of logs and it was right here in front of this fire that I spent my first winter in the new world. If you look in the porch you can see where the logs are still there. Of course it wasn't as big as it is now, and it wasn't shingled at first. The wind would sift through here in the dead of winter when one of those northeast gales would blow. It was enough to freeze you. All the heat seemed to go up the chimney and we'd huddle around the fire all together to keep warm. We lined the house with birch bark and shingled it the very next year. Spring seemed very far away.

"When I married your grandmother, I built her a pantry and when she had your Aunt Rebecca after the six boys, I built us the bedroom down here so that Rebecca could have our old room for herself. It wouldn't have been seemly for her to have slept in the same room with her brothers." He sighed. "They're all gone now except your Poppa."

"Where'd they go, Pa?"

Her grandfather was silent for a moment remembering the days when the house had echoed with the sound of his own children. "Rebecca and two of the boys, Ian and Murdoch, died from the fever one winter. Rebecca was only ten years old. She was such a bright little thing. Your Poppa doted on her, and she was always with him wherever he went."

Mattie counted on her fingers. "What happened to the others?"

"Angus went to the Boston States." The old man's voice held a note of pride. "He studied for the ministry. He was always a scholar."

"Is he there still, Pa?"

"Aye, and I wish I could see him once more."

"Why can't you?"

"'Tis a long way to Boston and a long way back home, but he writes."

"And what about Uncle Sandy?"

Mattie felt her grandfather's voice change. "Och, he was always a fly-by-night. Nothing like the others. He went to the west and hasn't come home. He could be dead for all I know. My heart is that heavy with his loss, for there was no need of it." He sat staring into the fire, lost in memories of his youngest son.

Mattie tugged gently at his beard. "I want to hear the rest about the house, Pa."

"Your Poppa dug the root cellar and built the porch when he married your Momma."

Mattie thought of all these stories in the days that followed, as she worked beside her mother cleaning the little house from top to bottom, then whitewashing it inside and out. New white curtains with red trim hung at all the downstairs windows, curtains that Mattie helped to make. Her mother washed and ironed her father's clothing and folded it into a neat parcel.

"Mattie, I want you to carry these over to the Johnsons' on the other side of the lot. You know where they live. They're too small for Tommy or for Mr. Martin."

"Do I have to Momma?" Mattie hunched her shoulders and held her breath. Her mother's wrath was not long in coming.

"Do as you're told, and none of your whining. Mrs. Johnson'll be glad to have these, there's still plenty of wear in them."

"But they're Poppa's."

"I know they are, it was me that made them for him, but he's dead now and we have to go on." Mrs. Cameron thrust the package into Mattie's hands.

Mattie looked at her mother with wide eyes darkened with pain. "But Momma …"

"That's enough Mattie. I know you miss him. I do too, but that's the way things are. The Lord giveth and the Lord taketh away, and we must be strong as He gives us strength. Now go."

Mattie trudged over to the other side of the lot with the package under her arm, and rebellion in her heart. The path through the spruce woods was sweet with the smell of sap and ferns. A squirrel chattered and scolded from somewhere overhead and in the near distance a locust buzzed in the still heat of the August afternoon. She made the walk last as long as she could, the red path cool beneath her reluctant feet.

Momma'll be mad at me again if I'm late back, but I don't care. She shouldn't be giving Poppa's clothes away. It isn't right.

"Would you want Mr. Martin to be wearing them, then?" The thought popped into her head as clearly as if someone had spoken it.

"NO!" She shouted the response aloud and began to run. She ran until the stitch in her side was so painful she was forced to stop. She sat down beneath a birch tree gasping for breath, and leaned back, resting her head against the slender white trunk.

Why don't I just throw these away? Momma'd never know that I didn't take them over there. Then no one would be able to wear them. Not Mr. Martin, and not Mr. Johnson, nor any of his awful children.

Be sure your sins will find you out. Her mother's tones echoed in her mind.

Mattie tried to ignore her conscience. If I just toss this behind these bushes no one'll ever know. And if I stay out here long enough, Momma'll think I took them all the way over to the Johnsons'.

She hefted the package and measured the distance to the spruce trees with her eyes. Her arm felt like lead and there was a knot in the pit of her stomach. What'll I tell Momma if she asks me about them? If I lie to her, she'll be able to tell. She always can. Mattie hefted the package again. I'll probably get the switch, but I don't care.

She tossed the bundle toward the little stand of new spruces. It missed and landed in front of the nearest one and lay there like an accusation.

She scrambled to her feet and picked it up. She raised the bundle again to throw it behind the bushes.

What would Poppa say? she thought. Her arm lowered, followed by her head, and she turned away, squashing the bundle beneath her right elbow. "I don't care if they do get wrinkled," she muttered toward the ground, and stomped away.

Mrs. Johnson wiped her hands on her grime-stiffened apron and opened the package. She was a woman of many children and few neighbours. "Come in, dearie. It's awful kind of your momma to think of us and send over these lovely shirts." She opened the bundle farther. "Oh, look. Underwear and trousers too. He'll be that pleased to have these, and in such good condition. Lots of wear left."

Mattie entered and stood just inside the door to the tiny house. As her eyes adjusted to the darkness within, she stared about in horror. The newly awakened housewife in her was appalled. A small fire burned dimly in the fireplace, and the hearth was unswept. Dirty dishes, not one of which seemed to be without a crack or a chip, covered the top of the rickety table, and there appeared to be a film of dust over everything. An odour of decay wafted upwards from the hard-packed clay floor. A grubby child in soggy diapers toddled up to her, raising its arms to be picked up. Mrs. Johnson scooped him up and nuzzled his sticky grey neck. "This is my youngest. The others are out with their father somewhere."

Momma would never let us go around like this, and she'd be ashamed to have anyone see her house in such condition, thought Mattie.

"Will you stop for a cup of tea, dearie?" Mrs. Johnson asked.

"No, thank you, Mrs. Johnson." Mattie prevented the lurch of her stomach from reaching her mouth. "Momma said to come straight home."

"I guess she's pretty busy, what with gettin' married again and all. She's lucky that she found a man so quick, and her with all those children. A good man he is, too. You're a lucky girl to have such a good man to be your Poppa. Of course, that's not to say that your own Poppa wasn't a good man. No, sir. One of the best, he was."

Mattie eyes filled with tears. "I have to go now,

Mrs. Johnson." She turned and almost ran from the house and out of the yard, setting the mangy, nondescript brown dog barking. He ran with her to the gate, his slobbery tongue hanging from the side of his mouth, and his tail wagging in delight to have someone to play with, if only for a moment. At the edge of the yard his tail drooped and he sat down on his haunches and watched her until she was hidden by the trees down the road.

How could Momma just hand over Poppa's good clothes to that woman, Mattie wondered when she had stopped running. He's only been buried a month. The tears threatened again. I don't know what I'll do when I see those dirty little Johnsons in Poppa's shirts.

She dawdled along the path toward home, mourning her father and longing for the old days. "It's just not fair," she sobbed, "everything's changed." That Mr. Martin. It's just not fair. Her grief returned in full force. She thought back to yesterday.

"Mattie, I want you to run over to Mrs. MacNeil's with this basket of blueberries, and mind you, wait for the basket," her mother had said after dinner. "She was saying how much she enjoys them but her rheumatism won't let her bend long enough to pick any amount anymore."

"Will you bring back that length of rope Mr. MacNeil said he had for me?" asked Mr. Martin. He filled his pipe and took an experimental draw on the unlit tobacco. "I meant to get it before this, but I've been too busy." He struck a match and settled the pipe more firmly between his teeth. "That well rope needs replacing soon, or we'll be losing a good bucket down there."

Mattie sighed hugely and picked up the basket of blueberries. She gave a sullen look out the corner of her eye at Mr. Martin, and went out the door.

"Mattie! You come back here!"

Mattie returned to the kitchen and stared at the floor. "Yes, Momma?"

"You answer when you're spoken to, like you've been taught. You know better than to be rude to your elders. Now, apologize to Mr. Martin."

Mattie looked at a spot on the wall behind Mr. Martin's right ear. "I beg your pardon."

"Sir!" interjected her mother.

"I beg your pardon, sir," repeated Mattie, still staring at the wall behind his head.

"Pardon granted, Mattie," said Mr. Martin.

"And I don't want to hear any more rudeness from you," said her mother. "Go on now, and don't take all afternoon."

Mattie turned on her heel and hurried out of the kitchen. Mr. Martin followed her.

"You know Mattie," he said, "I'm not trying to take your Poppa's place. Your Momma needs a husband, and I need a wife, and it's very fortunate that we're both here at the same time."

Mattie struggled to keep the tears from overflowing. She glowered at him, shrugged one shoulder, and turned away from him. "Fortunate for you, maybe," she muttered under her breath.

He sighed and said softly to her stubborn little back, "You know, it'll work out in the end."

Mattie pushed the troublesome incident out of her mind. It's not fair. She could feel her determination slipping. She quickened her pace. It's not fair. Oh, Poppa, why'd you have to go and die?

The scene over the well rope, and others like it, replayed themselves in her head. He really is trying, her conscience reminded her. Her determination took another dip downward. She marched along faster than ever. Her mother's scolding voice came back to her. "You know better than to be rude to your elders." Mattie squirmed. He's going to move into our house, she thought. And Momma never even asked us if we minded. It's not fair. I don't know how I'll be able to stand seeing him in Poppa's place. I don't know how Momma can stand it either. Momma's looking awful happy, for a new widow. It isn't decent.

She sat down on a stump at the end of the back lane and propped her chin in her hands. She stared at the ground watching a colony of ants building their nest. She put out one bare toe and disrupted the anthill to see how long it would take the ants to build it again. She sat contemplating the ants and the unfairness of life for so long that her mother sent Tommy out to look for her.

"Mattie!" Tommy called from some way away when he saw her. "Momma's looking for you, and she's gettin' savage. She said you should've been back long ago. Where were you?" He hastened up to her and sat down on the ground to catch his breath.

"Just here."

"What's the matter with you?"

"I miss Poppa, and I don't want Momma to get married again, and I don't want that man to move into Poppa's place, and everything's all changed, and I hate it." She set her face into a stubborn scowl, but the tears that had been lurking all afternoon spilled over in a veritable flood.

Tommy rooted in his pocket for his handkerchief. "Here Mattie, it's not clean but it's better than nothin'." He handed the crumpled item over to her, then leaned back on his elbows and waited for the flood to stop.

Mattie blew her nose and mopped at her face. "How can you stand it, Tommy?"

"I stand it because I have to, and Mr. Martin's a good man. He'll take care of Momma and the little ones as if they were all his own. It's really not so bad once you make up your mind to how it's going to be."

"How can Momma be so happy?"

"She's a very fortunate woman to have found someone so quickly. Some women have to struggle by themselves for a long time. Of course, she's a very eligible widow even with all us children. Now you know that."

"But why so soon? And why does he have to move in with us, and sleep in Poppa's bed and sit at Poppa's place at the table?"

Tommy answered her last question first. "He's moving in with us because we have the biggest house. All of us won't fit into his little house, and married couples share a bed, and where else would he sit at the table? It's the only place left. And he's moving in so soon because it's nearly fall, and if they don't do it now, they'll have to wait 'til spring, and there's the winter to get through, and since they're going to do it anyway, what's the point of waiting?" He stopped for breath.

"But how can you stand having him come in and just take over?"

"Look, Mattie, I'm happy to have him do that. I can't do it myself. That month of trying to keep things going with just Momma's help showed me that. I don't know enough yet, and neither does Momma. Besides, he hasn't just taken over. He always asks me what I want to do."

"Very clever of him."

"Yes, it is, and very considerate too, and it's about time you started to look at it from another point of view besides your own."

"What other one is there?" Mattie sniffed back another spate of tears.

"Oh, Mattie, dry up will you? Momma's point of view, of course. You and I aren't going to be here forever, you know that. We'll both get married and move somewhere else, and then who'll she have to help her? Ellie?"

Mattie gave a watery chuckle at the vision of Ellie working the farm. "That's easy for you to say, you're going to get the farm in the end anyway."

"I don't think so," replied Tommy. "Why should I?"

"Because I heard them talking about it."

"When'd you hear that?"

"The day that he proposed to her. I was in the porch washing up after weeding the garden, and I heard it all. He had it all figured out. He knew just the things to say to convince Momma. He said that if she'd marry him that they would save the farm for when you got married, otherwise it would go back to woods because right now you couldn't farm well enough to look after it all."

"Well, he certainly doesn't need to do that, does he? Besides, he's right, I can't do it by myself, and all Poppa's work would have been in vain."

"I could have helped you." Mattie scrubbed at her nose with the sleeve of her dress.

Tommy sighed in exasperation. "Grow up, will you, Mattie. You couldn't help me any more than Momma can, and it wouldn't last forever anyway. In a few years you'll be getting married and starting a home of your own."

"No, I won't." Mattie suddenly remembered the whole mysterious business of having babies.

"Yes, you will," insisted Tommy, "and sooner rather than later. Come on now, Momma's going to be sending a search party out for me too, if we don't get back soon."

Mattie mulled over the problem as presented to her by Tommy for the rest of the afternoon, and things began to take on a new meaning.

Mr. Martin was always nice to me when Poppa was alive, she reminded herself. He seems to really like William and Johnny, and he doesn't take anything off Ellie either. She tried hard to be pleasant at supper that evening.

But I can't call him Poppa, she thought, as she swept the floor after supper.

The change in her behaviour was noticed by her mother, and in a rare moment of privacy after the supper dishes were washed and put away she said, "So, are you feeling better now?"

"Yes, Momma." Mattie stopped sweeping and stood looking at her mother. "Momma, what'll happen to me once Mr. Martin moves in for good?"

Her mother stopped working on the sock she was knitting and looked at Mattie. "Why, you'll stay here with the rest of us. What else?"

"I don't know." Mattie began sweeping again as she remembered the way she had been acting since Mr. Martin had proposed to her mother. Maybe I don't deserve to stay here. She took a hard stroke of the broom and scattered the pile of wood chips, dust and ashes that she had just finished piling. I do so! It's him that doesn't belong.

"How can you marry so soon after Poppa?"

"It's what your father wanted." Mrs. Cameron's hands took up the rhythm of her work again.

"How can you know that?" Mattie stood with one hand on the broom and the other on her hip and scowled at her mother.

"Because he told me." Mrs. Cameron changed needles and continued knitting across the heel.

"When? When did he tell you a thing like that?"

Mrs. Cameron pursed her lips. "The night before he died. He was rational just long enough to tell me that he owed Norman two shillings for some seed he bought, and to marry again immediately."

"But why Mr. Martin?"

"Would you rather I married a stranger? Besides,

your father said it should be either him or Robert West."

"He really said that?" Mattie's stance lost its aggressiveness.

"He really said that," replied Mrs. Cameron. "In fact those were his last sane words to me."

Mattie sighed and began sweeping again. "I guess it has to be that way then, doesn't it. It being his dying wish and all."

The summer days continued long and sunny, just right for the harvest. Tommy worked with the men, thereby proving himself in the world without a doubt. Mrs. Cameron was free to take over the running of the household from Mattie again. After her chores were done, Mattie spent her days taking care of William and Johnny.

"Cows, cows," intoned Johnny, reaching his chubby hand toward the three cows in the pasture.

"No cows, they'll hook you." Mattie shifted his weight onto her other hip.

"No, I want cows," complained Johnny.

"You heard what Mattie said." William, at seven nearly eight, sounded very like his father used to. It brought a catch to Mattie's voice.

She cleared her throat. "Let's go see the calf instead."

"Calf. I want to see the calf." He squirmed out

of Mattie's arms and ran toward the barn. Mattie followed him into the sweet dimness.

"Can we take her outside, Mattie?" William stuck his feet through the bottom slat of the calf pen and hoisted himself up high enough to look over the top. "I heard Poppa say the other day that she was almost ready to be put out to pasture."

So it's Poppa already, thought Mattie. "What else did Mr. Martin say?"

"He said that he thought that he'd put her out on the home field where they've already finished cutting the hay." William climbed up another board and leaned over the edge of the pen to scratch the calf's ears.

"I see," said Mattie. "Well, I guess it'll be all right. Where's her rope?"

"Here." Johnny picked up a scrap of rope from the corner of the barn floor and stretched up tippy-toe to hand it to Mattie.

Mattie laughed. "No, silly, that's not nearly long enough. It won't even go around her neck, never mind make a good lead." She rummaged through a variety of ropes hanging from a peg on the barn wall and found one of a more appropriate length.

"There, that's better. Now she won't get away."

"Can I open the gate now?" William scrambled down from the edge of the pen.

"I want to lead her," said Johnny.

"You can help me lead her," agreed Mattie, "and

you can open the gate, William. Then run ahead and open the field gate."

Together they trooped across the barnyard leading the calf on the rope. She went tamely enough, given that this was her first time to be led, and her first time out of doors.

The home field was not large, and occupied the space directly across the fence from the back door of the house. It was shaded at the far end by two chestnut trees. Beside the chestnut trees the new mown hay had been piled into a plump yellow stack. The calf sniffed the air, took a few trial leaps then went gambolling away over the stubble. When it had exhausted its exuberance it nibbled at a wisp of hay lying on the ground, and found it to its liking. It began to graze.

"We'll have to fill the water trough for her," said Mattie. "That hay's pretty dry, and she'll soon need a drink. I'll bail, William, and you can carry the bucket and fill the trough. Johnny, you go and clean out the pen, and put down a nice bed of fresh straw for when we bring her back in."

I wonder how he'll do? thought Mattie. She watched Johnny trot manfully toward the barn, his hands in his pockets as he had seen Norman do. Mattie went to the well, dropped the bucket over the edge and listened for the splash. It came after a moment, for the well was not very deep. She cranked up bucket after bucket of water to fill the trough. William lost almost half of the water with each trip.

"Can we stop now, Mattie? I'm tired."

"So'm I," said Mattie dragging one more bucket of water over the well curb. "Let's see how full you've got it now." She picked up the full bucket and lugged it to the trough. "That's pretty good. She won't need that much to drink this afternoon." She poured in the remaining water. "Let's go and see how Johnny's getting along."

Johnny still struggled with the manure fork. "I piled it all in one spot, Mattie." He scooped up a forkful of manure and started toward the hatch with it. The load fell off half way there. He scraped it back to the pile in the middle of the pen.

"D'you want me to finish this for you?" asked Mattie.

Johnny shook his head. "The calf's mine, Poppa said. So I have to look after her." He continued working.

Alright," said Mattie, "but try taking smaller loads. We'll be over on the swing when you're finished."

Mattie spent a long time pushing William on the swing. The rhythm of the strokes brought some peace to her heart. The afternoon was warm and still. The locusts sawed away fitfully, their noise a pleasant accompaniment to the day. It was some time before she realized that Johnny hadn't joined them.

"We'd better go check on Johnny, he should be through cleaning that pen by now." Mattie hurried off to the barn with William a few paces behind her.

"Johnny? Are you still here?" she asked as her eyes adjusted to the darkness. Only the rustle of an escaping mouse answered her. The pen was empty, the new layer of straw smelled clean and fresh.

"He's certainly done a good job. Now, where could he have gotten to?" she wondered aloud. "Johnny! Johnny!" she called as she searched through the stalls and the storage room behind. She climbed into the hayloft where only dust and cobwebs and the first layer of new hay were to be found. She hurried out of the barn. "William. Come help me find Johnny."

Together they searched the farmyard over, looking in all the holes and spaces that had provided them with refuge during their games of hide and go seek. Johnny was not there.

"William, go down the lane and see if he's wandered down there. I'm going to go and search in the woods." Mattie hurried away into the cool shadows of the woodlot.

"Johnny! Johnny!" she called. Her voice was lost in the branches of the maple trees. Somewhere high up in the green branches a squirrel chirred at her for disturbing the peace. Except for that, the woods were silent, the birds having flown away at Mattie's noisy passage. Where could he be? He can't just have disappeared into thin air. "Johnny! Johnny!" She hurried on past the clearing where her father had cut last year's wood. Already it was green with new growth. Oh, Johnny, where are you?

She circled back to the farmyard and hurried once more across the yard past the well. The well cover was ajar. The well! I know I closed it. I wonder if he tried to draw water for the calf and fell in? "Oh, no," she moaned aloud. "Little Johnny!" She lifted the cover and shouted down the well. "Johnny! Johnny!" His name echoed from the shadowy depths, but there was no answer. A faint reflection of white showed against the dark water.

She slammed down the well cover and raced to the house, bursting into the kitchen. "Momma! Momma! Johnny's down the well and he doesn't answer."

Her mother's hands stilled at their task. "Go get Mr. Martin!" She dropped the darning she had been doing into the basket.

Mattie flew to the back fields. "Poppa! Poppa!"

"What's the matter Mattie? Is it your mother?"

"It's Johnny. He's down the well and he doesn't answer."

"Oh, my God!" said Mr. Martin. It was a prayer. He broke into a run, followed closely by Tommy and Mattie.

"Has he answered yet, Mary?" He peered over the edge of the well.

"I've called and called, and he doesn't even move." Mrs. Cameron's voice was sharp with fear.

Mr. Martin began removing the bucket from the rope. He tested the rope for strength, thankful that it was the new one. "This should hold me. I'm going down." He pulled off his shoes and swung his legs over the well curb. "Tommy, you take hold of the windlass and let me down easy."

"Yes, sir." Tommy grabbed the windlass and braced his feet against the well curb.

Mr. Martin squirmed over the side holding onto the rope. "I'll brace my feet on the sides as I go down so you won't have to hold on so hard."

"Oh, hurry! Hurry!" cried Mattie.

Mr. Martin eased his way down the narrow space until his broad shoulders stuck at the top. "Drat! I can't get through here, I'm too big. Can you do it, Tommy?" He squirmed his way out again.

"I can try, sir." He took his place on the edge of the well and slipped over the side. "I can't go any farther." His voice echoed inside the well. "I'm coming up." In a moment his head appeared at the hole. "I can get down almost all the way, but I can't move once I get down there. There's no room for me to bend over."

"Let me try," begged William. "I'm little enough, and I'm not scared."

Mr. Martin looked over at Mary. "What d'you think, Mary? He's your son."

Mrs. Cameron nodded. "Let him go. Just don't drop him." She closed her eyes. "I couldn't bear to lose a third one."

"I'm going to tie the rope to you," he said to William. "If you get in trouble or get scared just holler, and I'll wind you back up."

"Yes, sir."

"Are you ready?"

"Yes, sir." His eyes were enormous with excitement.

"Hold onto the rope, too." Mr. Martin lifted William over the edge of the well and carefully wound him down to the bottom. A few moments later William could be heard splashing about in the water. "Is he down there?"

"I can't find him." William's voice echoed from the depths.

"Look again," shouted Mr. Martin. This was followed by more splashing.

"He's not here."

"Can you reach the bottom?"

"Yes." William splashed around some more. "It's not very deep, but it's awful cold. He's not here. Can I come up now?"

"Hold on then," shouted Mr. Martin. "I'll have you up in jig time." He wound the dripping William out of the well.

"I c-could see the s-stars," said William through chattering teeth.

"You're sure he wasn't down there?" asked Mr. Martin.

William shook his head. "There's nothing down there except the bucket that Momma knocked in last spring, and the water's only up to here." He indicated the high water mark on his chest.

"Where is he then?" asked Mattie. "We've searched everywhere."

"Go in and put dry clothes on, William," ordered Mrs. Cameron. "The rest of you look some more."

They searched again through all the buildings, and the woods.

"Where could he have gotten to?" said Mattie. "There's nowhere else to look. He wouldn't have gone over to Mrs. MacNeil's, would he? He likes her pretty well."

"He doesn't know the way," replied her mother.

"The calf!" exclaimed Mattie.

"What about the calf?"

"We put her in the home field this afternoon, and you know what a pet Johnny makes of her. I don't see her in the field just now, I wonder if she's behind the haystack in the shade, and if Johnny's with her?"

She broke into a run. Her mother gathered up her skirts and hurried after her. They rounded the haystack together to find the calf asleep in the shade, and Johnny curled up between the its front and hind legs with his blonde head on the calf's belly. A wisp of hay was tucked behind one ear as he had seen Mr. Martin do for fun, and his thumb was in his mouth.

"Oh, the darling," said Mattie, her anxiety of the past two hours forgotten. "He was exhausted from cleaning out the calf's pen."

"That young imp. All the trouble he's caused." Mrs. Cameron bent down to pick up the sleeping Johnny.

"Now Momma, it wasn't really his fault, you know. He was just tired."

"And you. You were supposed to be looking after him."

"Now Mary, don't be too hard on Mattie, she's had enough punishment today, and it was only an accident that he disappeared like that. It's easy enough to do."

Mattie looked at Mr. Martin in wonderment.

"Accident? Accident!" exclaimed Mrs. Cameron. "He could have been drowned."

"Not in the well, he couldn't have," replied Mr. Martin. "He's too short to climb over the well curb, and if we'd been thinking straight, we'd have seen that immediately."

"Well, if Mattie had been doing what she was supposed to, none of this would have happened." She turned toward the house cradling a still drowsy Johnny.

"Just like you were when you knocked the bucket down the well?" he asked.

"Oh!" Mrs. Cameron stomped away over the field.

"Thank you for taking my part, Mr. Martin," said Mattie.

"You're very welcome, Mattie. You know your Momma's only letting off steam, don't you?"

"Yes, sir," replied Mattie. "That's how she does it most of the time."

They walked toward the house together. "May I call you Norman?" asked Mattie after a long silence.

"You may that," agreed Mr. Martin.

Chapter Five

The late summer morning was already hot and waiting. Three shepherd's clouds floated across the royal blue sky. A locust sawed from somewhere nearby, and from the distance the voices of the men at work in the fields drifted on the warm noontime air.

"Mattie! Mattie! Hurry up." William was hopping with impatience.

"Gu-um. Gu-um. We're going to get some gu-um." Johnny turned on his heel in a circle, digging a small trench in the patch of pink sand to pass the time. "Gu-um. Gu-um. We're going to get some gu-um."

The screen door bounced on its spring behind her as Mattie ran out to join William and Johnny under the spruce trees.

"Here she comes." William turned a cartwheel.

"Don't make so much noise, you'll scare the crows." Mattie hitched up her skirts. "Y'know this is the last year I'll be able to do this for you. I'll be sixteen next year and I'll be a grownup then. I won't be able to climb trees anymore. Momma doesn't want me to be doing it now." I can still hear her on the subject from the last time she caught me up there, she thought.

"Next year I can climb," said Johnny. "My legs be long enough, they be almost long enough now." He stuck one chubby, tanned leg out for Mattie's inspection.

"That's a fine leg, and next year it'll be able to climb to the top of the tree."

Mattie tucked her petticoats into the waistband of her apron, and began to climb. "I'm going after that big drop by the last big branch," she called. Her mouth watered and she swallowed hard.

That gum's been there for a long time, she thought. It should be good and ripe by now. She swallowed again, imagining its pungent perfection. She paused for a moment to catch her breath and to plan her next step. If I miss, it's a long way to the ground.

She reached her goal, hot and flushed, with sticky hands and bits of spruce twigs decorating her long braid. She pulled off the piece of gum and dropped it to the eager hands below. It was much larger than she had anticipated.

She looked up then, to take one last look around from her favourite vantage point. There hasn't been much time for climbing here this summer, and I likely won't be able to climb here again.

From this height she could see all across the farm. Below her was the barnyard, its grass worn down to the red clay from years of use.

The house looks so small from up here. It's hard to believe we all fit in it, she thought.

Her gaze took in the garden with its crooked rows where the pig had rooted. The plants were still smaller at that end. Beside the house was the home field where Johnny had fallen asleep with the calf just the other day. She looked out over the woods where the maples and the birches grew. They look just like big green pillows, she thought.

The path to the back of the lot wandered in and out among them. All the way to the Johnsons', she thought with a pang. The narrow fields, newly harvested, stretched as far back as she could see. She turned her head and gazed down the lane toward the track. A movement behind the little rise at the end of the lane caught her eye.

There's someone coming. She waited, watching until the distant figure came into view again. It must be important, he's wearing his Sunday hat. Hardly anyone visits us during the week. The hatted figure came closer. It must be someone for Norman, for I certainly don't recognize him.

The stranger strode steadily up the lane. He's a handsome one, she thought taking in the height and the breadth of him, then blushed at the unaccustomed turn of her thoughts. That's something Cora'd likely say, she scolded herself. Not a fit thought for a good girl. She continued to watch the stranger with curiosity. A bushy black beard hid most of his face, and the brim of his hat shaded the rest. He knocked on the screen door, and presently her mother came out to greet him and invite him into the house.

Mattie lost herself again in her surroundings, gazing about at the glorious August day. From here she could see the Northumberland Strait, its blue water sparkling and shining through the gap in Mr. West's woods. On the horizon lay the silhouette of Nova Scotia purpled by the distance across the Strait. The air carried a tang of salt with it, richly overlaid with the spicy green smell of spruce.

Her thoughts turned again to Cora. Mattie frowned thinking of the visit Cora had made just last week. I don't know what it is about her these days, she makes me so uneasy. She's not like the old Cora anymore. Mattie's frown deepened. She's turned into such a tease, and she's no fun anymore. I used to be able to talk to her, but now all she wants to talk about is boys and getting married and having babies.

Cora had breezed in about mid-afternoon to tell Mattie about her adventures in Charlottetown. She was carrying a parasol. Mattie had stared at her with wondering eyes.

"D'you like it? All the girls carry them in town. It protects their skin from the sun." Cora twirled the dainty pink sunshade on its handle for Mattie's benefit, and neglected to mention that all the girls were only Susan, the little girl who lived next door to her sister's house.

Mattie continued to stare at Cora, taking in all the changes that had been wrought in only a few weeks.

"Well, d'you like it?"

"I-it's very nice. You've put your hair up."

"Yes, Momma said I could while we were in town. It was so hot, I just had to get it off my neck. She said I was to take it down when we came home."

"But I see you didn't."

"Well-l-l, I did, but I wanted you to see it, so I told Momma that I was going to come over here and show you my new parasol, and I borrowed some hairpins from her dresser and put it up on the way over here. Is it up straight? I only had the brook to look in and I couldn't see very well."

"It's up straight. I suppose you're going to do that every time you're away from home now, are you?"

Cora simpered. "I just might do that. Momma'd never know."

"Not unless someone tells her."

"They'll be quick enough to do that, the old biddies."

"You look like a child playing dress-up." Mattie

inspected Cora's appearance. "Is that a new dress too?"

Cora nodded. "My sister had it made for me for my birthday. It's the latest from England. She copied it from a magazine that was only five months old and had the dress-maker make it for me."

"Ian must be doing well. That's a fine dress."

"Well enough. You should see their house, it has all the latest furniture. The living room is simply elegant. Here, d'you want to hold my parasol?" She thrust the handle toward Mattie.

Mattie backed away. "My hands are dirty, and besides I might break it. Come in and greet Momma, she'll be interested to see your new finery."

Cora hopped a few steps beside Mattie, then winced.

"Are your shoes hurting you?" asked Mattie. "You must be near roasted with stockings on, on a day like this."

"I got used to wearing them in town. You can't go bare-foot there." She hobbled a few more steps.

"Well, you're not in town now, so why don't you take them off?"

Cora scowled at Mattie. "It'd spoil my outfit, and besides you never know when you might meet a handsome boy and you want to look your best."

Mattie stared at her friend, as she mentally

inventoried the boys of their acquaintance. "I suppose so," she replied, "though I think your efforts'll be wasted on the likes of Danny and Sam and Willie."

"Oh, Mattie! I'm not interested in those children. Danny's nose is always running and he never has a handkerchief, Sam hiccups all the time, and stutters when he has to talk to a girl. And Willie! They don't call him Wee Willie for nothing. All those freckles and red hair. Can you imagine being married to any of those?" She hobbled a few steps farther.

"I see," said Mattie, "So you're out to get a husband are you?"

"Well, isn't everyone? Aren't you? Darn, I can't stand these shoes a minute longer." She sat down on the chopping block beside the woodpile with a thump, unbuttoned her shoes and took them off, then began peeling off her stockings.

Tommy's merry whistle stopped in mid-note as he came around the corner of the woodshed and took in Cora's toilette. He blushed as Cora scrambled to her bare feet.

"Hello, Cora. You're back are you?"

Cora batted her eyelashes. "We got back yesterday." She moved over to stand closer to Tommy and took his arm, thereby excluding Mattie from the conversation. "It's been so long since I've seen you."

"It was just last month in church." Tommy removed his arm from her grasp. "Is this the style in Charlottetown, then? Fancy dresses and umbrellas and bare feet?"

"Oh, you!" Cora turned on her bare heels and began stomping away across the barnyard.

"You forgot your shoes," called Mattie. She hurried after Cora, just as Tommy's chuckle came forth from his retreat in the barn.

It really had been quite funny, thought Mattie as she gazed toward Cora's house hidden by distance and trees. And that thistle she stepped on! I had a hard time to keep from laughing too. A chuckle escaped Mattie now.

"Mattie is that you up there? Get yourself down here at once." Her mother's angry voice at the foot of the tree startled her out of her reverie.

Oh, dear, I was hoping she wouldn't catch me. That's what I get for not paying attention. Mattie climbed down, acquiring a few more twigs in her hair and a three-cornered tear in the hem of her skirt in the descent.

"Just look at yourself. You look like a heathen. You should be ashamed of yourself, behaving like this at your age. Go and tidy yourself at once. Mr. Matheson wants to speak to you. Put on your Sunday dress."

So that's who it is, thought Mattie as she climbed

the stairs to the sleeping loft. Mr. MacDonald did say he'd be coming by sometime. I wonder what he wants with me? There was a funny fluttery feeling in her stomach and a strange ache of foreboding in her throat.

She splashed water into the china basin and washed her hands and face. She couldn't get all of the balsam off, her hands were still sticky in spots. She combed the twigs out of her hair and rebraided it. Wearing her Sunday dress made her feel better for a moment. The dress was dark blue and seemed to make her eyes more blue and sparkly in the sunlight.

Momma dyed this for me when she made it, and for once she didn't scold me for being prideful. It was a real surprise. Momma just opened her mouth to say something and then closed it again without a word and began filling the dye pot. That was last spring. It's getting tight on me now. Should I wear my shoes? I guess not. I'd better hurry before Momma yells at me. Her bare feet seemed glued to the floor and she came down the stairs slowly.

Mr. Matheson stood up as she entered the kitchen. The gesture unnerved her. Gentlemen only stand for grown-up women, not for children like me, she thought.

"Mr. Matheson has come for you. He wants to marry you today," said her mother.

The room tipped and swayed, then steadied. Mattie paled, then flushed. No! No! She can't mean it. Mattie was speechless.

"You'd better gather together the things you'll need for a few days. I'll bring the rest to church on Sunday," her mother was saying.

Mattie seemed to hear her from a long way away. "No!" she gasped, and turned and ran from the room. Where can I hide? Her eyes searched the familiar barnyard. The hay loft!

Her bare feet carried her swiftly across the yard. She hitched up her skirts and scrambled up the ladder into the sweet-smelling cobwebby darkness. Her heart pounded in her ears.

Marry Mr. Matheson? Whatever can they be thinking of? She waded through the new hay to the far end of the loft and buried herself in it. I don't even wear long skirts yet. Mr. Matheson and his big black beard that hides his whole face? How can they even think it? Her anxiety turned to fear. She tried to draw a deep breath and could not. I can't marry him. I just can't. I don't even know him.

"Mattie! Mattie!" The familiar anger began in her mother's voice. "Where are you, Mattie?"

Mattie sneezed.

"Is that you up there, Mattie?"

Mattie swallowed hard against the lump in her throat. "Yes, Momma."

Mrs. Cameron laboured up the ladder to the loft.

"Mattie, I want you to be a good girl and go with Mr. Matheson." She settled herself in the hay beside Mattie and tried to catch her breath. "He's a good man and he'll look after you well. You'll never have a better offer, you know."

"But Momma," Mattie protested, "I'm scared. I'm only fifteen."

"Nonsense, you're a big girl now, a woman these last three years," said Mrs. Cameron. "And besides that, it's an honour for him to ask for you. I've taught you how to cook and keep house. As for the rest, he'll tell you anything you need to know. You just do as you're told."

Rest? What rest? Mattie felt the fear expand in her chest. She held on tight inside herself. I can't panic. This is only a bad dream. It'll stop soon. Oh, Poppa! Poppa! This would never have happened if you were alive. Her father's face flashed into her mind. He was smiling his gentle smile like he always did, and suddenly she felt much calmer.

Her mother's voice penetrated her hearing from a long way away. "Now go and wash your hands and face, and go with him. Ellie's packing your things."

Mattie climbed down from the loft and did as she was told. The fear still clutched at her, and her heart was heavy and rebellious. How could

Momma do this to me? She just wants to get rid of me, that's all. She and that Mr. Martin. Oh, if only I had been nicer to him, she mourned.

All that talk about calling him Norman, and everything coming out right in the end. It's all a sham. It'll come out all right for them.

I'll miss the children. Tears started to her eyes. I won't see Johnny climb the gum tree or William turn cartwheels anymore. The tears overflowed. She swabbed them away and washed her face once more. She looked at her reflection in the wobbly glass of the mirror and stuck out her chin.

"I'll just show them," she whispered, as another tear escaped her lashes.

She swallowed hard against the lump in her throat and went downstairs. Ellie silently handed her a small bundle tied up with string. Her mother passed her her shoes and her bonnet. Mr. Matheson took it all from her and took hold of her cold little hand. No one said anything. Ellie and the little ones were crying.

"Hush, children," her mother scolded, "you'll see her on Sunday. She won't be that far away." She shook hands with Mr. Matheson.

"I'll take good care of her," he promised, his deep voice rumbling out from somewhere inside his beard.

They walked away together down the lane. Tears ran down Mattie's cheeks, the courage from a few minutes before gone with the salt breeze from the Gulf. I haven't even been properly introduced, she thought. He's Mr. Matheson, but for the life of me, I can't remember his first name. A fresh flood of tears ran down her cheeks. She held back the sobs by sheer force of will.

"I've built us a new little house," he said after the first two miles had passed in total silence except for Mattie's sporadic sniffs and hiccups. "I hope you'll like it."

They were passing Cora's gate. and she couldn't answer him for the lump of misery that was choking her throat. She looked up the lane to the grove of trees that sheltered her friend's house. I wish Cora was here. What do I know about being married? she thought. They walked on in silence for awhile. The village might as well be a hundred miles away as only five. She had to hurry to keep up with his long stride.

Mr. Matheson made another attempt at conversation. "I'm sorry to be so abrupt about this, but I had very little choice. I've just been offered the school at Orwell Cove on a permanent basis, but it's on condition that I marry. I wanted to court you properly, but you live so far away, and I don't have a buggy."

Mattie was little comforted by this revelation. She was still too shaken by the sudden change in her affairs. They continued their walk in silence.

§

They went first to the manse. The large grassy yard used to overflow with children, those of the minister and as many of the village children who could get out from under their mothers' eagle eyes for an afternoon. The yard was empty now since the last child had grown up and married. The grass, which for so many years had been worn down by the feet of all the children, was longer now and turning gold in the late August sun. Mr. Matheson opened the narrow white gate underneath the rose trellis for Mattie and together they walked up the narrow path to the house.

He rapped on the door. Mattie looked idly about while they waited. They seem a long time coming, maybe they aren't home, she thought.

The flower beds need weeding. Her thoughts wandered on. A half grown grey and white kitten pranced around the side of the house chasing a butterfly, and came to an abrupt stop at Mattie's feet. She stooped to pick it up. The kitten rubbed its whiskers across her chin and nuzzled her ear lobe. Mattie buried her face in its soft warm fur. It smelled of hay and sunshine and rich Island clay. Mr. Matheson smiled down at her but Mattie didn't see.

The door opened, and the rumpled figure of

Mr. MacDonald stood framed there. He doesn't look any tidier at home than he ever did in school, thought Mattie.

"Ah, Mr. Matheson. And Mattie, too. So you've finally come." He opened the door a little wider. "Come in. Come in." He stood aside to let them enter. Mattie disengaged the kitten's claws from the front of her dress, and followed them into the darkness of the house.

Mr. Matheson was led away into the parlour carrying Mattie's bundle. Mrs. MacDonald took one look at Mattie's unhappy little face and put her arms around her. "Come child," she said, "marriage isn't the worst thing that can happen to a woman, and Mr. Matheson's a good, kind man." She took Mattie into the kitchen.

"I guess so, but I don't even remember his first name," she said in a small voice.

"You don't."

"I heard it once when I was first in school, and Mr. MacDonald said it a few months ago, but I don't remember it now."

"His first name's ..." she glanced at Mattie's dress. "You must have had that rascally kitten up, did you? You've got red footprints all over your dress." She bustled around the room to get a wet rag, and mopped at the front of Mattie's dress leaving large wet spots where the paw prints had been.

Mattie lifted the soggy dress away from her small bosom and twisted her chin around trying to see the spots. I s'pose it's better to have it wet than spotted, she thought just as Mr. MacDonald stuck his head around the kitchen door.

"Any time you ladies are ready," he said.

"Hurry then, child," said Mrs. MacDonald, "you don't want to keep the groom waiting."

No, thought Mattie, but I still don't know his first name.

"Will you, David, take Matilda … " intoned the minister.

So that's his name. Mattie stared down at the floor, surprised to see her bare toes peeping out from underneath the hem of her dress. I forgot to put my shoes on! A blush of mortification crept up Mattie's neck, and she hastily tucked her feet out of sight, at least from the front. I don't even wear long skirts yet, she mourned silently as the blush faded from her cheeks.

"Will you, Matilda, take David …"

"I will," she whispered. The answer seemed to stick in her throat. What else can I do?

The rest of the ceremony went by in a blur leaving Mattie with a sense of unreality. It was finally over and Mrs. MacDonald was offering them refreshment.

"Thank you, Mrs. MacDonald, we still have a long walk ahead of us," said David. "A *strupach* will be much appreciated."

Mattie's appetite had reached a new low, and she sat and pushed the food around on her plate. Home, she thought, where's that? She sighed once, but there were no more tears.

They walked down the road past the schoolhouse. Mattie looked at the yard where she had spent so many happy hours not so very long ago. The swing hung empty, swaying slightly in the cool breeze from the Northumberland Strait. It was idle now, waiting for the new crop of students in the fall. The knot in Mattie's throat seemed to grow larger and she swallowed hard against it. The slender wedding band felt tight and foreign on her balsamed little paw.

They waved to Mrs. MacRae as they passed. She was taking in her washing. She waved back cheerily and dropped the clothes peg she'd been holding in her mouth. Mattie felt a little encouraged to see someone familiar, but the feeling ebbed as soon as they passed out of sight around a bend in the track. They went by Mrs. MacLeod's house. It stood silent in the afternoon sunshine. In the distance the sound of the blacksmith's hammer rang out on the summer air, and soon they were passing the forge. Sandy, the blacksmith, bellowed a greeting and never missed a beat with his hammer, his powerful arm rising and falling to his own rhythm. The store became visible through the trees, its whitewashed shingle walls stained pink with the red island dust, the narrow porch shadowed and inviting in the heat of the day.

"I have to stop at the store for a moment," said David. "You'd better come in with me out of the sun."

"Yes, sir." Mattie cleared her throat. Something still seemed stuck in it.

He held the door for her. "My name's David, not sir," he whispered.

I can't call you David, she thought, and ducked her head to avoid his gaze. She stopped to wait for him just inside the door, her skirt barely missing the spittoon. The interior of the store caught her attention for a brief moment. I always liked to come to the store with Poppa, she thought, and stifled another sob and gazed around at the wealth of goods contained in the small space. So many things, she thought.

Boxes and tins and sacks covered every avail-able surface. Lengths of rope, and harness parts hung from the rafters. A rack of new brooms stood to the side past the cabinet with the sewing threads and needles and buttons in it. It always smells like soap and tobacco and smoke in here, she thought. John Nicholson, the storekeeper, also known as John the Store, to distinguish him from his first cousin Little John Nicholson, stood behind the counter. An orange striped cat slept on top of the small stack of plain calico on the table. Momma'd never have a cat in the house, she thought.

"Mattie!" exclaimed Cora, appearing from the shadowy interior of the store. "What're you doing in town? I haven't seen you since ..." She stopped, remembering the last time she had seen Mattie and blushed. "How's your mother and the others?"

"Fine," quavered Mattie, and gulped back a sob.

Cora put sisterly arms around her as David went to complete his errand. "Come and sit over here and tell me what's wrong." She led the way over to some nail kegs.

"I-he-Momma," sobbed Mattie.

Cora patted her shoulder. "There, there now, Mattie, everything's going to be alright soon."

After a few minutes Mattie's sobs quieted to a sniffle. She rummaged in her pocket for her handkerchief and blew her nose. She scrubbed at her tears with the sleeve of her dress.

"Now, tell me what's wrong," insisted Cora. "Why're you here by yourself, and all dressed up, too?"

"I'm not here by myself." She blew her nose and sniffed hard.

Cora frowned. "Well, who're you with?"

"M-Mr. Matheson."

"Why're you with him?"

"B-Because, I'm M-Mrs. Matheson." Mattie choked back another sob, and stared hard at the splintery floor trying to maintain her slight composure.

"Oh!" For once Cora was speechless. She took Mattie's hand and patted it awkwardly. "How? Why? When did all this happen?"

Mattie sighed deeply. The tears seemed to have stopped for the moment. "Today. He came to the house this morning and Momma sent me with him. She said that I was being honoured, and that I'd never get another offer like this, and that he was a good man. We walked here and went right to the manse and got married, and I didn't even remember his first name." Her voice wobbled as tears threatened again.

"Well, didn't I tell you that he wanted to come courting?"

Mattie glared at her.

"Have you visited enough with Cora?" asked David as he returned with his purchases. "It's time to get going again, we still have a ways to go."

Mattie straightened her face and jumped up off the nail keg. "Good-bye, Cora," she called. "Come and see me."

"Where?" asked Cora.

"I don't know," said Mattie.

§

David led her to the right, down an old lane. The trees on either side arched their branches overhead to create a green leafy tunnel through the woods. Here and there a golden leaf announced the imminent arrival of autumn. Daisies dipped and swayed in the late summer breeze, and in the low part by the brook lady slipper and cowslips bloomed.

They walked on for what seemed to Mattie like many miles, occasionally passing the cleared fields of farms, their small whitewashed house and buildings gleaming in the late afternoon sun. It feels like I'm going to a foreign country, thought Mattie. Will I ever see Momma and Ellie and the boys again? Tears threatened once more, but she swallowed hard and tucked her chin down until the feeling passed. I'd even be glad to see Norman now. The thought surprised her, and she hurried to keep up with David's long stride.

At last they came to a white gate at the end of a path. David opened the gate and held it for Mattie to pass through. The path wandered through the trees and ended soon in a cleared area. The stumps of the former trees were still rooted in the yard, their truncated remains lush with the green growth of the leaves of the new potatoes planted about their roots. The only cleared patch was the garden, where carrots, peas, parsnips, turnips and onions grew in abundance. A small shed occupied one corner of the yard, with a privy close beside it.

In the centre of the clearing stood a frame house. It was a small house, only a story and a half. Its windows were open to the summer air. It had been freshly white-washed and trimmed in red. Some yellow marigolds were growing along the foundation. Mattie stopped so abruptly that David bumped into her from behind.

"I hope you like it," said David. "I've been planning this for over a year now. The land was my father's but it went back to wilderness when he went to town to live. The house had fallen down so I had to build a new one, but at least I didn't have to dig a cellar."

Mattie managed to find her voice. "It's lovely. When did you build it?"

"As soon as the snow went in the spring and the road was dry enough to haul the lumber on," he replied. "I didn't know what kind of flowers you liked, but Mrs. Nicholson had some of these to spare so she gave them to me. I hope you like them."

"They're beautiful," said Mattie.

He opened the front door and stood aside for Mattie to enter. The kitchen occupied the whole of the first floor, but it was still a small room.

A fireplace took up most of the space of one wall. In the far corner by the fireplace narrow ladder-like stairs led upwards into the dimness of the sleeping loft. A drop-leaf wooden table and two chairs filled the other corner, and in front of the fireplace sat two rocking chairs, one large, with arms, and one smaller, without arms. A lounge with a raised head occupied the dimness of the farthest corner. Beside the fireplace a doorway led into a small pantry, really nothing more than a place to keep the dishes and the flour bin. The tiny windows allowed only a little light to pass, and the whole room seemed as dark as night to Mattie's sun-blinded eyes.

"I made all the furniture last winter and stored it in Rory's barn," he said, "and we can buy some curtain material tomorrow if you like."

"Won't that be expensive?" asked Mattie. Momma always worried about the expense, she thought, I guess I'll have to, too.

"Don't worry about that for now. I've spent very little of my earnings these past three years so I have a little put by. We can afford curtains. I worked with Murdo Campbell this summer, putting in hay, so that helped, too. My own crops didn't take long to harvest. I only have a few hens. I hope you'll like your new home."

My new home, she thought. Will I ever be able to call it home?

"I'll be needing a churn," she said, remembering for no particular reason all the butter she had made this past summer.

"There's one in the back room. Mrs. Campbell gave it to me. It needed some repair, and it's small but it'll do fine for now, I think. We don't have a cow yet, anyway."

"Poppa'll likely bring one soon," she began and then stopped. "I mean Norman." She turned away from him. "Where can I put my things?"

"Upstairs," he replied. "Take care on the steps, they're steep."

Mattie climbed the stairs and laid her bundle on the wash stand. I don't even know what's in here, she thought. Heaven knows what Ellie would have thought I needed. She began opening the package and discovered the sheets that she'd woven under her mother's direction just that spring. She felt a little comforted by Ellie's unusual thoughtfulness.

It was probably Momma who told her to put them in, though, she thought.

Her two play dresses, her comb, her nightgown, a piece of hard soap, and a towel, made up the rest of the bundle. She made up the bed, hung the towel on the bar of the wash stand and laid her comb and the soap in a neat row beside the basin. She changed back into her everyday dress and set her shoes side by side beneath the washstand.

She hung her nightgown and her good dress on the hook behind the door beside David's Sunday shirt, then turned and surveyed the bare little room. A coolness seemed to cross her skin even though the loft was still hot from the heat of the sun. She shivered, then turned and hurried down the stairs.

"Shall I make us some supper?" She scrabbled about on the mantle shelf for the matches.

He took them from her and bent to light the fire. "Mrs. MacLeod sent us a pie this morning. It's in the pantry. There's milk and eggs and butter and some other things too. Mrs. Gillis sent over a loaf of bread." He showed her the hatchway to the cellar where everything was kept cool, then left her to her preparations and her thoughts.

So he's been planning this for a year, thought Mattie. It seems that everyone but me knew we were getting married. She sliced bacon and scrambled eggs and presently had a pleasant little supper ready for them, hardly a bite of which she tasted.

After supper they sat on the front steps. Mattie hugged her knees and sat as far away from David as possible, her thoughts in a turmoil. David puffed on his pipe. The smoke from it kept the black flies away.

"I want to build a front porch on here someday. Then we can have a swing. It'll be real pleasant on summer evenings," he said.

The light faded from the sky and a sliver of moon rose over the fir trees at the end of the lane. "Almost time for bed," David announced, knocking the ashes from his pipe against the sandstone step. He led the way into the kitchen and lighted a candle, then took down the Bible from the shelf. "We'll begin as we mean to go on." He selected a passage and began to read.

His voice rose and fell over the solemn passages. The soft musicality of the Gaelic slid gently from his tongue.

Mattie's mind refused to follow. How can I share a bed with this man? The enormity of her new status loomed larger and larger in her mind. She rubbed her stomach. I think I'm going to be sick.

David finished the reading and replaced the Bible on the shelf. Mattie rose and climbed the stairs. Her feet felt like lead. She made her toilette quickly, put on her nightgown, and rebraided her hair into its habitual night-time plait.

"Do you have to braid your hair like that?" he asked gently, appearing suddenly at the top of the narrow stairs. "I'd like to see it loose."

Mattie obediently stopped braiding and began undoing the plait with clammy hands. The candle light shone on the length of it showing the red highlights among the dark brown.

David reached out a tentative hand to stroke

the shining thickness. Mattie flinched away from his touch and climbed into bed. She wriggled over to the far edge under the eaves and faced the wall, screwing her eyes shut. Presently David blew out the candle and she could feel his weight on the straw tick as he stretched out beside her. She felt very hemmed in, and not just a little uneasy. David rolled onto his side. She could feel the soft warmth of his breath on her cheek. She jumped when his hand crept around her midriff. She curled herself into a tight little ball. The hand went with her. It began stroking her in little circular motions on her belly.

Is this what the girls at school were giggling about? she wondered. I wish Momma had told me something. Mattie shivered.

"Mattie, please don't be frightened," whispered David. "I would never do anything to hurt you."

Mattie felt a large cold lump in the pit of her stomach just about where the butterflies had been. I wish I could run away. But where could I go? Momma doesn't want me. She tried to squirm away from David and knocked her knee against the eaves. She stifled a yelp of pain and lay still. Why, I can't even get out of bed. The hand continued its circular motion and David curled himself around her stiff back.

She felt herself relaxing against him. A strange warmth was seeping into her limbs, and she felt a certain softness toward him beginning somewhere in the bottom of her belly. *What's happening to me?*

The hand roamed over her body, taking ever more liberties as it went. The other hand cradled her gently as her wilful body slowly uncurled itself and turned towards him in the darkness. His beard tickled her face as he pressed kisses on her blushing cheeks. Her hands ached to touch him back. She curled them into tight fists.

I'm a good girl. Oh, Momma. Oh, Poppa.

The hand had slipped up under her nightdress and had begun stroking her bare skin. A sigh escaped her tightly pursed lips.

"Will you take off your nightgown for me?" whispered David. The hand suddenly had an owner again.

"Oh," said Mattie in surprise. The languor in her limbs held her gently as David's hand continued its stroking. *Is this what Momma meant? Did she really mean that I was to do everything?* Mattie stiffened slightly. *Oh, Momma, I don't know what to do.* Her mother's scolding voice came back to her. "You just do as you're told."

Mattie sighed and sat up, and pulled her nightgown over her head. She lay back down in the curve of David's arm, willing herself to go limp. Her legs parted of their own accord as David arranged his long body over her. She cried out at the sharpness of the pain and tried to push him away.

"It's alright, Mattie," he whispered. "It won't always be like this."

Mattie held her breath against the moving pressure of his body. Presently he grunted and relaxed onto the stiffness of her frame.

She pushed him off and rolled as far away from him as she could get. Where's my nightgown? She rummaged around over the edge of the bed for the elusive garment. How could I ever have let this happen? I'm so ashamed. I'll never be able to face him again. She found her nightgown and slipped it on over her head, unaware that it was on backwards. I'll never be able to face anyone again. Oh, Momma. Oh, Poppa. I'm so sorry. Her misery increased as she reviewed the events of the past hour. Another more frightening thought flashed into her mind, I'll never be able to go home again.

Chapter Six

The next morning Mattie awakened to the sound of crows cawing from the spruce trees at the edge of the clearing. I wonder what the children will want to do today, she thought. I suppose we could go looking for blackberries in Mr. West's woods. They should be just about ripe by now.

She opened her eyes and was confused by her unfamiliar surroundings. A beam of sunlight found its way through the tiny window in the gable and memories of yesterday, and then last night, returned.

How could I have? Why didn't Momma tell me? I've disgraced myself. She'll never forgive me. How can I tell her that I did such a thing? Mattie's skin grew hot at the thought of confessing this shameful thing to her mother. She rolled over and buried her burning face in the pillow. It smelled of David. She rolled back to her own side of the bed and covered her face with her hands. "I just can't tell her," she muttered. Her face began to cool. "I won't tell her."

Downstairs a door slammed, and the rumble

of wood tumbling into the wood box reached her ears. David! How can I face him this morning? How can I face anyone? Everyone will know. They'll all look at me and know what I've done. I'm so ashamed. Her face began to burn again and she buried it once more in the pillow, but the pain and the shame remained. She heard David's tread on the stairs.

"Good morning, sleepy head, it's time you were out of bed. The sun's been up for an hour and so have I. Time to take up your role as a wife," said David.

Mattie couldn't bring herself to look at him as she hopped out of bed and went to stand by the washstand with her back to him. She blushed hotly, and then more hotly still, when she realized that her nightgown was on back to front, a sure reminder of this thing she had done.

"What's this, what's this?" David turned her around to face him.

Mattie hung her head and closed her eyes.

"You're not embarrassed about last night, are you?"

She nodded. He pulled her into his arms where she pressed her flushed face against the soft home-spun of his shirt.

"You don't need to be embarrassed or ashamed in front of me," he said. "We're married now and we have a right to it, an obligation even. The Bible says we're to go forth and multiply, and I'll never tell anyone about your nightgown."

Mattie groaned at David's soft chuckle.

"Come then, and we'll read and then you can make us some breakfast."

Mattie hurriedly dressed, grimacing as the comb stuck in the knots in her unbraided hair. I hope he won't want me to leave it unbraided too often, she thought as she worked the knots out one by one. Finally she was tidy and she made her way downstairs.

David sat in the small rocker with the Bible open on his knees. Mattie took her place in the large rocker and folded her hands, not rocking. The fire snapped in the fireplace and the kettle sang to itself on the hob. David leafed through the New Testament stopping now and then to scan a passage. Finally he smoothed the page and announced in serious tones, "First Corinthians, seven, verses one to five." He began to read. "Now concerning the things whereof ye wrote unto me: It is good for a man not to touch a woman. Nevertheless, to avoid fornication, let every man have his own wife, and let every woman have her own husband. Let the husband render unto the wife due benevolence: and likewise also the wife unto the husband. The wife hath not power of her own body, but the husband: and likewise also the husband hath not power of his own body but the wife. Defraud ye not one the other, except it be with consent for a time, that ye may give yourselves up to fasting and prayer; and come together again, that Satan tempt you not for your incontinency."

David cleared his throat and turned back to the Old Testament. Mattie began rocking quietly in her chair.

"Proverbs thirty-one, verses ten to thirty-one. Who can find a virtuous woman? for her price is far above rubies. The heart of her husband doth safely trust in her, so that he shall have no need of spoil." Mattie watched as David's finger followed down the passage's fine print. The thin paper crackled as he turned the page. The phrases in Gaelic flowed softly from his mouth. "Her children rise up, and call her blessed; her husband also, and he praiseth her. Many daughters have done virtuously, but thou excellest them all. Favour is deceitful, and beauty is vain: but a woman that feareth the Lord, she shall be praised. Give her of the fruit of her hands: and let her own works praise her in the gates."

David closed the Bible and bowed his head. "Oh, Lord," he began, "we thank thee for our many blessings." Mattie ducked her head and squeezed her eyes shut. "Bless thou this house and may Thou see fit to protect us from harm." David's voice rose and fell over the words of his prayer.

Mattie's mind wandered a little as he prayed for neighbours and friends. "Be with Angus as he recovers from his illness, give strength to Sarah as she mourns her husband." Mattie's attention was brought back as he began praying for their marriage. "Keep Mattie and me in Thy care as we begin our life together and may we always do Thy will. In Jesus' name, amen."

All Mattie's worries came rushing back. Was that really God's will? she wondered. If it isn't, how can I ever make up for it? It was hard to make breakfast go down. She was still not quite able to meet David's eyes. She choked down another spoonful of porridge as yesterday's misery returned in full force. Sunday's coming and I'm going to have to face the whole church, she thought. The porridge nearly came back up. She swallowed. At least, I'm going to have to look decent for church. The memory of Mr. MacDonald's sermon on whited sepulchres sprang to her mind, and she cringed inwardly. I'll just have to ask David. There's nothing else I can do.

She cleared her throat. "I'm going to need a dress before Sunday."

David frowned, and Mattie shrank back in her chair. "Why before Sunday?" he asked. Then he realized. "Oh, of course you do. We'll go to John's and you can pick out what you need for yourself. You'll need hairpins too."

Mattie released the breath she had been holding. At least I don't have to explain it for him.

After breakfast they set out for the village. David whistled a cheerful tune through his beard, and Mattie trotted along barefoot by his side. Her long brown braid swung from beneath her bonnet just as it had always done. The morning air was still cool, but the day promised to be fragrant with fall flowers and full of light.

"Do you want me to go into John's with you?" asked David. "He can be an awful tease when he wants to be."

"Yes, please. John always teased me when I went there with Poppa, this time probably won't be any different." Mattie smiled at the memory. Afterwards, John always had a treat for me hidden in one of his pockets. Her smile faded as they neared the store.

David held the door for her as they entered. "John, I'd like to present my wife."

John shook hands with Mattie. "How do you do, Mrs. Matheson? What can I do for you this morning?"

"I'm well, thank you." I sound like my mother, Mattie thought. "I need some yard goods and a few other necessities, please."

A twinkle appeared in John's eyes. "Shall

I include a licorice stick in that order, then?"

"No, thank you, just the yard goods."

"I'll get the missus to help you there then," said John, "I don't know much about dressmaking."

I don't either, thought Mattie.

That afternoon she spread the dress material out on the kitchen floor for want of any larger space. She surveyed the piece from all angles. Mrs. John said this would be enough, and I suppose it is, but how do I make it go from flat to round? She sat on the floor staring at it. Maybe if I just make it straight and tie a belt around it.

She was still considering this possibility a few minutes later when a knock came at the door.

"Anybody home?" It was a woman's voice.

Mattie scrambled to her feet and hurried to to the door. The woman stood on the sandstone step. Mattie stared at her, tongue-tied. The woman's head was topped by a thick coil of auburn curls that gleamed in the light from the sun, a plain straw hat perched on the top of the coil like a nest. Her broad face was smooth and plain, the creamy skin slightly freckled from the summer sun. Little wrinkles at the outside edges of her bright blue eyes came and went as she smiled at Mattie. Mattie found her tongue and her manners with difficulty.

"G-good-day," she faltered, "w-won't you come in?" I should know who this woman is, she thought racking her brains for the elusive memory.

"I'm Mrs. Anna Gillis. I think I must be your nearest neighbour."

"Please sit down." So that's who she is, she thought, pleased at being able to place her. She's been to visit with Momma before now.

"I thought I'd be your first visitor." Anna took a seat in the rocker at Mattie's invitation. "They say it's good luck to have a redhead for your first visitor."

"You're making that up." A chuckle crept into Mattie's voice, then a smile flitted across her face. "I've never heard such a thing."

"I haven't either, but there must be a saying somewhere about redheads. There's certainly lots to say about people with black hair." She looked at the dark blue material on the kitchen floor. "Dress-making, are you?"

"Trying to, but I don't even know where to begin." Mattie regarded the length of dress material now serving for a carpet. "Momma taught me lots of things, but this wasn't one of them."

"Well, I can see I came at just the right time. It's not hard to do, if you hold your mouth the right way."

"D'you make dresses?"

"I have to make dresses. There's no one around

to make them for me, and besides, even if there were, I still couldn't pay them to do it, so I have to make them."

"But you're always so well dressed."

"Why, thank you, dear. That's awful nice to hear, but if you look close you'll see it's only on the surface."

"Can you show me?"

"Of course I can show you. I'd be pleased to."

Supper was as silent as dinner had been. David seemed restless and ate his meal quickly, then hurried outdoors again. Mattie watched him go. I hope he's not sorry he married me already. The thought nagged at her mind as she turned to her task of clearing the table. It'll be an awful long time if he is.

The restlessness was still upon him when David came back in at dusk. The brooms he was tying for sale in Charlottetown could not seem to hold his interest that evening. Mattie sat opposite him in the large rocking chair casting on stitches for mittens. Her wooden knitting needles clicked softly in the quietness of the little kitchen. Mrs. Nicholson had included them in her package that day as a gift, along with a skein of grey yarn. A candle burned with a steady flame, adding its light to the light from the fire. Mattie watched David out of the corner of her eye, too shy to break the silence.

David arranged the straw around the stout broom handle and deftly tied it in place. Every few minutes his hands stopped and he appeared to be listening. His glance kept straying toward the little window.

What's he listening for? wondered Mattie.

Presently he got up and strode to the window and peered out into the darkness. A total velvety blackness enveloped the little house. Not one star shone to relieve the dark that even seemed to muffle the faint breeze that soughed through the trees. He sat down again and picked up another broomstick. The light from the fire cast shadows across his high cheekbones. His silhouette, with its great beard, flickered and danced on the wall.

Mattie stared over at him, remembering all the stories about witches and warlocks she'd ever heard. He looks devilish, she thought, as a whisper of fear gathered itself in her mind. She cleared her throat and bent her head to her knitting. Outside the wind had died down and except for the faint crackle from the fire, the tick of Mattie's knitting needles, and the rustle of straw from David's brooms, the silence seemed absolute.

The sound, when it came, was faint at first, barely a whisper. Mattie looked up from her work. The silence stretched on. David continued his work. It was nothing, she thought. She returned to her knitting. A muffled thump caused Mattie to jump and drop a knitting needle. David looked up from his task. He reached for the knitting needle and passed it back to her.

"Thank you."

David acknowledged her thanks with a nod and returned to tying brooms. "Soon time to read," he said, tugging hard on a knot.

"It is that." She glanced up at him. The fire flared and David's face lost its sinister look. She rolled up her mitten and stuck the knitting needles into the ball of yarn. As she rose from her chair a flash of white appeared at the window and was gone in an instant. She shrieked and dropped her knitting. The ball rolled under the lounge and the mitten skidded into the corner by the wood box.

David looked up in alarm. "What is it?" He jumped to his feet.

"A-a face! At the window!" Mattie was shaking.

David approached the window. Another thump and a muffled laugh disturbed the silence.

"Now you've done it!" It was a loud whisper just outside.

Mattie stared at the window with enormous eyes. A man's voice. Maybe it's the *bocans* come to get us. She squeezed her eyes shut as the little house was shaken by a mighty thump. The velvet silence of the night was broken by a cacophony of sound. Whistles shrilled through the darkness, the house vibrated to a regular beat, cow bells rang out, and over the noise and confusion the bagpipes struck up "Mairi's Wedding."

A shivaree! Mattie began to smile, then to laugh. A shivaree for us. She joined David at the window. "Who's out there?"

"Jamie bagpipe, at least," replied David over the noise. "I'll invite them in for a drop." He went to the door. "C'mon in boys, that's enough racket for this night."

The uproar ceased as abruptly as it had started and ten of the neighbour men trouped into the kitchen. There was hardly room to move. Mattie scurried into the pantry and got out all four of the glasses and the two teacups that she owned. They'll have to share, she thought, but that won't matter. She carried them into the kitchen where David was uncorking his new bottle of whiskey. So that's why he bought that today. He knew this was going to happen.

David poured the whiskey generously and Mattie handed the brimming glasses around to eager hands. Toasts were made and stories told, and Mattie blushed at the teasing and the insinuations that were made. In the midst of it all Jamie struck up the pipes and the noise in the kitchen was deafening. Mattie covered her ears.

"Jamie! Jamie! Have a heart, man." Rory leaped to his feet and waved his hands in Jamie's face.

"Take those things outside or you'll deafen us all."

Jamie turned and led the way outdoors to the tune of "Bonnie Dundee." The others rose and followed him. The tune changed to "Scotland the Brave" and the noise and the laughter receded into the distance as the men marched over the rise, warmed by the music and the whiskey.

Mattie and David watched them go. "You knew about this."

"Not exactly." David's beard was still parted by a huge grin. "I suspected they might try something of the sort, especially since we didn't have a wedding celebration in the usual way. The boys must have their fun. There's little enough of that in this life."

David worked around the little house all week, weeding the vegetable garden, chopping wood, and generally tidying the place for winter. His biggest project was to build a narrow porch across the back of the house. He whistled as he worked, and by the end of the week he had the back door enclosed in a solid porch with a wooden floor and room for storage. His hardest task in this construction was to move the sandstone steps to accommodate the new doorway, but Mattie helped with that and then returned to her sewing.

Mattie soon grew accustomed to her surroundings. Keeping house in so tiny a space did not require much effort. David is very easy to please, she thought. I hope I'm doing things the way he wants me to. He doesn't give me much direction except … She felt herself grow warm at the thought of their night time activities. I don't even mind that much anymore. The thought surprised her.

It doesn't hurt anymore, she thought in amazement. I wonder if other women do this with their husbands? I wonder if Momma and Poppa did this? I wonder if Momma and Norman will? Momma wouldn't do such a thing! Then she remembered the night last year when she had gotten up for a drink of water and crept down over the steep stairs so as not to wake anyone. She had heard her mother cry out, a soft mewling cry such as she herself had made only last night. Maybe Momma wasn't having a bad dream.

Mattie's mind leaped on to make other connections. It was just after that that I overheard Momma tell Poppa that there was going to be another baby, she thought, then frowned. But Momma never had another one. She never even got any fatter like she did with William and Johnny. What did she do with it?

Mattie continued to puzzle over the problem of the missing baby as she sewed. She sent us over to Mrs. MacNeil's that day last fall, and she was awful cross when I asked her before we left if there was going to be a new baby tomorrow. She just shooed us out the door and didn't answer me, but there was no new baby when we came home, and she was sick in bed for two days after that. Mrs. MacNeil said she was ailing, and we were to be real quiet around the house until she felt better. Maybe she wasn't really sick, maybe the baby just wouldn't come. Maybe it's still in there. No, that can't be it, that doesn't make sense. It'd have to come out sometime. But what did she do with it? Mattie's thoughts went round and round.

And that time that Poppa had Mr. Murchison's cow over to make friends with their bull. That's what Poppa said they were doing anyway, when he sent me back to the house with Momma. But I saw what they were doing, and it didn't look very friendly. Momma wouldn't even let me out of the house after that when Mr. Murchison's cow came to visit every fall.

Poppa always let Tommy watch though, and when I asked Tommy what they were doing, he got all red in the face and said I was dirty for even asking. She remembered the fight they'd had over that one.

"Don't ask such a dirty question!" Tommy's tanned features turned a dull red.

"Don't you call me dirty, Tommy Cameron!"

"Well, you are, for even thinking such a thing!"

"Am not, and you take it back!" She hurled her twelve year old body at Tommy and knocked him over onto the new straw on the barn floor. The attack was fierce.

"Take it back!" she shrieked in his ear. She had the advantage of surprise and was now sitting astride him with her skirts up past her knees, pinning his arms to the floor and screaming in his ears.

"Will not!" Tommy shouted back. "Get off me!"

"Take it back!"

"Get off me, or I'll tell Momma!" Tommy gave a violent heave and unseated Mattie, turning her onto her back in the straw. Suddenly it was no longer a fight for Mattie. She stared up at Tommy, her small, barely formed bosom, heaving, her eyes huge with wonder, as an exciting warmth began creeping over her body.

A strange expression crossed Tommy's face and he flung himself off her and jumped to his feet.

"I'm not dirty!" cried Mattie, but the energy of the fight was gone, and only a uncommon languor remained in her childish limbs.

The curse came soon after that. Momma seemed awful cross about it, even though it's never done anything except make me bleed every month. She said that it had to do with making babies, and that it'd keep coming regularly until I started making a baby of my own after I was married. Mattie frowned, remembering how angry her mother had been when she asked how babies got started before you were married.

"Never mind about that." Mrs. Cameron rolled strips of old sheets together to fashion a pad for Mattie. "Only tramps and bad women do things like that."

"But Momma, what about Christy? She had little Angus this spring and she was never a bad girl. You said so yourself last year. She always won all the prizes in school, and she always knew all her Bible verses by memory. You said how proud her Momma must be of her, and you said that you wished that I would apply myself like that too."

"That's enough, Mattie! You'll understand someday. In the meantime just keep yourself to yourself and you'll be all right. Here, go wash yourself and put this on." She shoved the pad into Mattie's hands and left the room.

But I still don't understand, thought Mattie, unless …? Maybe that's what David meant when he said that the Bible said that we were to go forth and multiply. No! Not that! She forced the thought to the back of her mind. Maybe Tommy was right. Maybe I am just dirty to think of things like that. She folded her new dress and went to make preparations for supper.

Sunday morning arrived too quickly, and Mattie had still not succeeded in arranging her long thick hair into a neat bun. It always looks so easy when Momma does it. She threw down her comb in exasperation just as David called up the stairs, "Hurry, Mattie, we don't want to be late."

"Oh, dear," she muttered, "Whatever am I going to do?" Her fingers began braiding of their own accord. "This'll have to do." She wound the two and a half feet of thick brown braid into a lump on the back of her head and secured it with hairpins.

She hurried downstairs and picked up her shawl and put on her bonnet. It perched on top of her head like an inverted basket.

"I can see we should have bought you a bonnet while we were at it," said David.

Mattie dragged at the bonnet strings, trying to pull it down to its accustomed place. "What am I going to do?" she wailed. "Momma'll be savage if I go to church without a hat." Her mother's voice echoed in her mind, "Every woman who prayeth with her head uncovered dishonoreth her head."

"Here, wear mine," offered David, "and I'll wear my old one." He took his Sunday hat from the peg behind the door and plunked it on top of Mattie's head. "A nice piece of cloth from that dress material and you'll have the best looking hat in the church. And there'll be room for your braid too."

Mattie ran to the mirror and surveyed herself in it. David's hat really didn't look too bad once the brim was folded down under the swathe of cloth she'd wound around it for a ribbon, and there was room for all her hair. She stuck a long hat pin in the back to secure it. "It'll have to do," she said. "I can't go to church without a hat, and I can't not go to church."

Together they walked down the path. David picked up Mattie's hand and folded it into the crook of his elbow. She marched along beside him. Squirrels chirred at them from the darkness of the fir trees at the end of the path. A grey hare hopped out of the bushes in front of them, raised up on its hind legs and stared at them for long seconds, then skittered back into the undergrowth. The leaves of the oaks, maples and white birches had the dusty darkness of late summer. Here and there whole branches had turned to gold or crimson. The sun shone with the golden mellow light of approaching autumn.

"School starts tomorrow," said David, "and I'll be gone all day. Will you miss me?"

"Yes." I will miss him, she thought.

David tucked her hand a little more closely into the crook of his elbow and patted it gently, his calloused hand warm on her fingers. "Good," he said.

They climbed the little hill to the church. The sanctuary and its slim steeple shone whitely against the dark fir trees behind it. The graveyard surrounded the church on three sides, its stones white against the dark green of the spruce woods.

Mattie could see her father's grave, the red soil of it still raw and new, heaped up and over-flowing from the space that the coffin occupied below. It doesn't hurt so much to think of him anymore, she thought in surprise. It seems like a such a long time since he died, but it's really only been ten weeks.

David interrupted her thoughts. "D'you know where I sit?" he whispered.

Mattie nodded. Her hands grew cold with apprehension.

"Are you ready?"

She took a deep breath and nodded again.

"Smile."

Mattie tried to turn her trembling lips upward but only succeeded in producing a grimace.

"Don't smile," David amended, "it's disrespectful of the Sabbath. Here, you have a smudge on
your cheek." He pulled out his clean white handkerchief. "Stick out your tongue."

Mattie obeyed.

David wet the handkerchief on her spit and
scrubbed at the smudge on her cheek. "There now,
you'll do." He tucked her hand into the crook of
his elbow again, and together they walked up the
aisle to David's accustomed place.

A few heads turned. The news of their marriage
had circulated slowly, and some of the people
who lived on the other side of the lot had not yet
heard. Mattie's mother frowned as she took in
Mattie's makeshift bonnet. Cora managed a tiny
wave before her own mother grabbed her hand
and pushed it back into her lap. Next week I'll
be sitting with the women again, she thought as
they slipped into David's seat with only seconds
to spare.

Mattie bowed her head. It seemed strange to
be looking at the pulpit from the other side of the
church, and stranger still to be sitting with a man.

The church was plain inside, and there was no
adornment except the mellow wood that finished
the walls and the ceiling. I always thought that
the walls went straight to heaven, and that the
people who sat in the gallery were already halfway there, thought Mattie. I always wanted to sit

up there, but I knew that Momma would never let us so I never asked. I spent my time during the sermons counting the narrow boards in the ceiling and turning them into roads. Momma always put a stop to that as soon as she noticed.

The pulpit was the focal point of the room, and over the years Mattie had absorbed the lessons almost by osmosis. The seats were hard and straight, and the congregation sat through the long sermons as still as statues, the women and girls on one side of the church and the men and boys on the other. Even the children were taught to sit still and pay attention at a very early age. Mattie wished with all her heart that she was sitting with her mother now.

"Happy the Home When God is There," announced the precentor. He chose a pitch and began to sing.

There was no accompaniment. One by one the congregation straggled into the song. The melodious cacophony rose and fell, each person offering his own version of the common tune. Notes glided into notes, as if on a swing. The voices wove in and out with each other until the whole was more beautiful than its many parts.

Mattie sang along softly. It was one of her favourite songs. It told of the ingredients for a happy home and this morning the verses struck her as particularly apt to her situation. I wonder if that applies to me? The thought overwhelmed her and she had a difficult time controlling her voice around the lump in her throat.

The hymn plodded on, and gave Mattie some encouragement. That's what David said, thought Mattie. The lump in her throat began to dissolve.

Mattie was greatly encouraged as she sang. Lifting her head, she sang out the words with the others. She looked around the church. It was almost full. Latecomers had entered quietly and had joined the singing with the others. The song came to an end in joyous praise. At ten o'clock Reverend MacDonald pulled his watch out of his waistcoat pocket, inspected it for the time, then rose to take his place behind the pulpit. The service began.

The Psalms were sung line by line after the precentor. Mattie joined in the singing with the others, her small soprano voice still childish and light beside David's rich baritone. She peeped up at him from under the brim of her makeshift hat. A faint smile ghosted across David's face, but reverence for the Sabbath was so deeply ingrained in him that he quickly suppressed it. She ducked her head and lost her place in the Psalm.

Mattie sat through the sermon without moving. She was acutely aware of her mother's disapproval. I can tell by the set of her head that I'm going to catch it for wearing David's hat, she thought. Well, at least I have a hat on. She shifted her position slightly. If I sit up straight and still, maybe she won't be so hard on me. David's hand tightened on hers. She blushed again at having been caught squirming.

After the last Psalm, David escorted her to her mother who was standing with the other ladies outside the door, then went to join the men under the chestnut trees.

"This is my oldest daughter, Mattie Matheson," said her mother, staring at Mattie's unusual bonnet. Mattie was uncomfortably aware that it was her introduction into the world of women, even though they had all known her almost since she was born.

"There's Mattie," said William in a loud whisper, and the two boys walked quietly over to greet her. They stopped suddenly, overcome by the change in her appearance.

"Is that really you, Mattie?" asked Johnny.

"Of course it's Mattie," said William. "I'd know her anywhere."

"Come and play with us, Mattie," said Johnny. "We've found the best puff balls over by the stables."

Puff balls were Mattie's speciality. She was the one who could really make them pop and send their dark brown spores floating on the breeze to make more puff balls. Immediately she forgot her new role and the Sabbath, and made a move to go for a romp with them, but her mother's hand on her arm and the little shake of her head restrained her. Her changed status was brought home to her, and her face saddened. I won't ever be allowed to play with the children again, she thought.

"You children behave yourselves." Mrs. Cameron's attention was diverted from Mattie's hat for the moment. "It's almost time to go home now. Just look at you. And on the Sabbath too. You know better than that. You're all dusty." She began brushing Johnny down with the flat of her hand. "I wish you two'd leave those mushrooms alone. William, get some of that dust off you. Mattie, help him, will you? Mrs. Smith has invited us all to dinner, and I can't take you there looking like that."

Chapter Seven

Summer seemed to end with the beginning of school. Mattie picked the last of the late blackberries that the birds had missed, and made a little jam for the winter.

She admired the four bottles of purple jam on the cellar shelf next to the three bottles of apple jelly that her mother had brought to church for her last Sunday. I'm glad Momma gave me some of that jelly I made last month, or I would hardly have a thing for David, she thought.

Mattie's days were filled with new responsibilities. The cow, Pansy, mother to Johnny's calf, had been delivered to the school one day. David led Pansy home. He milked her in the morning while Mattie got breakfast ready, and Mattie milked her every evening before David arrived home from the schoolhouse.

I know that it's customary, but I'm awful glad that Norman and Momma *tochered* me with a cow of their own. Perhaps they haven't forgotten me after all, she thought, as she skimmed the cream off the top of the milk the next morning.

Mattie churned the cream into butter and soon

had a dozen pats of it, each marked with the design of the thistle from the butter press Cora had sent to her for a wedding present.

The milk they were unable to use she allowed to curdle and made cheese. She wrapped it tightly and pressed it in a wooden tub under a large piece of sandstone. The pale pungent rounds were a great source of satisfaction to her. The cupboard in the cool darkness of the cellar became full to overflowing.

"Will you fetch me a bottle of jam from the cellar, please?" Breakfast was late that morning, or Mattie would have gone down for it herself.

David went to the cellar to fetch the jam. He opened the cupboard door and discovered a battalion of ants covered in grease marching up and down the wall.

"Mattie!" he shouted, his great beard trembling in outrage. "We have ants!" He began rooting around on the shelves. "What's this?" He pulled out a package of butter. "Mattie! Come down here at once!"

Mattie hurried down the steep steps and stood speechless in front of David.

"What are you doing with all this butter?"

Mattie licked her dry lips. "I-I made it."

"I can see that. Whatever for?"

"I didn't want to waste the cream."

"Did you really think we'd use all of this?"

"I-I don't know. I guess I just didn't think very far."

"I'll say you didn't! Just look at those ants!" He reached for her hand to pull her around to where she could see.

Mattie took an involuntary step backward and tripped over a basket of potatoes, upsetting them and herself onto the floor. Potatoes rolled into the darkest reaches of the cellar and Mattie curled herself into a protective ball.

"D-don't be angry with me," she whimpered. "I was only trying to save things." She began to cry.

He bent down to help her to her feet, but Mattie cringed away from him.

"Don't smack me." She wriggled out of David's reach.

David stared down at her in amazement. "Hit you? Hit you? What makes you think I'd hit you?"

"I-Momma-I." Tears continued to run down Mattie's face.

"Is this the sort of thing you'd get smacked for at home?"

Mattie nodded.

David knelt on the clay floor beside her. "Well, this's your home now, and I won't hit you. Not now, not ever, not for anything." He held out his hand to her and assisted her to her feet.

"Whatever made you think I'd hit you?" he asked.

"You were so angry, and your beard ..." She sniffed and scrubbed at her tears with the sleeve of her dress.

"What about my beard?" He handed her a clean handkerchief.

"It's so big and black and ..."

"And what?"

"Fierce," she whispered.

"Fierce?"

Mattie nodded and then said in a rush, "It hides you, and I can't tell what you're thinking. I never know what you want."

"Oh."

"It makes me afraid."

"And afraid of me too, I suppose."

Mattie nodded.

"Well, that explains a lot of things." He reached over and picked up the potato basket. "We'll talk about this later. In the meantime, we have to do something about all this butter." He dumped the remaining potatoes into a heap on the floor.

"What are you going to do with it?" She scrambled to her feet.

"Carry it upstairs in this and see what's not spoiled of it and feed the rest to the hens."

There wasn't much that wasn't spoiled, reflected Mattie later as she scraped the last of the butter into the hens' trough. The hens clucked and rustled around her feet. I guess I really didn't think. I should have sent it in to the store, John might have been able to sell it for me, or at least I could have given it away. Old Mrs. Finlayson would have been glad of it. She's too old to look after a cow anymore.

"Good morning, Mattie." The sweet voice was raised just enough in pitch so that Mattie couldn't recognize it. It seemed to come from just beside her right ear. She shrieked and dropped her spoon. The voice giggled.

"Cora Smith! You scared me half to death!"

"It was such fun doing it, too," giggled Cora. "You were so unaware. What're you doing, anyway?" Cora peered into the trough. "That's butter, isn't it?"

Mattie sighed. Trust Cora to notice, she thought. "Yes, that's butter." She clamped her lips shut.

"Why're you feeding it to the hens?"

"Because it spoiled."

"That's too bad, maybe you could have sold it. Does David know, or didn't you tell him?"

"He knows."

"Oh, so we've had our first fight, have we?" Cora watched Mattie's face.

"No, we haven't, and it's none of your business anyway." Mattie suppressed a gasp. It feels strange to be talking to Cora this way, she thought. She turned away toward the house to hide her discomfort.

Cora hurried after her. "Well, waste not, want not, I suppose." She tossed her head and changed the subject. "Nice place you have."

"Thank you," replied Mattie. "What brings you here today? Aren't you supposed to be in school?"

"I 'm playing truant. It's not any fun since you left and all the boys graduated." Her eyes brightened. "Did you hear? Some relative of Andrew MacMillan's in the States sent word that if Andrew wanted to, he could come and live with him and he'd pay his way through college."

"Well, that's good luck, isn't it? Andrew's always wanted to go to college." Mattie recalled Andrew's earnest, freckled face framed in its mop of untidy auburn hair. His spectacles always seemed to be sliding off the end of his nose, she thought.

"He wants to be a doctor," said Cora. "I'm sorry now that I was so mean to him in school. He'll be a good catch in a few years."

"Cora!" exclaimed Mattie. "Is that all you ever think about these days?" She opened the door to the house, then stood aside to allow Cora to enter.

Cora stepped inside. "Well, a girl has to be thinking about her future." She looked around the tidy kitchen. The last of the breakfast fire was glowing in the fireplace, and the kettle, filled and shining, was warming over the embers. Snow white curtains with red trim now framed the tiny windows. "My goodness, Mattie, your future certainly looks bright."

"As long as David's able to teach, I'm secure." I am secure, she thought. I really wasn't secure living at home. I've never thought about it that way before. She shut the door behind herself. "Make yourself at home, Cora. I'll just boil the kettle and we'll have some tea."

Cora pulled the big rocker closer to the fire. "You're turning into quite the hostess, too, I see."

"I do my best." Mattie stirred up the embers and added a stick to the small flame that flared, then pushed the kettle over the fire. "How's your mother, these days?"

"Oh, you know Momma, she's only as well as she thinks she is. She's having a bad day today. She went back to bed as soon as the breakfast dishes were done."

"So that's how you got out of going to school."

"Oh, I went to school." Cora tossed her black head. "I just didn't stay. I'm glad they built the school so close to Neil's back lane. All I had to do was climb through the fence behind the outhouse and no one could see me for the bushes, although I think I tore my dress getting through the wire." She made a face. "Momma'll want to know how that happened for sure. I ran into George O'Brien on his way to the store and walked with him for a ways."

"Cora, you know that your Momma doesn't want you associating with those boys. They have a bad reputation, and besides, they're Cath'lics." Mattie said the word as if it left an unsavoury flavour in her mouth.

"I only walked with him in broad daylight. It's not as if it was the middle of the night, for heaven's sake."

"It won't take the middle of the night to get people talking about you."

"Old biddies!"

"Cora! It's in your own best interest." Mattie got up to make the tea.

Cora looked at her from the corner of her eye. "Speaking of best interest, did you hear about the tramp who surprised Mrs. MacKinnon when she was hanging out her clothes the other day? He near scared her to death. She has that weak heart, you know."

Mattie missed the look. "You don't say. What did he want?"

"She never found out. I guess she ran screaming into the house and slammed the door."

"Oh, Cora, I don't believe that. She'd never do that. She's the soul of kindness. She'd probably offer the poor fellow a meal."

Cora shrugged. "It's true. I heard Momma

telling Poppa last night after I went up to bed."

"How could you hear that if you were in bed?"

"I wasn't in bed. I was sitting on the floor by the stovepipe hole listening. They were in the kitchen down below having tea before they came up to bed themselves. Poppa said that Momma should keep the doors and windows locked from now on."

"Is that how you hear all the things you tell me about?"

Cora nodded. "Didn't you ever do that? You hear the most interesting things if you just listen."

Mattie shook her head. "Cora, it's bad manners to listen to other peoples' conversations. Now you know that."

"But Mattie, how else would I find out what's going on?"

"Maybe you don't need to know. There're some things that just aren't anyone else's business."

"Oh, and I suppose you know so much. After all, you're a married lady for at least a month."

"No, Cora, I always knew that."

"Y'know Mattie, you've changed." Cora watched Mattie's face from under drooping lids. "I don't know if I like you anymore."

Mattie looked at Cora in silence for a moment. "There's not much I can do about that, then." She got up to pour the tea.

"How's Tommy these days?" Cora blew on her

tea to cool it.

"I don't know." Mattie did likewise. "I never see him except at church, and then I don't get to talk to him because I'm always with the women."

Cora sipped her tea. "That's too bad, you two were always so close." She watched Mattie's expression. "I saw him yesterday at the store. He's certainly growing into a fine-looking man. Does he ever come here to visit you?"

Mattie blinked. "No, why would he? He doesn't have time with all the work he has to do." I don't suppose he'll ever come and visit me, she thought. Probably none of them will.

"I suppose he'll be getting married someday soon. I hear he's been seeing John's Annie." Cora watched Mattie's expression out of the corner of her eye.

Mattie suppressed a gasp. Tommy and Annie? It doesn't seem right somehow, she thought. She took another sip of tea to settle her thoughts. "Annie's much too young," she replied. "Besides, they've always been friends." She could not hide her frown. "We're practically related anyway." She took a large gulp of tea and burned her mouth.

Cora kept an interested eye on Mattie, "I could certainly go for him if I had the chance."

"You're not likely to get it," said Mattie, "the way you behave around him."

The visit did not last long after that. Cora drank

her tea in almost complete silence and refused the second cup. She left soon, declining Mattie's offer to accompany her to the gate.

Mattie watched her from the doorway until she disappeared into the trees at the top of the path. Cora's changed, she thought. I'm not sure that I like her much either. She went in and closed the door. She's much slyer than she used to be, and she keeps trying to bait me about things. I wonder how much of what she said about Tommy is true? And that story about the tramp, I wonder if it's really true? There never used to be tramps around here, we're too far from town.

By the end of the week Cora's visit had retreated to the back of her mind. I must set bread today or we'll have none for the Sabbath, she thought as she stirred the inevitable pot of porridge for breakfast. David's taking an awful long time at the milking this morning, I hope Pansy isn't sick.

She laid the table with a spoon and a knife at each place, and sliced up the last of the loaf of bread. A noise at the kitchen door caused her to look up. A tall, dark-haired man stood looking at her. She gasped and clutched her knife more firmly in her hand.

"W-who're you? What d'you want?" She backed into the corner by the wood box.

"Now who d'you think I am?" The stranger's eyes seemed to glitter.

Mattie bent to pick up a good sized piece of wood, all the while keeping her eye on the intruder. "Don't you come a step nearer, or I'll scream!"

"That'll do you no good." The stranger stepped forward a pace. "There's no one to hear." There was a teasing note in the man's deep voice.

Mattie was perplexed. I know that voice, she thought, and brandished the knife. "My husband's in the barn and he'll hear me, so don't you try anything." It's his eyes, they look familiar too. The eyes seemed to mock her.

"Your husband's not there any more." He took another step forward.

A picture of David lying dead and bleeding on the barn floor flashed into Mattie's overwrought mind. Her control broke and she rushed at the tall dark man waving her stick and slashing with the knife. "What have you done with my David?" The knife swished past the man's chin. "You've killed my David!"

The man grabbed her arms and pinned them to her sides. She began kicking and screaming. "No, but you will if you don't stop swinging that knife," he laughed. "Ouch!" he exclaimed as Mattie landed a random kick on his shin. He wrestled the stick of wood from her hand and threw it back into the wood box. The knife soon followed. "Will you settle down!" Mattie stopped struggling and tried to get a look at him. He turned her around to face him and held her at arm's length.

The rage drained out of Mattie and she stood still looking up at him. He has eyes like David, she thought, taking a deep breath to renew her fight. She paused. The fresh clean scent of the man mingled with the sweet smell of milk from the barn. He smells like him too. She stared hard at him. "Is it you, then?"

"Yes, it's me."

"What happened to your beard?"

"I shaved it off."

"For me?"

"Yes, for you. Who else? I'll probably freeze this winter. I haven't been without a beard since I've been able to grow one, but if that's all it takes to please you, I'll do it."

Mattie stared up at this handsome stranger, then reached out a tentative hand to touch his face. "It's really you?"

"Of course it's me." He pulled her into his arms. "Now you don't have to be afraid of me any more."

"Well, now!" A smile of delight whispered across Mattie's face and was quickly gone.

"So I'm your David now, am I? I'm sorry I scared you so."

"You probably wouldn't have, if Cora hadn't been telling me wild tales about tramps the other day." Mattie turned to give the porridge a stir, then ladled out two steaming bowlfuls and set them on the table.

David sighed. "What did Cora have to say on the subject?" He pulled his chair in to the table.

"She just said that Mrs. MacKinnon was scared by one the other day." Mattie pulled up the other chair and scooped some sugar into her bowl.

"Och," said David, "trust Cora! That happened at least three years ago, and it was only Old Danny, and he's dead now."

Mattie smiled. "I remember him. He was just like one of us children, he was that simple. He was always so kind. I heard that he died but Momma would never tell us what happened to him."

"He got caught in a blizzard a couple of years ago and froze to death. They found his body out by the brook in Murdoch's back field when the snow melted in the spring."

"Oh, dear-o," said Mattie, "and he never hurt anyone."

As the days grew noticeably colder she harvested the garden, pleased with the abundance of the little plot of ground. She stored everything in the cellar. My back aches so, she thought as she stood, holding her candle, regarding the work she had accomplished in the last few days. She stretched her back to ease the ache. I'm glad all this is finished. I should try and spread the manure so David won't have to do it on Saturday, but I'm just too tired to do it right now. She turned and climbed the stairs.

Now that the work was finished, the days seemed twice as long. Her time was spent more and more indoors. It was not difficult to keep the house clean and neat, so time fell heavily on her hands.

I suppose I could start knitting again, she thought. I don't like to knit, but David needs new socks. I just darned the darns the last time. There'll be nothing left to darn the next time they wear through. She got her double-pointed knitting needles from her workbasket and began casting on stitches.

I'm glad Momma made me knit all those socks for the boys last fall. Mattie's thoughts flitted here and there. I'm so lonely. I wish Cora would visit again, but she'd have to skip school to do it, and that wouldn't be right. I miss the boys. I miss David, too.

The days passed and her loneliness increased. Mattie fell asleep over her knitting more than once. David's socks grew slowly. I don't know why I'm so tired these days. I'm not sick, but I have no energy. I wish it'd go away.

October crept by, and Mattie turned into a silent

little shadow. David looked at her with concern until a bout with nausea and vomiting put her to bed for the morning. He brewed her a pot of clove tea and the next day she was up and about as usual, although her silence and her pallor were not improved.

One day in late October, David made a suggestion to her.

"Mattie, how'd you like to have the boys and Ellie here for Saturday?"

Mattie's eyes lighted up, then immediately lost their sparkle. "Momma'd never let them come."

"If I could persuade her, would you like that?"

"It'd be wonderful. I've missed them."

"Good then. They can come home with me after school on Friday and go home with your mother after church on Sunday."

Mattie waited anxiously. At last, on Thursday, they received word that the boys could come but that Ellie was needed at home. Mattie had to be satisfied with that. She cooked and cleaned all day Friday to make the time go faster. Finally she heard them coming down the path, William and little Johnny. She ran to hug them.

"My, how tall you've grown Johnny, and you too, William. And it's only been two months."

"I can climb to the top of the spruce tree now," bragged Johnny.

"Momma will let you do that?"

Johnny shrugged and ducked his head. "She don't know."

"I can turn two cartwheels in a row," piped William. "Just watch me."

He turned his two cartwheels then announced as he righted himself, "I'm hungry. What's for supper?"

Mattie laughed. "Come inside and wash your hands, supper's all ready to go on the table. Tomorrow we'll go exploring in the woods."

Saturday dawned. The Indian summer was mellowing into the coolness of late autumn. Mattie put on her old dress. I must be getting fatter, she thought. This dress is tight in the seams now, and it feels awfully short. Oh, well, it'll have to do, and I am only with the children.

Mattie and the boys played, and wandered, and talked and teased all day. The air was fresh and heavy with the scent of the dying year. The trees were nearly bare of their golden leaves, their branches naked against the brightness of the sky. It's a perfect day, thought Mattie. It's just like old times.

"Are there any good gum trees around here?" asked William.

"There's a row of them down by the house," replied Mattie, "only the gum is pretty high up, we'll have to climb for it."

"Come on, then," he shouted, "last one back's a rotten egg."

Mattie walked slowly. Where is my energy these days anyway? she wondered again. "C'mon Johnny, William's waiting for us."

William was hopping back and forth from one leg to the other when they got there.

"Hurry up you two," he shouted. "I tried to climb this one but the branches are too far apart and there's a great gob of gum up there that's just waiting for us. You can get it, Mattie."

Mattie looked to where he was pointing. I guess I can climb up there, she thought, that gum looks just ripe enough. She gathered up her skirts and began to climb. It only took a moment to pry the gum loose and drop it to Johnny. She then began the careful descent. Reaching the lowest branch she jumped to the ground, landing at the feet of her white-faced husband.

"Don't you ever do that again!" he said. "Not only is it dangerous for you but what would have happened to our baby if you'd fallen? Don't you have any sense?"

Baby, what baby? she thought. She remembered the strange bout of nausea the other morning soon after David had left for school. I lost my breakfast but I was fine the rest of the day and I didn't think any more about it. It was there again the next day but the tea seemed to settle me, and it didn't come back. Cora … ! Suddenly it all made sense.

That's what's wrong with me, why I've been so tired and sickly lately. But women die having babies. I'm going to die! Her mind went numb. She turned on her heels and began to run. She ran and ran, past the little clearing where they had been playing not an hour before, through the woods on the other side, and across the fields, coming to a stop by the river which barred her way.

I'm going to die! She sank to her knees in the damp brown grass and began to rock back and forth. I'm going to die. She stared unseeingly across the river and gradually her mind began to work again.

I think I've figured out how babies get started. Poppa was so mad at me the day I peeked around the edge of the barn to see what they were doing with the bull. Momma was that cross when she found out about it. The bull was just climbing onto the cow's back. Daisy was bellowing, so she couldn't have liked it much. That's when Poppa caught me. I've never seen him so angry, and Momma too. If that's what they do, I guess it's no wonder they didn't want me to know about it. Mattie lay back into the tall grass oblivious to the cold, river-wet earth underneath.

And those ladies at the quilting frolic. They sure

were ashamed of themselves when they discovered
me in the corner listening. They kept apologizing
to Momma. Momma was cross that time, too. The
quilting broke up right after that. I don't think
Momma's finished the quilt yet. I wonder if all
those stories were true? They must have been, or
why else would Mrs. MacKenzie have said that I'd
have to know sometime. She said, "Tell the truth
and shame the devil." Momma just gave her a
dirty look and said that there was no need of me
knowing things that I didn't need to know, and
she shoved me out the door. Mattie sighed. But
I'm still not sure how they get out.

"Mattie!" David's voice broke into her thoughts
from a long way away. "Mattie!" She raised her
head and he hurried over.

"Oh, Mattie, I'm so thankful I've found you."
He knelt down beside her on the grass and lifted
her up to lean against him. "You didn't know,
did you," he said. "Your mother never told you."

"No." Mattie sighed. "She was always too busy.
Am I going to die?"

"Die? Whatever put that idea into your head?

"I heard the ladies talking once when they were
in for a quilting frolic with Momma. They were
saying that women die having babies. Cora said
that too."

"Mattie, women have babies every day and very
few of them die. The ones that do usually have

something else wrong too. A strong healthy young woman like yourself shouldn't have any problem at all."

"I'm so afraid. I don't know anything about having babies."

"Weren't you there when your mother had the younger children?'

"No, we were always sent to Mrs. MacNeil's, and when we came home there was a new little baby in the cradle. I could never figure out how she knew to send us away. I thought we must be like the animals, they always seem to know when it's time."

"Mattie, do you know anything at all?"

"Not much, I guess." She sighed again. "What else do I need to know?"

"I think you'd better ask Mrs. Gillis. She's a mid-wife and she'll tell you better than I can." David rose to his feet. "Come on now, let's go home, it's getting chilly out here."

A few days later Mattie accompanied David on his way to school. He left her at the top of Ian Gillis' hill field. "It'll be alright, Mattie, you'll see." He patted her thin shoulder then turned and walked on toward the school house, still three miles away.

Mattie watched him go. When he was out of sight she turned and trudged down the path to the house. The day was dark and chilly and Mattie's shawl did little to keep out the cold. She shivered.

This house is larger than our house. I think it's even bigger than Momma's house, she thought as she wended her way up the muddy red path. The dead stalks of last summer's weeds caught and pulled at her skirts.

The house had been added onto higgledy-piggledy by earlier residents and it now sat hunched in the curve of the spruce grove like a hen with all her chicks under her wings. One white birch shone out from the darkness of the spruce trees. Dead marigolds and chrysanthemums still decorated the flower beds along the foundations of the house.

I wonder if those are good gum trees, she thought as she waited for someone to answer her knock. I guess I'll never know now.

The door swung open. "Why Mattie Matheson! What a pleasant surprise. Come in. Come in. You must be half frozen. It's as cold as Greenland out there." Anna Gillis hustled Mattie inside and led the way through the dark porch to the kitchen.

"Come in and sit by the fire, and I'll put the kettle on. A cup of tea'll warm you nicely. Have you made any more dresses?" She beamed at Mattie, her faint wrinkles deepening into the cheery lines they would become in her old age.

Mattie felt the loneliness of the last few months

drop away from her. She settled herself beside the fireplace and looked around. The kitchen was similar to her mother's and just as tidy. It felt warm and comforting.

"No," replied Mattie, "but I made a pair of curtains for the kitchen a few weeks ago." She lapsed into a tongue-tied silence.

"So what brings you out on such a cold day as this?"

Mattie remembered her errand and blushed. "David said that I should come and talk with you." She stopped and couldn't go any farther.

Anna's sharp glance took in Mattie's wan face and the tightness of her dress. "I see," she said. "Are you in the family way, child?"

Mattie could only nod. Her blush deepened.

"Never mind, dear, it happens to all of us sooner or later. Have you been keeping well?"

"Yes. No. I don't know." Her voice was barely a whisper.

"For goodness sake, you're either well or you're not." Anna bustled around the little kitchen filling the kettle from the bucket on the shelf by the door and setting it over the fire to heat.

Mattie ducked her head. "I was sick the other week for a couple of days, but not since then." Her voice was a little stronger.

"What did you do for it?"

"David made me a cup of clove tea and it went

away after awhile."

"He's a wise man. That's the best thing he could have done."

"I've been very tired lately too, and my back's been aching an awful lot."

"D'you know when you're due?"

"Due?"

"When will the baby come?"

"I don't know." Mattie's head drooped again and she stared into the fire. "Am I going to die?" she asked in a very small voice.

"Of course you're not going to die. Whatever put that idea into your head?"

"Cora ... ," Mattie began.

"That young scamp doesn't know what she's talking about. She heard all she knows from her mother and that sister of hers in Charlottetown, and it isn't much. Why, her sister thought, well, never mind, that's not important now."

"It wasn't just Cora."

"Well, I expect it was the older girls, was it?"

"No. It was the ladies the day they all came out home to help Momma quilt. They were all talking about Christy and how she'd shamed her family and how her mother and her aunt had had a hard time having babies and how their mother had died having the last one of them and how Christy was so much like her grandmother that she was lucky she didn't die too." Mattie stopped for breath.

"But she didn't die, did she."

"No-o."

"And you're not going to die either." She rose to pour out the tea. "Here, drink this. It'll put some warmth into you. I declare, I don't know how you got so thin. I only saw you last Sunday and you looked fine to me then." She pushed a steaming mug into Mattie's hands. "Are you eating right?"

"I-I think so. As much as ever I do."

"Well, you don't look it. You have to eat for two now, you know." She plumped herself down in the other rocking chair next to Mattie.

"I do?"

"Yes, you do. You're growing another person inside you and that takes a lot of energy."

Mattie visualized a miniature person floating around somewhere inside her stomach along with all the other vital organs known and unknown to her, and gulped.

Anna rocked vigorously. "What did your Momma tell you about having babies?"

"She said that it was hard work and that it hurt but that it was our lot in life." Mattie took a sip of tea and burnt her tongue.

"D'you know how they get started?"

Mattie blushed. "I think I do."

"I see." Anna gave her a keen look. "So she never told you that either."

"The children were always coming in and

interrupting and then Poppa died and there didn't seem to be any more time, and all of a sudden I was married."

"Well, dear, whether you know for sure or not, you're going to have it when it comes. When did you come around last?"

"Come around?"

Anna shook her head. "When were you last unwell?"

"In August, I think. So much has happened I don't remember anymore."

"So your baby will come in April or May next year. That'll be good. You won't have to work hard while you're carrying. Winter's always an easier time to be in the family way." She poured more tea into Mattie's cup. "How's your Momma keeping these days? She's due at the end of May."

Mattie gasped. Her pale cheeks went paper white.

Anna looked at her in alarm. "You didn't know?"

Mattie leaned her head against the back of the rocker and closed her eyes. "No. I didn't know."

"Does it matter so much to you?" asked Anna.

"It's so soon. It hardly seems decent." Her voice was barely a whisper.

"Well, it is true that your Poppa was just buried a few months ago, and that she and Mr. Martin were only married at the first of September, but Mattie, your Momma's getting along in years, and it soon won't be possible for her to have babies anymore, and he likely wanted one to call his own. Most men do, you know."

Mattie tried to imagine what it would be like to have another little brother, but couldn't quite manage it. She tried to imagine her mother and Norman in her father's bed like she and David were. She felt faintly sickened by the idea and pushed the image away. I can't believe she'd do that. And with Norman, too!

She thought of him and his brown flannel shirts and the old rags he used for handkerchiefs during the week. He only has one white one, and it's for Sunday, she thought. She thought about his ragged moustache, the white patches in it stained yellow from the tea he drank. His bright blue eyes looked out at her from his kindly face but she shut her mental eyes to that part of the picture. "I can't believe it," she muttered.

"What's that you say?" asked Anna.

"Excuse me, I was just thinking out loud." Mattie opened her eyes.

"I'm surprised your Momma hasn't told you yet."

"I haven't seen Momma, except at church. Anyway, she never told me before when she was expecting another one, why should she have told me now?" A bitter edge had crept into Mattie's voice.

"Are you angry with your Momma?"

"I don't think so."

Anna smiled slightly. "Well, it doesn't matter right now. Things'll …"

"… Work out all right in the end," chorused Mattie. "That's what Norman kept telling me, too."

"Well, it's true. It may not be the way you expect it to, it almost never is, but it's always good in the end." She poured Mattie some more tea.

"I don't see that Poppa dying was such a good end," said Mattie. "All it did was break up our family, and nothing'll ever be the same again." She fought back tears.

Anna patted Mattie's hand. "Perhaps the changes aren't finished yet. In fact, I'd be willing to bet they're not."

Mattie swallowed hard at the lump in her throat. "How do you mean? I don't know if I want to see any more changes." She gulped at her tea.

"I mean that you're bringing another life into the world to replace the one that was lost. You have David now, and he's a good man. You have your own home already. Lots of young couples have to live with their families until they can afford a place of their own. I'd say you were really pretty fortunate."

Mattie thought these things over in silence for a few minutes, especially the part of having her own home. The idea of living with David and her mother and Norman all at the same time was not a pleasant one. She frowned. Momma'd know everything we ever did, she thought. Even the things we do at night. A blush rose from somewhere and she took a hasty sip of tea. "Where did you live when you were first married?"

"With Ian's parents right here in this house. We lived with them until they died. My children were born before they passed on. I missed my mother a lot those days."

"Did your Momma deliver your babies?"

"No. Old Annie did. She was the midwife here then. She taught me almost everything I know about delivering babies. She's very frail and forgetful now, although Edith says she still has some good days. Old Annie was a great healer and not everyone appreciated her. She'd been here since shortly after the settlement began and for a long time she was the only one who could cure serious illness. Then Dr. Moore came."

"What happened then?" asked Mattie.

"When he came, a lot of Annie's clients deserted her and went to him for advice, and she was forced into living very frugally, but she still delivered the babies. Dr. Moore trusted her. He's a wise man." Anna sat lost in thought for a few moments then rose to her feet. "Well, this won't buy boots for the baby. I expect you're famished by now. I'll just make us a *strupach*."

Chapter Eight

"Did you have a nice visit with Mrs. Gillis?" asked David as they walked home in the greyness of the late afternoon.

Mattie pulled her shawl up over her bonnet to shield it from the heavy mist that had just begun. "Very nice."

"Did she clear up the matter of having babies for you?"

"Hm? Babies?"

"Yes, babies. That little thing in there." David reached over and patted her round belly.

"Don't! Someone might see." Mattie pushed his hand away.

"Who's going to see besides the squirrels? We're out in the middle of the woods."

Mattie returned to her thoughts.

"So did Mrs. Gillis help you any?" persisted David.

"Some."

"Mattie! What's the matter? I thought a visit with Mrs. Gillis would settle your mind, but you're farther away now than you ever were."

"Momma's going to have a baby, too."

"And?"

"And nothing." Mattie kicked at a pebble in the path.

"C'mon now, Mattie, what's wrong?"

"It just doesn't seem right, that's all." She pressed her lips together and scowled.

"What doesn't seem right? That she's having another baby?"

"Any of it. How could she? Just, how could she?" Mattie swiped at some brown oak leaves that were hanging in the way, sending a small waterfall down her back.

David watched Mattie's angry face. "How could she do what we do?"

"Yes, that. And with Norman, too!" Mattie reminded herself again of the handkerchiefs. "It isn't decent."

"What's not decent about it? Your mother's his wife."

"It just isn't decent." She stomped on down the path. "She never told me, either." She turned in at their gate slamming it behind her and leaving David on the other side.

David pulled open the gate and hurried after her. "So that's what's wrong. She never told you."

"No, and she never has."

"Did you tell her yet that we've started a family?"

"We-ell, no. I haven't really seen her except at church and you know what that's like."

"Does she know yet that she's going to be a grandmother?"

"She's got eyes hasn't she?"

"So do you. And you've got a tongue in your head, and you can talk to her if you want to."

"How can I do that? She lives half way to the other side of the lot. I didn't even get to go to her wedding. I didn't even know about it until it was all over. Besides she wouldn't tell me anything anyway. She never has."

"Would you like to go home for a visit on Saturday?"

Mattie considered this in silence for a few minutes. "She could at least have told me," she muttered.

"It'll probably be your last chance to go before the snow flies, and think how nice it'll be to see Ellie again. You haven't seen her since August."

"I'll think about it."

The heavy mist turned to rain and continued all week. Mattie mulled over the problem every day, but in the end the decision was taken from her. At ten o'clock on Saturday morning a knock came at the door. She went to open it.

"Hello, Momma." Mattie stood looking at her mother. I'd forgotten how little she is, she thought. She looked beyond her mother to the woods. Why,

I'm taller than her.

"Aren't you going to ask me in?"

Mattie stood staring at her mother in bewilderment. "I was going to visit you today."

"Mattie, it's cold out here, and you're letting it all into the house. I taught you better than that. Now let me in before I freeze to the step." Mary Cameron Martin took a step closer to the door.

Mattie came out of her reverie, and sprang aside. "I'm sorry, Momma, come in and get warm. I'll just put another stick on the fire."

Mattie scurried about the kitchen straightening things that didn't need to be straightened, and brushing at bits of dust that weren't there.

"You might take my coat." Mrs. Martin was still standing in the middle of the kitchen.

Mattie helped her mother with her coat. "I'll just hang it here by the fire to dry," she said. "Can I get you a cup of tea? It'll take the chill off."

"May I sit down?"

"Yes, of course, you don't need to ask. Pull the rocker nearer to the fire." Mattie swung the kettle over the fire to come to the boil, then picked up the mending she had been working on.

"How did you get here?"

"Norman had business with Sandy today and he took the truck wagon, so I came too. He's going back mid afternoon so I'll have to be back at the store by then."

"Where're the children?"

"Ellie's minding them. She's a great help these last few months since you went away. You'd hardly recognize her anymore."

Mattie got up to put down the tea. "How's Tommy?"

"Humph! He's well, and I hate to say it! He's taken up with that Colleen O'Brien from Iona. It'll be the shame of him, and us too. She's no better than she should be, and a Cath'lic besides. The priest'll be gettin' him yet."

"Well, he's old enough to make up his own mind."

"Yes, and he knows better than to make it up that way. The next thing you know, I'll be having Cath'lic grandchildren."

"Well, it won't be the babies' fault."

"I see you're in the family way yourself." Mary's glance was sharp. "When's it to be?"

"May."

"You didn't waste any time then, did you."

Mattie got up to pour the tea. "I didn't know anything about it, and it's well you know that. David had to tell me the difference." She handed her mother the cup. "I've never been so shamed!"

Her mother sighed. "Aye, well, isn't that the way it always is for good girls, and so it should be. There's no need of them knowing about babies and such things before it's time." She clamped her lips shut.

"And I suppose it isn't time yet for me to know about my new brother either."

"Who told you about that?"

"Never mind. I just heard it."

"Don't you speak to your mother like that, Mattie Cameron! If someone's been gossiping about me I want to know."

"My name's Mattie Matheson now Momma, and no one's gossiping about you." Mattie's heart fluttered in her chest. I've never defied Momma before, she thought. She hunched her shoulders to ward off the verbal blow, but it didn't come.

Mary glared at her daughter and changed the subject. "Where's Himself today?"

"Over at Minister MacDonald's. There's some kind of church meeting for tomorrow, and he and Mr. McRae have to prepare for it. I don't envy Mrs. MacDonald, they'll be there all morning, and for dinner too."

"It'll be company for her, though."

"If you call a kitchen full of men company."

Mary looked around. "You have a nice little house here. Enough room for two and a place to add onto when the time comes. You've done well for yourself, Mattie."

"You mean you've done well for me!"

Mary looked surprised. "And what else could I have done? Aren't you happy? Isn't he good to you?"

"He's good to me."

"What else could I have done, then?"

"It doesn't matter any more. I have a home and a baby coming. What else could I have wanted better than that?" She was silent for a few minutes. "When're you expecting?"

"Sometime in May. Norman's that pleased you'd think he was growing it himself." A smile crossed Mary's features.

You're looking pretty smug yourself, thought Mattie. She got up and gave a hard poke at the fire, sending showers of sparks up the chimney. "I suppose he wants a boy."

"I don't think it matters to him much right now. He's just too pleased to think he's fathered anything."

"D'you think about Poppa ever?"

"Sometimes."

"I think about him a lot."

"It's not good to think too much. It'll make you melancholy. Besides, he's been dead five months. It's time to stop thinking about him as if he was just here."

"But he was your husband!"

"I know that, and better than you do. But things have changed. How do you think Norman'd feel if I went around with a long face pining after your father everyday? Norman's a good steady man and deserves better. Of course I miss your father, and I probably always will. We were going to do great things together after you children were grown, but his days were cut short and Norman stepped in to take his place and I'm glad of it."

"But how could you?"

Her mother's face saddened. "A woman does what she has to do."

A few hours later, Mattie watched her mother out of sight up the little path to their gate. An intense longing for home overwhelmed her at the sight of her mother's short sturdy figure disappearing through the trees. Oh, Poppa, I miss you so much. She choked back the tears. Nothing's the same anymore. I'm so lonely.

She turned back into the house and picked up her shawl from its hook behind the door. She wrapped it around her head and shoulders and walked across to the shed that housed their cow and the three chickens. The cold east wind whipped colour into her pale cheeks and tugged at the ends of her shawl. The icy rain stung as the wind flung it against her skin. She quickened her pace.

At least I can start the chores before David gets back.

She entered the sheltered dimness of the barn. Pansy turned her head to look at her, her jaws working rhythmically on her cud. The hens clucked softly to themselves and regarded her out of baleful yellow eyes. Somewhere a mouse squeaked. Mattie put a generous forkful of hay in front of Pansy, then went and inspected the bin where David always put the grain for the hens. The bin was almost empty, and an ugly sight met her eyes. Rats! Three big ones! She shrieked and dropped the lid.

What am I going to do? I can't let them eat all the grain. She still had the fork in her hands. She lifted the lid and peered over the edge of the bin. There they were! Letting the lid fall back against the wall she lifted the hay fork over the edge of the bin and began stabbing at the cornered rats. Suddenly she began stabbing with all her might at the scurrying squealing beasts. "It's not fair! It's not fair!" she screamed at the rats. "Why'd you have to die, Poppa?" She felt the fork go through a soft belly. "I don't want to be a wife!" She shook the grey furry body off the end of the fork and continued stabbing randomly inside the bin. "I don't want to be a mother!" The strength of her rage seemed enormous to her. "I'm so afraid!" She gasped for breath but kept on stabbing. The fork crunched through a hard skull. "I'm going to die! I wish I was dead!" At last all three rats lay dead and bleeding in the bottom of the bin and Mattie collapsed, sobbing, on the hay beside it. "Why couldn't she have just stayed with making jelly."

The barn door opened and David's tall figure briefly darkened the grey light of the rainy day. He hurried over to Mattie and lifted her out of the hay. "Mattie! Mattie! Hush now, everything's going to be all right." After a few minutes Mattie's sobs quieted. David mopped her face with his handkerchief.

"I heard you scream up at the gate. Whatever happened? I got here as quick as I could."

Mattie opened her eyes and gazed up at him barely seeing him. "Rats," she whispered. "They're in the feed bin."

Mattie roamed listlessly around the kitchen that evening. My back aches, she complained to herself. I hope this isn't the way it's going to be for the next six months. She sat in the rocker and rocked for a few minutes, then got up and fussed at the fire. I don't feel well. She sat down again.

David looked up from his book. "What's the matter, Mattie?"

She shrugged. "I don't know, I just don't feel well this evening."

"Why don't you go up to bed. We can skip the reading tonight. I'll be along in a few minutes." He marked his place and put down his book. "Between your mother and the rats, you've had a hard day."

Mattie nodded and climbed the stairs. Her cry a few minutes later brought David up to the bedroom two steps at a time.

"What's wrong?"

"I'm bleeding!"

"Very much?"

"Yes! No! I don't know." Mattie began to whimper.

"I'll go fetch Mrs. Gillis."

"Don't leave me!"

"If I'm to get help, I have to. I'll be as quick as I can." He disappeared down the steep narrow stairs, and a few seconds later the door slammed and Mattie heard his footsteps running across the yard.

Mattie lay on the bed praying as hard as ever she had prayed in her life. The dull backache eased somewhat and she fell asleep.

It was a heavy aching sleep, more a stupor than real sleep. The light from the candle flickered in a draft from the window. Mattie shivered. "So cold," she muttered, and tried to cover herself with the corner of the quilt. She slipped into a dream about babies with little rat faces. They were running everywhere on their hind legs, and she and her mother were trying to catch them. "You can't have them, they're mine!" She reached for the rat-faced baby that her mother was holding and gasped. Her mother had a rat face too!

"Oh, no," said her rat mother, "they're mine."

Mattie grabbed for the baby and pulled its leg off. "Now look what you've made me do!" she cried. "Now I'll never be able to walk."

She stirred restlessly as the door banged announcing David's return. The dream faded, and she opened her eyes to find Mrs. Gillis standing over the bed.

"Hello, Mattie," said Anna softly. The candle she was holding wavered in her breath. "I hear you're having a little trouble."

"My baby. I'm bleeding."

"Very much?"

"I don't know."

"Let me see."

Mattie rolled onto her back.

"Not much. Have you passed anything yet?"

"I don't think so."

"You'd know it if you had. Let me help you get ready for bed. Maybe a good night's sleep will put things right again." She pulled Mattie's shoes and stockings off. "David tells me you've had a hard day today."

"Yes." Mattie struggled out of her dress. "Momma came and we had words."

"Oh." Anna dropped a clean nightgown over Mattie's head. "He only told me about the rats."

Mattie sighed. "That too."

"Well, you lay down now. I've brought some

tea that should help to calm your womb. That and a few days rest should be all you need. David's boiling the kettle, I'll send it up with him." She covered Mattie with the quilt and arranged her pillow. "I'll stay the night and see how you are in the morning."

Mattie opened her eyes to the greyness of another misty dawn. November seems to go on forever, she thought, and then remembered yesterday. My baby! She lay very still, afraid to move. She patted her belly tentatively. It was still round and full. She sighed. At least it's still there.

David stirred beside her and opened his eyes. "You're awake, are you?"

"Yes."

"Did you sleep well?"

"Yes. Whatever was in that tea made me relax."

"Good. Are you alright?"

"Yes."

"And the baby?"

"It's still here."

David smiled. "Good. I'll just get up now and send Mrs. Gillis to you."

Mattie was confined to bed for several days. Anna made gallons of tea and chatted endlessly on about everything.

Mattie wasn't fussy about the tea because it

made her sleepy, but she was grateful for the company. At last she was allowed out of bed, and Anna went home after admonishing Mattie to take care of herself and not to do any barn work like killing rats. "Leave that for David. It should all be man's work anyway."

What's man's work? thought Mattie as she watched Mrs. Gillis disappearing through the trees. Every woman I've ever heard of has done barn work, and not just once either. She thought of her mother's red, work-roughened hands. Hands as big as her father's had been. She looked down at her own, still faintly brown from last summer's sun. They were cracked and dry around the edges. Mine'll soon look like hers, too. A tremendous sadness overcame her. Is this all we're good for? she wondered. Working and making babies?

She moved restlessly around the little kitchen. A log hissed and snapped in the fireplace accentuating the silence. Loneliness rushed in once more, and the weight of it was a burden she could hardly bear. Unconsciously she braced her shoulders, her mother's words repeated themselves in her mind, "A woman does what she has to do."

Mattie sank into a melancholy so deep that for several weeks she did nothing but sit and stare into the fire all day. She barely moved to attend to her bodily needs. Dust settled in the little house and the hearth went unswept. She roused herself long enough to make meals for David, but ate very little herself. David came home from school one day to find that she hadn't even combed her hair.

"Mattie, whatever's wrong these days?" he asked.

"I don't know." Mattie answered him lifelessly.

"Are you sick? Is the baby alright? Do you need for me to get Mrs. Gillis again?"

Mattie's heart lightened for a moment, then fell to its previous level. "No, she has her own work to do."

"Would you like your mother to come?"

"No!"

"What then? What can I do?"

Mattie rocked in silence for a few minutes. "You can get Cora for me." She nodded. "Yes, that's what you can do."

Chapter Nine

The next day Mattie swept out the fireplace and laid a new fire. I'll have to set bread, she thought. What I made a few days ago is down to the heel. And a cake! I'll make a hot milk cake. She stoked up the fire. I don't know how I could ever have let my house get into such a mess. Momma would be ashamed of me. Cora'll think she taught me nothing.

The day following this was grey and mild with a hint of sunshine. Mattie paced the small kitchen as she waited for Cora. She's a long time coming, she thought and stopped to stare out the window at the path to the gate. At last she saw Cora through the trees and hurried to meet her.

"It's so good to see you," they shrieked in unison, and fell into a hug, giggling happily.

"You're looking well," observed Cora. "I heard you were sick for awhile and that Mrs. Gillis had to come. Nothing to do with the baby, I hope?"

"That was a few weeks ago. I'm fine now. Come into the house." Mattie turned and led the way back down the path.

"Oh-h, this is so-o nice," squealed Cora. "Just

look at it! Real flower beds, oh and a real barn. I came across the fields the last time and I didn't have time to appreciate it. Do you have a cow too?"

"Yes, and that's real too."

"Oh, you!" Cora tapped Mattie's arm.

"Come in, then, and I'll show you the inside."

I don't remember her squealing so much, thought Mattie after Cora had squealed over the pantry, the sleeping loft, the kitchen, the wood box with the design that David had painted on the lid, and finally, the jars of jam in the cellar. This is about the dozenth thing she's squealed over since she came.

"Come up, then, and I'll make some tea." Mattie led the way upstairs. "I made a cake for us too." She pushed the kettle over the fire to heat. "We'll have that later."

In a few minutes they were settled in front of the fire with cups of tea in their hands and their feet stuck out close to the hearth. The fire crackled like another friend.

"Such a darling house!" exclaimed Cora. "You're so lucky. Why didn't you show me all this before?"

"You didn't give me much chance to."

Cora sipped her tea, ignored Mattie's tone of voice and changed the subject. "Didn't I tell you he wanted to come courting?"

"I guess you did, indeed."

"And are you happy?"

Mattie blinked. "I suppose so, I hadn't really thought about it."

"Well, surely you'd know if you were happy or not."

"Why wouldn't I be happy? I have everything I could want."

"So what's it like to be married?" Cora took another sip of her tea, and watched Mattie while she considered the question. The answer was several minutes in coming. "Well?" prompted Cora at last.

"It's pleasant enough. It took me a long time to get used to him though. He used to make me nervous."

"And you're all over that now?"

"Oh, yes, long ago. Well, not really that long ago. It's been easier since he shaved his beard off. I can see better what he's thinking about now."

"I saw him in church. I didn't recognize him. Did it tickle?"

"I don't know if it tickled him."

"No, silly! I meant, did it tickle you?"

"No, yes," Mattie blushed when she realized what she had just admitted to. Cora could always do that to me, she thought. I'll have to be more careful.

"So it did tickle!" Cora giggled again at Mattie's discomfort.

"Have some more tea."

"So, what's it like?"

"What's what like?"

"You know," said Cora, "what married people do."

"Cora, you brazen thing! That's none of your business!" She dumped tea into Cora's mug so energetically it almost overran the cup.

"You mean you won't tell me either?"

"No, I won't. That's private. Besides it's also very embarrassing."

"Oh, you married women, you're all alike. Sarah won't tell me either." Cora made a face.

"Well, if your own sister won't tell you, did you really think I would? Besides," she pursed her lips, "a good girl doesn't need to know these things until it's time."

"You sounded like your mother."

Mattie looked alarmed. "I did, didn't I. Well, she was just here the other day."

"You looked like her too, the way you made a mouth."

"D'you think I'm turning into my mother?"

Cora shrugged. "I don't know. Maybe. Your mother always seems to be cross, and you don't smile much these days."

"She is, isn't she. Always growling about something. I can't ever remember her not having something short to say about almost everything. Is your mother cross like that?"

Cora giggled. "She had her moments. Sarah and I'd get into it, and she'd get cross, and then we'd do it all the more just to keep her going. Poor Momma. It always took her a while to figure out what we were up to." She giggled again. "Then, of course, she'd have to laugh, and it'd be all over 'til the next time. Of course, she's not like that now."

"Well, I just hope I'm not like that with my children."

"How many children do you want?"

Mattie shrugged. "I don't know. I've never thought about it. As many as I have, I suppose. What else can I do?"

"Ah, me," sighed Cora, as if she knew, "and isn't that always the way."

Mattie laughed. "Now who sounds just like her mother?"

"I guess we can't escape it. They feed it to us with our porridge." Cora's grimace was fierce this time.

"So, d'you want to see our 'real' barn now?" asked Mattie. She set down her empty cup.

"And your 'real' cow?" giggled Cora. "Sure, I like barns. You never know what you'll find in them." Her rosy face took on a sly expression.

Mattie rose and handed Cora her shawl. "And what d'you mean by that?" She looked at her friend sharply.

"The last time I was in a barn I had company,"

Cora replied, then giggled again.

"And whose company was that, and what barn?"

"The church barn, and never mind whose company, but it was awful nice."

"Oh?" Mattie opened the door for them and they strolled across the yard.

"He tried to kiss me."

"And did he succeed?"

"Not right away. I made him work for it."

"How long were you in the barn, anyway?"

"Long enough."

"Did your mother know?"

"No! She didn't go to church that day. She was having one of her spells. A good thing, or she'd have skinned me."

"She'd have been right, too." Mattie swung the barn door open. "You'd better be careful, Cora, or you'll end up like poor Christy. A new baby, and no father, and the talk of the neighbourhood."

"And what am I to be careful of if no one'll tell me?"

"Never mind, just don't be going into barns with any unnamed males." Mattie picked up the fork and lifted hay into Pansy's stall. "This is Pansy. Norman sent her for us. She just had her first calf last summer, but she was extra. The children made kind of a pet of her from the time she was a calf, so she's nice and gentle. Get over, Pansy!" The cow obediently moved and Mattie cleared out the old straw and put down a fresh bed for her.

Cora watched from the cobwebby dimness just inside the door. "Should you be doing that in your condition?"

"I suppose not. Mrs. Gillis said that I wasn't to do any heavy lifting 'til after the baby comes, and after the trouble I had a few weeks ago, I guess she's right." Mattie went to the feed bin to scoop up a dish of grain for the chickens. The rats were gone, but a faint dark smear near the bottom of the bin made her shudder.

"What trouble?"

"I started to bleed after I killed some rats out here in the barn."

"Bleed?" Cora curled her lip.

"Yes, you know, like when you have the monthlies."

"Oh, so that's it." Cora's face brightened. "That's really how they get out. Is that how they get in, too?" Cora's inquisitive bright eyes watched Mattie's discomfort.

"Yes, that's how they get in, too. So now you know, and that's why you have to stay out of barns with the boys!"

Cora digested this bit of news for some minutes in silence. "I'd never do that!"

"Humph," said Mattie, "just see that you don't."

"So why'd you start to bleed?"

"I went to feed the chickens and there were

three big rats in the feed bin and I killed them with the pitchfork, and it was too much for me. I was afraid I'd lose the baby."

"Whatever would you have done?"

"I don't know." Mattie thought back to the dreadful night. "I was that scared."

"He'd have disowned you."

"No, he wouldn't have disowned me. He'd have been plenty upset though, but not at me." Mattie shivered. "Let's get back to the house, it's cold out here."

The girls settled themselves in front of the fire again. Mattie poked at the fire with the poker, sending a shower of sparks up the chimney. "So who were you in the barn with?" She sat down opposite Cora.

Cora blushed a little and would not look at Mattie. "Charlie."

"Charlie! Cora Smith! You can do better than that!"

Cora tossed her head. "Yes, well, the best's already taken."

"Oh, Cora!" Mattie couldn't help the look of smugness that stole across her face. "There's lots of nice men around. You don't have to be stealing kisses with the boys. You'll get yourself a reputation, and then no one'll want you."

Cora sighed. "I know."

"Well then, why do it?"

"Oh, Mattie, you sound just like my sister."

"Well, at least she has some sense."

"And I don't, I suppose."

"Sometimes you don't act like it." Mattie gave the fire another poke.

"And I suppose you had sense when you were killing rats in the barn and making yourself bleed. A person'd think you didn't want a baby."

Mattie's eyes filled with tears. "I didn't until I thought I was going to lose it," she admitted. "Now I don't know what I'd do if I did lose it. I've been in the depths of despair these last few weeks just thinking about it."

"Now, now, Mattie, you didn't lose it after all, so there's no use crying over it."

"No, but I might have. I was so angry that day. Momma'd been here. She's expecting too, you know, and she's that smug about it! Her and that man! You'd think they'd have the decency to wait until Poppa was cold."

"D'you miss your father?"

"Every day. If he hadn't died, none of this would have happened."

"None of what?"

"Norman and Momma and another baby that isn't Poppa's."

"And David and Mattie and the baby that is theirs."

"That would have happened anyway likely, only not so soon." Mattie sniffed and rummaged in her apron pocket for a handkerchief.

"Maybe it would, and maybe it wouldn't have. Did you know that Rachael had her sights set on him?" Cora watched Mattie out the corner of her eye.

Mattie's heart bounded in her chest. "No, I didn't. How d'you know?"

"I heard Mrs. John tell Momma one day at the store right after we got back from Charlottetown. Rachael was just seething. She heard that he was building a house, because he used to go up and spend time with her father. They're great friends, you know. Anyway, I guess she thought it was for her." Cora's chuckle was tinged with malice. "She's not getting any younger, and she's starting to feel it."

"She's a couple of years older than David, isn't she?"

"Something like that. I guess she took to her bed for three days when she heard."

Mattie chuckled. "She's probably sorry now that she turned down Geordie."

"Och, that was ages ago. He's happily married to Elizabeth now. They have three little ones and another on the way."

"Babies, babies, and more babies." Mattie sighed.

"And what's wrong with that?"

"We're either avoiding having them or having them hand over fist, that's all. How'd your mother only have the three of you?"

Cora shrugged. "I don't know, and it's for sure she'd never tell me. All I know is that she and Poppa fought a lot."

"I never knew that. They always seemed so …"

"So what?"

"I don't know. So friendly, I guess."

"Only at church. The rest of the time, the only time they weren't fighting is if they weren't speaking."

"Oh, my! Momma and Poppa were never like that. As cross as Momma was all the time with us children, she was never cross with Poppa. She was stern with him, and I'm not sure that she liked him much, but she never went against him and they never fought." Mattie sighed. "It must have been really unpleasant for you."

"Well, it wasn't too bad until James died. After that it got a lot worse. I think Poppa wanted her to have another one and she didn't want to. She developed this condition, whatever it is, just about then, and things have finally settled down, thank goodness. At least they don't fight anymore. Whenever Momma doesn't want to do something she takes to her bed and that ends the fight right there. Poppa doesn't even bother much anymore."

"And this all happened since James died? D'you still miss him?"

"Not exactly. It was awful at first. He was my best friend in some ways, even though he was five years older than me. It was real strange not having him around anymore. It was like there was a giant hole in my life that wouldn't go away."

"How long did it take you to stop missing him?"

Cora stuck her lip out while she considered this for a few minutes. "Probably a whole year. Once the anniversary went by, things didn't seem so empty anymore, and by that time Momma had stopped talking about him all the time, so I wasn't reminded about him every day. It helps to keep busy, I think. I had school, and you and I were always up to something afterwards. You just need to fill your time, and not dwell on it too much, that's all."

"I see."

"Well, I'm hungry," said Cora. "Where's that cake you said you made?"

Mattie jumped to her feet. "I'll just get dinner ready." She began bustling in and out of the pantry.

"Let's just have cake for dinner," said Cora. "I've always wanted to do that."

"We'll probably make ourselves sick."

"It'll be like when we used to play house, except we'll have real cake."

Mattie chuckled. "We always fed our babies on cake, didn't we."

Mattie walked up the path to the gate with Cora. The day had gotten progressively colder, and the fitful sunshine had given way to a heavy overcast. The smell of snow was sharp in the air.

"You'll have to hurry if you want to get home before dark." Mattie gave Cora a hug. "I wish you didn't have to go, I've enjoyed your company so much today."

"I hope the snow keeps until I get home," replied Cora. "I suppose I'll meet David on the way."

"Oh, likely. He comes home about this time every day." A snowflake drifted to the ground. "You'd better hurry, the snow's starting."

Cora gave Mattie another hug and started up the road.

"And stay out of barns," called Mattie. She turned and walked slowly back to the house, her sense of isolation accentuated by the visit. I've got to stop this, she thought. It was lovely having Cora here, but I can't have company all the time. I wish David would come. She went into the house and closed the door against the snow and cold.

She added a stick of wood to the fire and began peeling potatoes for supper. I'm sorry I ate all that cake for dinner. I don't feel like eating supper, but I suppose I have to. Mrs. Gillis did say that I should be eating for two. I hope you liked the cake, baby. For myself, I think it was too much of a good thing.

She rinsed the potatoes and put them into the cast iron pot. She added a dipperful of water and hung the pot over the fire. I'm glad I saved a piece for David, though I don't think I'll want cake again for another year. She peeled a few carrots and sliced some turnip. That Cora could always talk me into things without me hardly knowing it. Her lips curved into a warm smile at the thought of her friend. She's so silly about so many things, but she cheers me up. The kitchen door banged and a gust of cold air blew into the room.

"I'm home." David hung his coat on the hook behind the door.

Mattie ran to him. "I'm so glad." She stopped short and hung her head.

David drew her into his arms for a hug. "I'm glad too," he replied. "Why're you hiding your face? Have you done something you don't want me to know about?"

"N-no." Her reply was muffled in the folds of his shirt.

David tipped her face up. "What then?"

Mattie's blush was hidden in the shadows of the gathering dusk. "Am I being too bold?" Her voice was barely above a whisper.

David began to laugh. "Too bold? To come and greet your husband at the door? I don't think so. I'm glad you did. I've been wishing for this day for a long time. Whatever made you think you were being bold?"

"Momma never greeted Poppa at the door."

"Not in front of you children, maybe, but let me tell you, my mother always greeted my father and it was nice."

CHAPTER TEN

The storm increased in intensity all evening. The wind whined through the trees surrounding the house, and drove snow through the cracks in the porch door to lie in small drifts on the floor. The draft from the porch was frigid even though the door between was closed. The frost crept up the panes in the window until it reached the top, but it didn't matter, because there was nothing to see in the howling darkness outside. A particularly vicious gust of wind shook the house. Mattie shivered and pulled her shawl closer to her neck. It sounds like the *bochans* are trying to get us, she thought, and shivered again.

"Are you cold?" David looked up from the broom he was tying by the light of the fire.

Mattie shook her head. "I've just never been by myself in a snow storm. It sounds evil when you just sit and listen to it."

"Och, Mattie, it's just a storm, and you're not by yourself now."

"No, but before there were the other children. We'd always be doing something so there was plenty of noise around and I couldn't hear the storm. It's so quiet here in the house with just the two of us." She picked up her knitting. "How can you be so calm? It's this kind of night that witches walk."

David laughed. "I think they'd be mighty cold and wet if they were out walking tonight."

"How can you joke about that?" Mattie crossed her fingers. "If they heard you they might come to get you, and then where would I be?"

"Now Mattie, you don't believe all that stuff, do you? It's all just tales told by old women to frighten children into being good."

"But Momma told me about an old man from the Head of Montague who laughed at the witches and they came to get him. She said that he went to the barn to do chores one evening and never was heard from again."

"I heard that story too." David pulled hard on the knot he was making. "And he didn't just disappear, he went to the Boston States to get away from his wife. She was a terrible nag and made life miserable for him. He left to get away from her. He milked the cows and did up the chores and as soon as it was dark enough, he left."

"I don't believe you. You're making that up. How can you be so calm about it all?"

David frowned. "You don't really believe all that do you?"

"Momma told me, and anyway, it's in the Bible."

Mattie closed her lips.

"I see," said David, "Momma and the Bible. I guess I can't beat that."

Mattie looked over at him, catching the last of the smile that had ghosted across his face. "Well, it is!" she said. "Just look at Saul and the Witch of Endor, and Minister MacDonald is always warning us about having anything to do with the powers of darkness."

"Saul called on the Witch of Endor for his own purposes, and I don't think that was quite what Minister MacDonald was meaning when he mentioned that last week." David's smile was plainly visible now.

"Oh! You're laughing at me. How can you be so disrespectful? They'll be coming to get you the next thing you know, and then you'll not be laughing."

"Mattie, those things are all a figment of your mother's imagination, and I think that you need to forget about them. I certainly don't want you teaching such nonsense to our children."

"How can you say that? What if they meet one someday? How'll they know to protect themselves?"

David sighed. "Those things are not real."

"How do you know that?"

"My mother was an Englishwoman and she told me." He clamped his lips shut and returned to his task.

Mattie bent over her knitting in silence for some minutes. A gust of wind hissed snow against the window panes. "I hope Cora got home alright. It's a fair walk from here, and it was just starting to snow when she left."

"Did you have a pleasant visit?"

"It was lovely to visit with her, but you know, she's changed somehow." Mattie frowned. "She's giddy or something."

"She always was giddy. I met her on the road just down from the store and she seemed the same to me."

"She said that Rachael had set her sights on you. She said that she went to bed for three days when she heard that we'd gotten married."

David blinked. "Rachael who?"

"You know, 'my-sister-Rachael,' from Flat River."

"Oh, that Rachael. I know her father well." David held a finished broom up and inspected it for workmanship. "How'd she ever get such a strange nickname?"

"Her little sister was very attached to her and always wanted to know where my sister, Rachael, went to, whenever she wasn't in plain sight. So she was always called my-sister-Rachael to distinguish her from the other four Rachaels, especially her cousin Rachael, because they always used to be together."

"And I suppose the cousin is my-cousin-Rachael?"

"Oh, no. She's Rachael Sandy because she married Sandy MacPhail, and Sandy's brother William married one of the other Rachaels, so she's Rachael Willie because he goes by Willie more than he goes by William."

"And the other Rachael?"

"She was the first Rachael so she's just Rachael."

The wind shook the little house once more, sending a shower of snow down the chimney. It hissed in the fire and then evaporated.

David rose, went to the window and rubbed a hole in the frost. He peered outside into the darkness, the faint light from the kitchen barely illuminated a very small patch of the yard. "It's really piling up out there. I hope we're not snowed in. I'll need to get to the schoolhouse in the morning."

"I don't think they'll be expecting you if it snows too much. Hardly any of the children'll be able to come anyway. Most of them live too far away and will likely be snowed in too." Mattie's knitting needles clicked as she knit the cuff on a pair of socks.

"I'm glad I banked the house so well," said David, "it'd be a lot colder in here if I hadn't." Another shower of snow came down the chimney. David rearranged the fire with the poker and added another stick of wood. "I wish I had something to put in front of that door to keep the draft out. It's so cold in the porch that the snow's not even melting." He sat back on his chair and began to work on another broom. "So did Cora have any other news?"

"Not much. We mostly talked about babies. She giggled a lot and marvelled at us living in a 'real' house with a 'real' barn, with a 'real' cow in it." Mattie's face grew serious. "I'm worried about her though."

"Why's that?" David frowned, concentrating on his task.

"Charlie persuaded her to let him kiss her in the church barn the other day, and Cora's just the one to let things get out of hand and get into some real trouble some day."

"So that's who Charlie was talking about."

"They're talking about her already?"

David looked up from his work. "No, they weren't talking about her. I just overheard Charlie telling Donald Peter about it. I had no idea it was Cora they were talking about, and I don't think Donald did either. Charlie was being very secretive."

"Even so, she took a risk. I just hope she doesn't do it again. Charlie's far too young for her, and so are any of the other boys she knows."

"Well, I hardly think a kiss is a reason for a wedding."

"Well, you know, one thing leads to another,

and it's never very far to the altar that way."

David swallowed a chuckle at Mattie's knowing air. "I don't think it's likely to happen again," he said, "Charlie said he didn't like it."

"That's as may be, but he'll soon get used to it if he keeps practising."

"And wanting more besides?"

Mattie lay awake for a long time that night listening to the storm. The wind whistled in the eaves, driving the snow wetly against the small window panes. The curtains moved in the slight draft that seeped in around the sash, and occasionally she could hear the branches of the spruce trees striking the house.

I'll have to get David to trim those back when the weather's fit again. I wonder how much snow's down now. She rolled over and curled herself into David's back.

Mattie awoke the next morning to a still whiteness. She lay for a few minutes listening to the muffled scrape and thunk of David's shovel as he cleared the snow from the back door. The grey light of dawn filtered into the loft bedroom.

It's not sunny out, I wonder if we're to get more?

She eased herself upright onto the edge of the

bed and shivered as the cold air struck her warm skin. She gasped from the shock and her breath curled on the still air and then evaporated.

I can see my breath, she thought.

She grabbed her clothes and stuffed them under the warmth of the bed covers while she attended to other needs. Steam rose from the bowl.

Good grief, even that's frozen! she thought. She dressed hurriedly and went down the steep stairs into the kitchen.

Good! David's put a stick on the fire already. She rubbed a spot through the thick frost on the window pane, and peered out with one eye. A blank whiteness filled the hole on the pane. She blinked and tried again to see outside.

Is the snow over the windows? she wondered. It can't have snowed that much.

She grabbed her shawl from the hook and wrapped it around herself as she opened the back door. David had cleared the red sandstone step, and was now a few feet into the deep drift that separated the house from the barn. The grey clouds were thick and threatening, and the smell of snow was still on the wind. David paused for breath, and leaned on his shovel.

"We must have gotten three feet last night, and by the look of that sky, there's more to come."

"Well, at least we'll have a white Christmas." Mattie pulled her shawl over her head.

"A good thing, too. You know what they say, 'green Christmas, fat graveyard.'" He turned back to his work. "You'd better get yourself indoors where it's warm."

Mattie returned to the kitchen and began preparing breakfast. David'll need lots of food today, she thought as she chipped through the shell of ice on the water bucket. I should have set the bucket on the hearth last night. Well, at least it hasn't frozen all the way through. She dropped a wedge of ice into the pot and set it over the fire to melt. I'll pour a little water in too, that should help it along.

Presently she had the porridge cooking, and the table set. The back door thumped, and she heard the scrape of the shovel as David set it down against the wall. He stamped the snow off his feet before entering the kitchen.

"It's a cold one." He hung his coat on the hook behind the door. "I wish I had a pair of snowshoes, there must be six or eight feet where it's drifted." He held his hands out to the warmth of the fire.

"Breakfast is ready, sit in." Mattie ladled porridge into two large bowls. "How soon before the next one, d'you think?"

"A few hours, not much more." David blew on his porridge. "Just about time enough for me to get to the barn and tend the animals."

"Poor Pansy sounds in distress."

"Aye, well, she's usually milked and fed long before this. If I had snow shoes I could have gotten to her first, and then shovelled a path for convenience's sake. As it is, I still have to shovel out the barn door before I can get in." He ate his porridge in large spoonfuls.

"It's still blowing out there."

"That I know. For every shovelful of snow I move, there's a half a one blows back in. It's almost a losing battle." He swallowed the last of his tea. "As soon as I get Pansy attended to, I'll bring in some more wood and water. We have a good deep well, so it won't have frozen."

Mattie helped him on with his coat and watched him trudge across the yard to tackle the last of the snow drift. He'll have to find the well first, she thought. There's not even a dimple in the snow to tell him where it is.

The day grew minimally brighter for a brief period, but by late afternoon the snow had started again. In the interval between storms David and Mattie filled the wood box to overflowing and stacked more wood in the little porch. Pansy had been fed and watered and milked, and then fed and milked again before the first flakes of the new storm had begun falling. David cleared the snow away from the windows in an attempt to let in a little more

light, but the frost had so coated the inside that
it made very little difference. At last everything
was made snug, and they relaxed in front of the
fire for awhile.

"We'll probably get three more feet," said David.
"Just you listen to that wind! I'm glad I did the
roof myself. I was going to get Herman to do it,
but his roofs don't always last."

Mattie chuckled. "D'you suppose the story's
true about them having Sunday dinner with company and all, the other year, and the roof blowing
off in the wind?"

"It was John, the store, who told me about it.
He said he and Mrs. John were there when it
happened. It's that house they're living in now,
and Mrs. Herman was awful eager to move in,
so Herman hurried to get the roof on, intending
to go back later and put a few more nails in it.
Well, he forgot about it, and with one thing and
another, he never did get to it, and one Sunday
in November there blew up an awful storm off
the Atlantic and lifted the roof right off the house
and left everyone with their heads bare to the
heavens. Minister MacDonald was there that day
too, and had just finished blessing the roof over
their heads in such a storm."

"The whole roof?" asked Mattie.

"Well, the part that wasn't well-nailed down.
Mrs. Herman's mother was staying with them

for awhile, and she hasn't stopped talking about it since."

"I heard Momma say one time that Mrs. Herman's mother never liked Herman."

"No, she thought that he wasn't good enough for her daughter. He was just getting on the good side of her with the new house and all, when that happened, and her worst fears were confirmed as far as she was concerned."

"But they'd been married for years by that time. For heaven's sake, their children were all grown by then."

"I know, but that's the way her mother is. Besides, she's had her nose out of joint for years because of something that Herman's father had done to her when they were young."

"Och, well, people are funny, aren't they."

David smiled. "Indeed they are! How about some supper for a hungry man?"

Mattie jumped up. "Is it that time already? I'll have to light a candle, it's that dark in here."

That night new snow fell on the previous day's snow, and the wind piled it all into deep drifts. We'll not get out until spring, thought Mattie, as she stood on the doorstep gazing across the blank whiteness of the yard the next morning. The barn is practically buried! She turned her head and looked at the house. A sense of claustrophobia rushed over her. Snow covered the house on this side, half way up the roof. She couldn't see the other side from where she stood. Her stomach clenched. What if something goes wrong with the baby? She pulled her shawl more tightly around herself and shivered. I wonder where David's got to? The rhythmic sound of his shovel sounded from somewhere close at hand. Presently he emerged from a drift almost in front of her.

"What're you doing out here with just a shawl on? You'll catch your death of pneumonia. Get back inside where it's warm."

"I couldn't see you," said Mattie.

"No wonder. The drifts are over my head. I'm just making a tunnel through. It must have blown a gale overnight. Now, get indoors before you freeze."

Mattie did as she was told. "I wish I wasn't with child," she muttered to herself, poking at the fire, "then I could go out and shovel too."

She thought back to winters at home. It was such fun. When it stormed so much like this Momma'd let us take blankets and build a tent and pretend we were the settlers just newly come to the Island. I suppose they're doing that just now if Norman'll let them.

It was strange, but Momma was never cranky during snow storms. She said one time that she liked snow storms because they made her feel safe with everyone home and indoors, and the fire going. She even let us picnic in the tent one day. Of course, that was only once, and Poppa was still alive. He played with us that day, too. He said that we'd taken up so much of the kitchen with our tent that he had to join us. He tried to persuade Momma to come in too, but she wouldn't.

Mattie gave the fire another poke, and sighed. I guess I'd better not think about that anymore, Momma said it'd make me melancholy, and I've certainly had enough of that.

She idled the morning away in front of the fire, not even picking up her knitting. I've still got plenty of time to finish the baby sweaters, she thought. We'll be here for a week at this rate. She pushed the kettle on its hook over the fire with the toe of her shoe. David'll be in soon and likely freezing. He'll be wanting a cup of tea.

The kettle began to boil just as the back door slammed. Mattie could hear David stamping the snow off his boots. Presently he came into the kitchen, his face red with the cold. "Can you mend these? I've shovelled a hole in them." He held out his mittens for Mattie's inspection.

"You have, indeed," agreed Mattie. "I'll do what I can, though it may not be much, there's not much left of them." She stuck her hand into a mitt. "I'll just make you some tea and a bite to eat. You must be 'gant' by now."

"I am that. Shovelling's hard work." He settled himself by the fire and held his hands out to its warmth. "At least the wind's died down. I don't have to shovel the same snow twice now."

Mattie put the tea down to steep, and cut thick slices of bread from the loaf and buttered them. "Have we seen the last of it for awhile?" She set the bread on the table, and poured the tea.

"For a few days, I hope. I'll have to fashion myself some snow shoes to get to school next week. It's certain that I won't be getting there anymore this week. I should have thought of this before."

Mattie carried the glass of molasses to the table, and stuck a spoon in it. "A person can't think of everything," she consoled. "Where are you going to get wood to make snow shoes out of?"

"I have a couple of nice pieces that I've been saving down in the shed. There's enough for a pair in them, and they're about the right size and thickness. All I have to do is bend them." He spooned a generous helping of molasses onto his bread and let it soak in before taking a bite. "You should put on your coat and come out and see what a nice tunnel I've built to the barn and the well." He took a bite of bread. "It's a little bit crooked because I didn't know exactly where I was going until I got there." He sipped at the dripping molasses and some dribbled down his chin.

Mattie laughed at him. "You need sideboards for that."

After David had finished his lunch, Mattie put on her coat and followed him out into the yard. She marvelled again at the beauty. Except for the deep paths and tunnels that David had dug to the barn and the well, the whole yard was an unbroken carpet of white. It sparkled and winked in the feeble November sun.

The roof of the barn was nearly covered at the front. The tall spruces at the edge of the yard were covered to six feet up their trunks, their branches were weighted down with snow. A crow cawed in the top of the tallest one, and flapped his wings, sending down a shower of snow that glinted in the sunlight on the way down. Mattie was delighted.

The edges of the drifts were curled and scalloped by the wind. "We could build wonderful snow houses," she exclaimed, turning in a circle to take it all in. The house was covered nearly to the eaves in white drifts. Icicles hung like great fangs at the far corner of the roof where the snow hadn't drifted so high. "Oh, I wish the children were here!"

"Let me show you the way to the well and the

barn," said David taking her arm. "At first I was only going to shovel a path, but the snow was so deep, I ended up just cutting a hole through the drifts." He led Mattie to the entrance of the tunnel.

Mattie stepped inside. Sunlight filtered through the snow and lighted the interior with a soft diffusion of light. In places there were holes to the outside where the snow was less deep and David's shovel had broken through. She walked forward, marvelling at the translucent blue inside the tunnel. "It feels warm in here," she said in surprise.

"That's because it's sheltered from the wind and snow's an insulator."

"What did you do with all the snow from inside?"

"Threw it out the holes in the roof. The roof'll keep it from getting snowed in again in the next snow storm too."

"It won't fall in?"

David shook his head. "It shouldn't. By that time it'll have had a chance to settle and get stronger. And if it does, at least I'll have the worst of the snow moved out of here."

Mattie walked the length of the tunnel. She opened the barn door and looked into the blackness within. Pansy turned her head to look at her, her dark eyes gleaming against the whiteness of her face, all that was visible of her in the gloom. "It's really dark in here. You must need the lantern to see by."

"I did this morning. I'll need to get a supply of candles and matches down here."

"I'll be glad when I have enough fat saved to render for candles."

David looked at her in surprise. "D'you know how to make candles?"

She nodded. "I've helped Momma make them ever since I was eight, and last summer I had to make them all by myself because Momma was working in the fields with Tommy, and we'd run out sooner than she expected, what with using them all up when Poppa was so sick."

"Weren't you a little young to be working with hot fat like that?"

Mattie shrugged. "I guess Momma didn't think so. Of course, I just set the wicks and tended the fire when she had to see to William. I was too short then to stir the pot, and I never poured the tallow."

"I see," said David. "Well, we'll have lots of fat next fall. I've made a trade with Sandy for a cow to butcher. He thinks he'll have an extra one and I can give him a day's work for it."

"Oh, good, then I can make soap too."

He looked at her in surprise. "I guess I got a better bargain in a wife than even I imagined."

Chapter Eleven

Christmas'll soon be here, thought Mattie some days later. David had gone off to school that morning on his new snowshoes. Mattie had watched him go. What if it snows again? What'll I do all by myself? She paced restlessly around the kitchen.

I can't panic, that would only make things much worse. She peered out the window. The sun was shining. I wish everyone wasn't so far away.

She forced herself to do her morning chores, stopping every few minutes to check on the sun. It was always shining. I'm being silly, she scolded herself.

She finished her chores. The house was tidy again, but she was still restless. I wish the children were here, we could have so much fun. She went to the door and looked out into the yard. We could build a snowman, or a fort, or make angels in the snow. It's not even very cold out today, the icicles are dripping. She put on her coat and wrapped her shawl around her head and shoulders. I'm going out anyway even if I can't do all those things by myself.

The day was fresh and clear. The sun sparkled

and danced on the snow. It was dazzling to her eyes. She picked up a handful of snow and formed it into a ball. We could have made a snowman. This snow's just right for it. If only the children were here.

Mattie threw the snowball with all her might across the yard. It hit one of the spruce trees by the fence. A small avalanche of snow fell from its limbs with a sparkling thump. A squirrel chirred at her from its branches.

She made another snowball and threw it at the barn roof. It flattened itself against the peak. Inside, one of the hens cackled. Mattie threw another. It arched white against the brilliant blue sky and buried itself in a snow drift.

Snowball followed after snowball until she could throw no more. The drifts were pocked with little holes where each one had landed. She paused for breath, stretching herself upward toward the brightness of the sun. I'm going to make myself a snowman, she thought. I don't need any help.

For an hour she pushed snow around, building three balls in graduated sizes, carefully lifting each one on top of the last one to form her snowman. What'll I do for a face? She stood back and studied her creation, then hurried down into the cellar and returned moments later with a small potato and a carrot. These'll do for eyes, she thought, cutting the potato in half and sticking them, peeling side out, on the snowman's face. She trimmed the carrot back a little, and tried it for a nose, then trimmed it again. "You look just like old Rory MacRae," she chuckled when she had applied a mouth of bark from the wood pile.

"This has been such fun!" she exclaimed aloud. She flung herself backwards into a snowdrift as she used to do, and began swinging her arms and legs back and forth to make an angel. She lay there for a few minutes staring up at the sky. The deep blueness of it was now marred by grey clouds. The stillness of the day had a waiting quality, and the air felt damp and colder.

It's going to snow again! She jumped to her feet. The anxiety of the early morning returned. I've got to get ready! I hope David can make it home.

She hurried in and out gathering wood, filling the wood box to overflowing. She went to draw water from the well. It was much darker in the snow tunnel than it had been the other day when the sun was shining. She fed and watered Pansy and the hens, then ran outside to check the sky once more before she started milking. It seemed darker but there was still some blue. Her anxiety communicated itself to Pansy and she was difficult to milk.

"C'mon Pansy, cooperate," complained Mattie, forgetting that it hadn't been that many hours since David had milked her last. Finally she gave up and carried the half bucket of milk into the house. She checked the overflowing wood box again, just to make sure that the wood hadn't gone anywhere in her absence, then hurried back to the barn to check on the animals one more time.

She closed the barn door and propped the stick of wood against it to secure it. The wind had picked up and the smell of snow was sharp in the air. She shivered, and pulled her shawl more closely around her shoulders. I hope David gets home safely, she thought. She looked toward the track willing David to be coming, then hurried back to the house without even a glance for the snowman, and slammed the door against the gathering cold.

The stillness of the darkening day was oppressive. Mattie hung her coat and shawl beside the fireplace and poked at the glowing embers with the poker, sending sparks flying up the chimney. She put another stick of wood on the fire and watched as the greedy little flames took hold of the bark and the fire came to life casting its warmth into the kitchen. She shivered as the cold in her bones ebbed away.

I shouldn't have stayed out so long, she thought. I was foolish to waste my time on childish things. I'll be paying for it yet.

I'm hungry, too. She poked around in the

porridge pot with the wooden spoon, then added a little water to the remains of breakfast. This'll do, she thought, giving it a vigorous stir and setting it over the fire to heat. I'm glad now that I saved it, instead of giving it to the hens. She paced restlessly around the room while the porridge heated, stopping now and then to peer out the window at the gathering weather.

The porridge bubbled and she ladled it into a bowl and scraped the pot. Some brown sugar and the cream still warm from Pansy made her dinner. Anxiety made it hard to swallow. She jumped up several times to peer out the window when some stray sound from outside caught her attention.

The afternoon stretched endlessly in front of her. I've got to stop this! she thought. David has sense enough to stay at school if it storms. He can always go home with one of his pupils or stop at John's or at Angus'. He knows that I'm safe and warm here. She made herself sit in the rocker by the fire for five minutes without moving. It was agony. I know what I'll do! I'll make him a pair of mitts. It'll help pass the time, and he needs a new pair. She hopped up in search of some suitable wool and her knitting needles. By five o'clock she had one mitt done and the cuff of the second one started. Her anxiety had not decreased.

I wish he'd get here. Her nerves were jumping. The storm still waited, although the day had turned dark, and dusk was falling. The stew she had taken the time to make earlier bubbled in the pot over the fire. She pulled it out and lifted the lid. The rich smell of game and vegetables filled the air. She stuck a fork into a carrot testing for doneness. Her mouth watered. I haven't eaten since noon, she realized. She dropped the lid back on the pot with a clang and pushed the stew to the side of the fire to keep warm while she waited.

She looked out the window once more into the gloom of dusk. The snow had started. "Oh, I wish he'd hurry!" she cried. She forced herself to sit down in the rocker and pick up her knitting. Back and forth she rocked as her knitting needles flew faster and faster. Her feet began leaving the floor with each swing of the rocking chair until she hung suspended for a brief moment on the back points of the rockers, bringing her awareness back to reality. Over half the mitt was finished.

I'd better slow down before I fall over, she thought in shock. I didn't know these things could rock so far. She jumped to her feet and hurried over to the window again. There was nothing to be seen except the blackness of the night and the snow driving against the pane.

It's going to be hard for David to find the house in this darkness. I'll set a candle in the window for him. I hope, now, that he stayed where he was, he'll never find his way.

She sat down in front of the fire again, her hands idle in her lap. I can't go through this every time it snows and he's not home, she thought. At least Momma never had to do this. Poppa was always home. Except that one time when he had that church meeting and it started to snow. What did Momma do that time? I was only little, and I don't remember. Of course, she wasn't by herself, she had us. Mattie began to rock gently. Ma used to sing to us when it stormed. I was even littler then.

The sound of her grandmother's scratchy voice came back to her and the memory of the rocking and singing brought comfort to her. I would sit on her lap and she would sing hymns and old songs in Gaelic. Mattie hummed one of the tunes that she remembered her grandmother singing. For another hour she rocked and sang every song she could remember by heart. She was just starting them over again when there was a thump in the porch and she flew to the door with a glad cry.

"It's yourself!" She flung herself on his snow covered body. "You came home! You're safe!"

"Safe, and as hungry as a bear," he replied. "Something smells good. Let me get in and get these clothes off. I'm that cold and wet." He knocked the snow off his boots and stood his snowshoes in the corner. Mattie just stood and stared at him her relief was so great.

David walked to the kitchen door. "Come in

then, before you catch your death of cold, and then who would I come home to?"

Mattie followed him into the kitchen. "I'd just about given up hope that you'd be home this evening."

"Well, if it wasn't for your candle in the window, I'd be halfway to Nova Scotia by now, it's that dark out." David hung his coat by the fire to dry. "What's for supper?"

"Stew," said Mattie.

The storm blew itself out overnight. Mattie woke the next morning to the muffled stillness of drifted snow. The sunlight was muted by the snow on the window panes into a blue translucence which softened the bare, unfinished boards of the bedroom walls into something almost beautiful. She lay staring at the rafters for a few minutes before steeling herself to climb out of bed into the cold that awaited her. Leaning out of bed she grabbed her clothes off the chair and pulled them all into bed with her to get warm before she put them on. She shivered as the chilled materials struck her warm skin. Outside, she could hear the soft scrape and thunk of the snow shovel as David cleared the snow from the back door. She got out of bed and dressed, her breath hanging mistily in the air around her. She hurried downstairs.

David had already tended the fire, and it was sending its warmth to every corner of the kitchen. Mattie filled the kettle and pushed it over the flames to heat. She filled the porridge pot half way with cold water and added the oatmeal and a little salt. She hung it over the fire and soon the porridge had thickened and was steaming and bubbling. I'll fry up a few of those potatoes from the other day, and some bacon, too, she thought. He'll be hungry with all that shovelling. She set to work.

The back door thumped and Mattie could hear the hollow bump as David kicked off his boots before entering the kitchen.

"It's a cold one," he said as he closed the kitchen door behind himself and hung up his coat on the hook behind the door. "I'm glad I made those snow tunnels, it saved me a lot of work."

"Your cheeks are just red with the cold," said Mattie.

"How about a hug." David caught Mattie in his arms and rubbed his icy cheeks against her warm ones.

Mattie squealed and struggled. "Stop it, David, you're freezing me!"

"Now if I'd been allowed to keep my beard, none of this would have happened," he teased and rubbed her cheeks again.

"Stop it now, breakfast is ready."

David released her and sat down at the table. "Bring it on, I'm starving!" He said grace and then ate in silence for a few minutes. "Will you be alright here by yourself today?"

Mattie looked away. She braced her shoulders. "Of course I will." She forced a smile. "It's not going to storm today too, is it?"

"I don't think so, unless the wind changes again. I have to go to school. If the children get out of the habit of taking lessons it'll be hard to get them started again. They'll have forgotten a good deal of what went before, and I'll have to back-track too far, and I'll have wasted a lot of time."

"If it storms again," said Mattie, "I want you to promise to stay where you're safe. I'll be fine here. I can fill the wood box and draw the water and feed the animals before the storm gets here, and I'll be safe. It will ease my mind considerably if I know that I don't have to worry about you, too."

"Were you worried about me yesterday, little Mattie?" David watched her face.

"Of course I was worried about you. You're my husband aren't you? What would I do without you now?"

"What would you do, indeed." David turned back to his porridge.

§

After David had gone that morning, Mattie put on her coat and shawl and went outdoors to survey the sky. There was not a cloud in sight and the bright blueness of it dazzled her eyes. "Just like yesterday," she muttered to herself and went to fill the wood box and draw water.

"Hello, Rory," she said to the snowman as she passed him on her way to the well. "You don't look very much like Rory anymore with that mountain of snow on your head." She brushed the snow away from his shoulders. He stared blankly back at her with his potato eyes. She brushed the snow off his head.

"You still don't look like him." She pushed him over, breaking him into several pieces. His head rolled away and then lay still, staring back at her with the same blankness that was almost accusing. "Don't look at me like that!" she said and kicked the snowman's head into oblivion. "It was foolishness for me to make such a thing." She stomped away toward the well.

Chapter Twelve

There was no more snow in the weeks before Christmas. Mattie finished the mitts for David and went back to making baby clothes.

They sure need a lot of things, she thought as she sewed in small stitches on a belly band. I'm glad I've still got five months to go or I'd never get all this finished. "Ouch!" She sucked on her finger where she had pierced it with the needle.

"This is all for you, child, I hope you appreciate it." She regarded her round belly, tight inside her dress. I'll soon have to let the seams out. She inspected her finger for blood and picked up her work again. "I hate sewing!"

Mattie's thoughts wandered on and her hands idled to a stop. Christmas is just next week. I should make something nice for David to eat. I wonder if I have enough raisins, I could make him a pudding, and some brown sugar sauce. He likes sweet things. I'll make a boiled pudding. There's just enough time left for it to season a little before we eat it.

Mattie laid aside her sewing, stoked up the fire and added another stick. She filled the porridge pot with water and hung it over the flames to heat, then went into the pantry to rummage in boxes and bins for ingredients.

She mixed dry ingredients and added the spices. M-m-m, I love the smell of cinnamon and ginger, she thought as she added them to the cake. She poured cream into the mixture and stirred it all together. Pansy's milk is getting poor these days. I suppose in a month or so it'll be time to rest her until spring. Mattie popped a few raisins into her mouth, then dumped the rest into the batter and folded them in.

I don't have a pudding cloth, I'll have to make do. I hope it'll be alright. I can't stop now. She wrapped the batter up in a cotton dishtowel and tied the top securely, then carried the whole package to the kitchen and dropped it into the pot of boiling water.

The house was redolent of spices when David came home that evening. "You've been baking," he said, "I can smell it."

"Maybe," she said. "Supper's almost ready, you'll need to wash up. I've already attended to Pansy and the chickens."

"Only two more days of school," said David, sitting into his place a few minutes later.

"I'm glad," said Mattie. "It"ll be nice to have you home for a few days."

"So you miss me when I'm not here, then?"

Mattie looked at her plate. "Sometimes." She took a hasty bite of potatoes.

"Mattie. Look at me, please."

"Yes, sir." Mattie sat up straight and swallowed her mouthful of potatoes. She watched David with wary eyes.

David sighed. "I'm sorry, Mattie. I shouldn't have said that like that, but you know, it's alright to miss me, and I'd like to know it if you do."

Mattie's eyes returned to her plate.

"I miss you when I'm not with you." David's voice had a softness Mattie had never heard there before.

Mattie's eyes opened wide. "You do?"

"Well, of course I do! Now eat your supper."

Mattie ate the rest of her supper in silence, mulling over David's words. So I am important to him, she thought. He didn't marry me just so he could keep the school.

"So, are we going to have some of whatever smells so good?"

Mattie shook her head. "It's a surprise for Christmas."

Christmas day dawned icy bright like all the other days for the past week. Mattie hopped out of bed and cringed as her feet struck the cold floor. She dressed quickly without warming her clothes and shivered as the chilly material touched her warm skin. She brushed her hair and rebraided it, then hurried down to the warmth of the kitchen. David was just in from the woodpile.

"Good morning, sleepyhead." His armload of wood clattered into the wood box.

"Good morning, David. I'll have breakfast ready in a few minutes." Mattie bustled about making the porridge. "There's only a little bread, a 'bonnick' will have to do."

"It'll be fine. I have to see to Pansy. I'll be awhile."

In a few minutes Mattie had the *bannoch* baking and the table set. She took David's mitts out of their hiding place and set them by his plate.

I'm glad I saved that bit of crottle so I could dye these, she thought. Brown is so much prettier than sheep white. She admired her work.

I did a good job with the thumbs this time. The ones I made for the children last year were a little holey. Momma said that I didn't keep my wool tight enough when I joined it. Oh, well, they were good enough for play, and Johnny was forever losing his. I guess practice really does make perfect. She gave the bubbling porridge a stir, then thumped the top of the *bannoch* for doneness.

Presently David came in with the milk. "Pansy's not milking so well anymore. It'll soon be time to let her rest until she calves." He handed Mattie the bucket and hung up his coat behind the door.

Mattie set the milk in the pantry. "Sit in to your breakfast, then, it's ready," she called.

David pulled up his chair and sat down at his place. "What's this?" A smile spread across his face as he picked up the mitts. "A Christmas present for me?" He tried them on. "These are just the ticket. The darns are wearing through from shovelling on my old ones. Thank you, Mattie." He beamed across the table at her.

Mattie smiled back. "I'm glad you like them. I made them the day of the storm."

"Your fingers must have been flying."

"They were," said Mattie. "I was that worried."

"Eat your breakfast, then, I have a surprise for you, too."

"You do?"

"Yes, I do." David chuckled. "Now eat your breakfast. You're going to need your strength."

By the time breakfast was over and the house tidied, Mattie was almost beside herself with excitement. David watched her and smiled.

"I've finished my work," she said at last.

"Good. Put your coat on, you're going to need it."

Mattie hurried into her coat, and wrapped her shawl around her head and shoulders. "I'm ready."

David shrugged into his coat and opened the

door. "It's out in the barn." He lead the way into the snow tunnel.

Mattie's face was pink with excitement.

David opened the door. Pansy turned and regarded them with her elegant brown eyes, and continued chewing her cud.

"I'll have to light the lantern, it's too dark in here to see it properly." David struck a match and applied it to the wick of the candle. The barn was bathed in the glow of candle light magnified by the reflector on the lantern.

Mattie gasped. "Oh, it's beautiful! We can go coasting!" She ran her hands over the smooth finish of the sled. "When did you make this?"

"I didn't. I had Herman make it for me. I swore him to secrecy. Mrs. Herman thought he was making it for their grandson, so he had to make two just to keep her satisfied."

"When did you bring it home?"

"The night of the storm. That's why I was so late. He was just finishing it, so I thought I'd wait and take it home with me then, and I wasn't paying close enough attention to the weather. It was already snowing when I left his place. It got dark fast that night."

Mattie frowned. "You might have gotten lost and frozen to death."

"Not a chance. Well, at least not a very big chance. The trees grow so close along the track

I couldn't walk anywhere else, and once I found our gate I was practically home."

Mattie shivered. "Please don't do that again."

"Don't worry, I won't. By the time I got to our gate I was tired, so I decided to ride the sled down the hill. The snow is right up to the eaves on that side and I missed the end of the path and went right over the roof of the house and upset in the snowbank on the other side."

Mattie shook her head. "It's a wonder you didn't kill yourself. Is that why you were so covered in snow when you came in?"

David chuckled. "I had to roll off the snowbank because I'd lost one of my snowshoes. I didn't find it 'til the next morning when I went out to shovel. I had to poke around for it and I thought for awhile that I wouldn't find it. Now enough about that, let's take this out for a test run." He extinguished the candle and pulled the sled out through the snow tunnel. "Want to start at the top of the path?"

Mattie nodded. She hurried toward the slope where the path used to be.

"Wait, you, Mattie, 'til I'll get my snowshoes on. I'll pull you to the top. We'll both ride down on it. I had him make it big enough for all three of us."

Mattie stopped her rush and turned around. "All three of us?"

"Yes. You, me and the baby. He'll be just old

enough to enjoy a ride on a sled next year." David tugged at the straps on the snowshoes. "There, I'm ready."

Mattie sat well back on the sled against the smooth wooden back, her arms resting on the arms of the seat. David pulled steadily up the moderate incline to the road. The flat runners whispered across the white snow, the only sound in the sparkling silence of winter. Even the crows were quiet. Mattie could see them silhouetted against the bright blue of the sky above the spruce trees at the end of the path.

David pointed the sled downhill, and unfastened his snowshoes. "You're going to have to let me sit behind you." Mattie slid forward and he squeezed in behind her, leaving his snowshoes on top of the snow on either side of the sled. He picked them up and handed them to Mattie. "You'll need to hold these on the way down. Now remember, you have to lean to steer this thing."

Mattie nodded, and settled herself more comfortably between David's knees.

"Are you ready?"

"Yes." Mattie's eyes were bright with anticipation.

David pushed off. The wind whistled past their ears. The snow sparkled and flashed beneath the runners as they gained speed. Mattie shrieked with delight startling the crows into noisy scolding. "Lean right! Lean right!" shouted David.

She leaned, and in seconds they were slowing to a stop by the back door of the house.

"That was wonderful!" Mattie's breath came in gasps.

"Want to go again?"

"Oh, yes, please!"

David pulled her to the top of the incline again and climbed on behind her. They flew down the hill, the snow spraying out behind them. "Lean left!" David shouted.

Without thinking, Mattie obeyed him, then realized they were going over the roof. The sled gained speed as they neared the bottom, their momentum carrying them up the slight incline of the roof and over the top. For a moment they were airborne and Mattie shrieked in panic as the ground fell away from beneath them. Her heart seemed to go with it. With a soft thump they landed on the other side on top of the snowbank. Snow sprayed everywhere and Mattie fell off the sled and lay still, her mouth and eyes covered in snow. It choked her breath and she struggled to sit up but only managed to dig herself in deeper. Her heart pounded with the effort of her struggles.

"Lie still, Mattie!"

David's voice came from a long way off. Mattie stopped struggling and raised her head gasping for breath. The snow melted and ran down her face. David was putting on his snowshoes. Anger surged within her, and she began to struggle again.

"Lie still, Mattie! You're only making things worse." He tightened the strap on his snowshoe and stood up. "Now, roll over onto your back."

Mattie rolled, and David pushed the sled closer to her.

"Sit up now, and give me your hands, and I'll help you onto the sled."

After a brief struggle against the soft yielding snow Mattie was seated upright again on the sled. "You might have killed us!"

"I'm sorry I frightened you, Mattie, but it seemed like it would be such a lot of fun. We were airborne for a few seconds, did you know that?"

"But you might have killed me and the baby," she repeated.

"I don't think so. The snow's too soft. I just scared you and I'm sorry. We won't do that again this winter."

"I want to go in now," said Mattie.

The rest of the day passed in silence. Mattie was too shaken by the experience to have much to say. She sat in the rocker and rocked silently for a long time that afternoon. David sat in the other rocker and poked idly at the fire, or paced the room.

"Mattie, did you get hurt this morning?" he

asked when the silence had become more than he could bear.

"No, I was just frightened. Angry too. You should have told me you were going to do that."

"I know, and I'm awfully sorry. I never thought anything would happen to us. After all, I went over it the other night in a raging blizzard."

"I know, but you aren't with child. I have to think for both of us all the time. It becomes a habit."

Fear shadowed across David's face. "The baby's alright, isn't it?"

Mattie shrugged. "I'm not bleeding, and I'm not in pain, so I suppose it must be. There's no way of telling." The picture of their baby being born missing an arm or a leg because of their foolishness crossed her mind and she shuddered. His foolishness! she corrected herself and forced the picture out of her mind.

"I'll make supper now." She rose from her seat and stirred up the fire.

The flames leaped to life, and she pushed the kettle of water over them to heat for tea. Supper was a hash of turnip, potato, and carrot mixed with a little of the gravy from the stew from last Sunday, and flavoured with a slice of onion. She made her brown sugar sauce, and while they ate she set the boiled pudding over the fire to heat again.

"Is this your surprise?" asked David, when she

placed his pudding in front of him.

She nodded, and offered him the pitcher of sauce. Somehow it doesn't seem like such a great surprise anymore, she thought.

Chapter Thirteen

The days between Christmas and New Year's Day remained cold and sunny. David persuaded Mattie to come on the sled again.

"We won't do any coasting," he promised.

"And how are we to get down off the hill? Everything's up from here."

"Well, just that one hill on the way back, and I promise I won't go over the roof again."

Mattie regarded him suspiciously.

"I promise."

"Alright." She went to get her coat.

Mattie settled herself on the sled. The air is so cold and crisp, it feels good on my face, she thought. She arranged herself more comfortably on the sled and watched David fasten the straps on his snowshoes.

"Are you ready?" He picked up the tow rope.

Mattie nodded, tightening her grip on the arms of the seat.

David trudged up the hill. The snow squeaked and hissed beneath the runners of the sled. Somewhere in the silent woods a squirrel chattered and then was quiet while they passed. The tracks of small animals covered the surface of the snow, their makers in silent hiding while the humans were about.

"Want to go visiting?" asked David.

"I don't think so. Where would we go?"

"To Mrs. Gillis'?"

"Oh, no, I couldn't go there looking like this. Dear knows who'd be there, too." She firmed her lips taking on her mother's expression.

I am just longing to visit with another woman, she thought, but I'm not dressed for it. Why, I haven't even taken off my apron.

"I'd be ashamed to be seen visiting in my work clothes," she said. "Besides, it's an awful long way to drag me on this contraption. A turn around the field'll do just fine."

"That sounds like your last word on it."

"It is."

Two turns around the field, just to show her that he could, and a gentle coast down to their back door to prove that he kept his promises, completed the outing.

"Want to build another snowman? I had very little time to admire the other one before he fell over."

Mattie blushed and looked away.

"He looked a lot like Rory MacRae. He had just the right tilt to his eyes, and that side root on the carrot looked for all the world like the wart on Rory's nose, hair and all."

Mattie looked back and nodded. "I thought so, too."

"So, shall we make another one?"

"I don't think so. It's all a lot of foolishness, and just for children." She got up off the sled and shook out her skirts. "I'm going in and start supper." She went into the house, almost banging the door behind herself.

David looked after her and shrugged. "Well, I'm going to make one," he muttered, and stood the sled up against the side of the house.

Mattie watched him through the pantry window. It's all childish foolishness, she thought. It just takes a person's attention away from the real things in life.

She watched David roll a large base and set it on its side beside the entrance to the snow tunnel. It's going to be a nice snowman, she thought, much better than I could make myself.

She forced herself away from the window, and took a turn around the kitchen, stopping to give the fire a poke and add another stick. The sound of David thumping about outdoors called her back to the window. He had almost finished the snowman's middle.

I wish ..., she thought, and looked out the window again. She watched David struggle to lift the second ball onto the first. It roll off the back side of the base. David looked up and waved at her before going back to his task. She raised her hand to return the wave then put her hand behind herself without completing it. She stood watching for another minute.

I suppose I could go and help him, she thought.

She took another turn around the kitchen. Her feet stopped of their own volition in front of the coat rack.

"I guess this means that I've given in," she muttered as she put on her coat and shawl and went to join David in the yard.

"I'm glad you decided to join me." David smiled so happily down at her that she had to smile back at him. Together they lifted the snowman's middle into place and packed snow into the spaces to hold it there.

"D'you want to roll the head?" asked David.

"No, I'll make the face. I can't bend very well anymore." She patted the roundness of her belly.

In a few minutes the snowman was complete, and they stood back to admire their work.

"He looks for all the world like Herman, the roof, this time," laughed David. "Did you do that on purpose?"

"Sort of," she shrugged. "I used to draw the neighbours' faces for the children when they were little. It was a good pastime on rainy days."

"You're very good. I draw like I'm holding the pencil in my foot."

Mattie ducked her head. "I always liked to draw."

David put his arm around her and they stood in silence for a few minutes. "Mattie, why didn't you want to make a snowman with me before?"

Mattie considered this for a moment. "I think because the last time I made a snowman, I got so involved with it that I didn't see the storm coming, and it frightened me. I could have frozen to death out here all by myself."

"You're a funny little thing. Why would you have frozen to death?"

"Momma always warned us to be ready for storms and things. She always kept the wood box and the water bucket full, and made us stay around the house when we went outside to play. Not that we could have gone anywhere anyway, the snow was always too deep."

"I see," said David. "I don't think it's as much of a danger as she thinks, if you take proper precautions. It's people who do foolish things who freeze to death. Anyway, how could you have frozen to death? You were right here by the house. The wood box was overflowing and you had plenty of food."

"Yes, but I had to get ready before the storm came."

"Mattie, Mattie, the wood pile is right outside the door. If it was a raging blizzard out here you couldn't have missed it. I think you're letting your mother's fears rule your life."

"Maybe. But that's all I have to go by."

"Put on your Sunday dress, we're going to a *ceilidh* this evening," said David on New Year's Eve.

Mattie clapped her hands. "Where are we going?"

"Well, I heard there's to be one at Ian Gillis' and that everyone's invited. They'll be needing a dark haired man to first foot them on the New Year."

"Have you got a lump of coal? You can't first foot without that."

"No, a stick of wood'll have to do, and after all, that's what coal is made from."

Mattie wrinkled her forehead. "But what if it snows?"

"It's not going to snow, and if it does, we'll just stay there. Now hurry and get dressed."

Mattie hurried. I'm glad I set bread today. I'll take that and some butter and a bit of jam with us, she thought as she rebraided her hair and pinned it into its bun. My, this dress is getting so tight I'll soon not be able to wear it.

She hurried downstairs and packed a basket with her bread and butter and jam, then shrugged into her coat. "Oh, David, how're we going to get there," she wailed. "I don't have any snowshoes. I can't go."

"Now, Mattie, why do you think I've been pulling you on the sled all over the yard? I've been building up my strength for just such an occasion. Now go and make yourself comfortable while I get ready."

Mattie went out and sat down on the sled and pulled her feet up under her coat. I think I'm going to need a second shawl, she thought. It's cold out here.

Presently David joined her carrying a heavy blanket and her other shawl. "Here, put this on, it's pretty cold out tonight." He handed her the shawl. "I brought you this old blanket to wrap up in so you won't get cold. It's a fair walk on snowshoes." He tucked the blanket around her. "I banked the fire so it should stay 'til morning if need be." He picked up the tow rope. "So, are you ready?"

"I'm ready." She snuggled down underneath the blanket.

The night was still. The snow squeaked beneath the runners of the sled, and with David's every step. Mattie took a deep breath of the crystal air. It was so cold that it stuck her nostrils together. She wiggled her nose. It always feels so funny, she thought and pulled her shawl up over her face.

Overhead a vast drift of stars shone with cold brilliance, their light almost equalling the light from the moon. The snow reflected back the light and the whole countryside seemed alive and breathing. The trees along the narrow road stood sentinel to their passage, their silhouettes dark against the shining heavens.

"The going'll be easier once we're up the hill." David stopped for a moment to catch his breath. "It'll be almost a straight run to their house then." He picked up the tow rope again and trudged onward. They soon crested the hill and it seemed like a very short time before the lights of their nearest neighbour's house shone through the darkness. Mrs. Gillis opened the door to David's knock.

"David and Mattie! Come in and welcome! How'd you ever get here?"

"On the sled." David pointed to where he had stood the sled against the house.

"How clever! You pulled and Mattie rode. And it's such a lovely night for it. Let me take your wraps." She stood aside to let them enter, then closed the door behind them.

"The men are all in the kitchen telling stories, and the ladies are in the parlour. Jamie brought his pipes to pipe in the New Year, and Robert brought his fiddle. We'll have some music in a little bit." She led the way into the parlour.

"Good evening, Mattie." The other women greeted her.

"Good evening." Mattie felt the rush of colour in her cheeks. She took a seat in the corner and sat quietly listening. Talk ebbed and flowed around her. It felt good to be in the company of women again. The parlour was soft with their voices. The fire crackled and glowed in the fireplace, and was reflected off the vase of dried flowers on the side table. A worn rag rug of immense dimensions warmed the floor, its colours softly blended by time. The work-weary faces of the women were muted and blurred into beauty by the candle light. Mattie sat absorbing the peace and companionship. Mrs. John smiled across at her and she smiled back. Snippets of conversation entered her awareness. Recipes shared, household tips, bits of gossip. Well, not really gossip, she thought, just the news.

"… that young imp of mine." Mattie's ears focused on the sound of Rachel Sandy's voice. "… kissing in the barn!"

Who was kissing in the barn? Alarm feathered its way through Mattie's chest. Not Rachel Sandy's "young imp," he's too young. Mattie tuned her ears more closely.

"And the church barn at that!"

"Well, she'd better not be at that too often. She'll be making a name for herself." Mary Peter's voice was grim. "I'll bet her mother doesn't know."

"Not likely, but it wouldn't make any difference anyway. My Cora can do no wrong." Rachel Sandy's voice took on the tones of Mrs. Smith.

Cora! They were talking about Cora! Mattie strained her ears but a burst of laughter from the kitchen covered the end of the conversation, and the talk went on to other things.

Mrs. Gillis came and went, ushering in newcomers and directing the flow of people.

"Hello, Mattie." Mary Cameron Martin pulled a chair over next to her daughter and sat down. "I hope you're in better humour this evening."

"Hello, Momma." Mattie tried to smile. I wish she wouldn't put it like that, she makes it so hard. "I see you brought Tommy with you."

"Aye, well, he wanted to come, and he's a man now, so there wasn't much I could say."

"He is indeed," agreed Mattie. Momma looks tired, she thought. "How's Ellie?"

"She's home tending the little ones. She's turning into a grand girl. She's gained at least two inches in height this fall. She's taller than I am now, and such a help."

As if I never was, thought Mattie. "The boys'll soon be coming after her, too."

"Not yet." Mary's voice was stern. "It's bad enough that Tommy's racketing around the countryside, without his sister following him."

"Is he still going to see Colleen?"

"I'm not sure it's Colleen he's seeing."

"Well, who would it be, then?"

"Those brothers of hers."

"But why would he want to keep friends with them, they're Cath'lics."

"I don't know, for the life of me, what the attraction is, but I don't think it's Colleen. It started off with her, but I don't think it's her anymore."

"And I suppose Tommy won't say."

Mary sighed. "He's terrible secretive these days. I can't get a word out of him."

If you get at him the way you get at me, thought Mattie, it's no wonder. Her thoughts were interrupted by Mrs. Gillis.

"Come out to the kitchen then, and have a cup of tea. Robert's just about to tune up. Bring your chairs." She led the way into the kitchen. "Find yourselves a place. It'll be close quarters, but kind of cozy anyway." She disappeared into the pantry.

Mattie found herself a space not far from the fireplace. The kitchen was bright with candles, their greasy tallow smell hanging heavy on the air. A cheery fire blazed in the fireplace pouring its warmth into the room. The large black kettle whispered and sang to itself on the hob. In the middle of the room Robert tuned up his fiddle and tried the opening bars of "Morag of Dunvegan." He tuned the D string again, then plucked at the

E string, and soon music poured out of the fiddle, tune after tune with hardly a break. Mattie's feet tapped of their own accord.

I'll be dancing yet if I'm not careful, she thought, and hooked her heels into the chair rung, earning a look from her mother across the room. She returned her feet to the floor and clamped her knees together, but her toes continued to wiggle inside her shoes. David came and sat at her feet. She looked down at his dark head and a tightness filled her chest. She reached out a tentative hand to stroke his hair, then pulled it back. This will never do! And in public, too! she thought. Robert played all the old tunes: jigs, reels, and hornpipes. Marches and slow airs straight off the Scottish moors recalled the anguish of the Highland clearances. Talk quieted as the old men remembered the stories of their parents and grandparents.

"Play something gay!" commanded Mrs. Gillis. "'Tis a new year almost here, and you're turning this *ceilidh* into a funeral!"

"How about 'Maggie Cameron'? Is that gay enough for you?" The notes of the strathspey danced out of the fiddle, and the somber mood lifted.

"Help me set the table, please, Mattie." Anna's voice in Mattie's ear startled her.

Mattie jumped to her feet and followed Anna into the pantry.

"You pass and I'll put," said Anna.

Together they soon had the long table set to overflowing with golden loaves of crusty bread brought from many kitchens. Rosy jellies glowed in the firelight as if releasing the stored light of the summer sun. A pale moon of creamy cheese, aged since the early fall, and a dark loaf of potted meat shared space at the foot of the table. A ham, newly roasted and pinkly juicy, crowned the head of the table. Mattie had never seen such abundance, and the pantry shelf still held three cakes.

The fiddle music ceased. "It's a beautiful sight, Anna. My mouth is watering." Robert laid down his fiddle in the case.

"Come and help yourselves," said Anna as she filled teacups and passed them to Mattie. "Mattie'll bring your tea when you sit down."

Mattie looked around at the rosy glowing faces. David's was not among them. I wonder where he's gone, she thought before her attention was taken up with serving tea.

Jamie was in the porch tuning his bagpipes. He had foregone the supper until after he had piped in the New Year. The pipes wailed momentarily, and then settled into the mellow drone of well-tuned bagpipes. He tried a measure of "Rowan Tree," adjusted the inside tenor drone, then satisfied, with the chording and tuning, he marched into the kitchen to "Bonnie Dundee," and stood in front of the fireplace. Straight and tall he stood, his shaggy grey head regal in the candle light, as tune after tune poured out of the pipe chanter. Everyone sat and listened. They could do little else, but the sounds were the songs of their ancestors, and brought to life the stories of the old people. Indeed, Jamie's piping was so magical they could almost smell the heather on the hills.

A knock came to the door as Jamie paused for breath.

"Is it that time already!" exclaimed Ian with a twinkle in his eyes. "You'd better go and see who it is, Anna."

Anna hurried to open the door. David entered carrying the traditional lump of coal. He bent and kissed Anna on the cheek and wished her a healthy and prosperous new year. He handed the lump of coal to Mr. Gillis.

"You'll have a drop suitable to the occasion," Anna offered.

"To be sure, and thank you." David accepted the dram of whiskey, he tipped it back and swallowed it in one gulp. The ritual of first footing was complete.

Talk and laughter erupted again. David joined Mattie by the pantry door. "Where'd you get the coal?" she asked.

"Peter brought it back with him from Nova Scotia last year when he was over visiting with his brother in Stellarton. That storm came up on the way back and he lost most of his belongings overboard, but the coal he had in his pocket, and there it stayed even though they were almost drowned. He was warned against trying to make the crossing in such a small boat with a storm coming on, but he wouldn't listen."

"He was a fortunate man."

"Foolish, more like it. But he's here and safe and a year's gone by." David smiled down at her. "There's Hector over there, and I still haven't greeted him. I'll be back in a few minutes."

Mattie began carrying empty plates into the pantry.

"It's a grand *ceilidh*!" said Elizabeth. "It's a shame Anna doesn't have room for some dancing."

Mattie looked at her, startled. "Dancing?"

"Yes, I was quite a dancer in my younger days, and Mr. MacDonald was a wonderful sight with the 'fling,' and the 'sean truibhas.'"

Mattie suppressed a giggle. The vision of chubby, cherubic, Mr. MacDonald trying to kick the imaginary seams out of his trousers was almost more than she could cope with. I still don't understand why the British thought they could subdue us Highlanders just by making us sew a seam in our kilts to make trousers.

"You're looking pleased with yourself," said Tommy as Mattie scuttled out of the pantry still trying to keep a straight face.

She was instantly serious. "Oh, Tommy!"

"Yes, Tommy," he said. "I didn't think you were going to greet your big brother tonight, and it's already the new year."

"I'm sorry, Tommy. It seems like I've been busy ever since I got here. How are you?"

"I'm fine. And you? I see I'm to be an uncle."

"Yes, in May." Mattie blushed. "I hear you're seeing Colleen O'Brien these days."

"So it would seem, though that's not quite the story of it."

"That's what Momma says. She's worried that she's going to have a Catholic daughter-in-law, and Catholic grandchildren."

"She would worry about that now, wouldn't she?"

"And so?" Mattie waited for an answer.

"And so nothing, little sister. Neither you nor she need worry about that."

"Shall I tell her that you said that?"

"If you like, but it soon won't be necessary. I'll come and visit you some time." Robert was tuning his violin again and Tommy drifted away to the other side of the room.

He's changed so, thought Mattie, harder somehow, and more secretive. Not at all like he used to be. Scenes from their childhood when Tommy had been her best friend passed through her mind. He never did tell his business, she suddenly realized, even to me! I always told him everything. She felt suddenly lonely and cold. She stared across the kitchen at him, trying to see in his face the man he had become.

He's a fine looking man, she thought with a small burst of pride. It's no wonder Colleen finds him attractive. He looks harder too, not at all like Poppa anymore. Poppa always had a twinkle in his eyes and a softness about his mouth that Tommy doesn't have. Tommy's more like Momma, kind of stern and distant. He's filled out since last summer, too. He's not so long and lanky as he used to be. It's like I don't even know him anymore. Maybe I never did.

"Thanks for all your help, Mattie." Anna's voice broke into her thoughts. "I couldn't have done it all without you." She smiled at Mattie. "Why don't you sit down, you must be about worn out."

Mattie smiled back. Mrs. Gillis can make me feel so good, she thought. She accepted the chair that Anna held out for her. "I am getting a little tired."

"They get heavy about now, don't they."

Mattie nodded and sighed, her attention caught again by the conversations around her now dominated by the voices of the men.

"… a good crop of oats this year …"

"… broke my plough blade on that chunk of sandstone in the shore field. I had to wait a month for a new one."

"A month, you say. Well, well, that's a long time when there's work to be done."

"Well, it wasn't broken altogether. I straightened it but it didn't work as well anymore, the pesky thing."

"… call another one?"

"Aye, they'll have to do something after the mess they made of the last one."

"Indeed, yes! It's a terrible thing when a man can't go to the polls without being harassed. They frightened away a good many voters that day."

"Och, the government'll have to do something about it. It wasn't fair a'tall, a'tall."

"Well, they'd better do it soon, is all I can say."

The mens' voices rumbled on. The soft music of the women's voices floated and mingled among the heavy tones. The whole was supported and overlaid by slow airs on the fiddle. Mattie's eyelids drooped.

"Did you have a good time?" asked David as he tucked Mattie onto the sled for their return home.

Mattie sighed. "It was wonderful."

David started down the road, calling goodnight to their friends and neighbours. Mattie waved and called goodnight too, then snuggled farther down beneath the blanket.

Their way was lit by a cold white moon shining

high in the sky. So much less friendly than stars, thought Mattie.

David trudged up Ian's hill in silence, and Mattie was soon nearly asleep. Her head rolled a little with the rocking of the sled over the small humps in the snow; her eyelids drooped. A curious touching crossed the inside of her belly then stopped. She was instantly alert, waiting for it to come again. It was a long time coming and she fell into an almost sleep. There it is again! she thought. I feel as if I'm being touched from the inside. She sat very still on the sled all the way home, but the sensation did not come again.

Chapter Fourteen

Mattie lived on the pleasure and companionship of the *ceilidh* for several weeks. Her loneliness and isolation faded for a brief period. School started up again and David was away all day until another snowstorm kept him home. The storm did not last and not much snow accumulated so he returned to school after a day. Mattie's loneliness came back wider and deeper than ever.

After her chores were done she sat in the rocking chair in front of the fire and looked with distaste at her belly. It seemed enormous to her. She had altered her dresses to accommodate it, but it continued to grow.

"I'll have to let the seams out again," she said aloud, then sighed. Talking to herself seemed to ease the absolute quiet. "I don't think there's much seam to let out anymore. If only Mrs. Gillis would come and see me." Mattie picked up the poker and rearranged the logs on the fire.

"I wish I knew what that queer feeling in my belly is. It's happening a lot more often now. I don't like it." She sighed again. If I could only talk to Momma, she thought. But it wouldn't do any good. Momma would never talk about such a thing. Mattie stared into the fire. Why couldn't she have been more like Mrs. Gillis? The stab of guilt caught her by surprise and she jumped up and thrust the poker back into its holder with a clatter. She pushed the thought away and collected up her sewing equipment, then settled herself by the fire with her other dress.

"If I'm going to let these out, I'd better get at it." She began threading her needle.

I wonder where Cora was the other evening. She never wants to miss any fun. Her mother too. Neither one of them was there. Maybe Mrs. Smith was having one of her spells again, or perhaps she found out about Charlie and Cora. Mattie examined a seam.

"I'm going to have to put a piece in this," she muttered and snipped at the thread.

Her thoughts returned to Cora. If her mother knows about her antics in the barn she's likely being kept home in disgrace. Mattie chuckled out loud. Mrs. Smith wouldn't like that any better than Cora would. I expect that Cora'd be awful hard to live with if she was being punished. Mattie sighed. It'd be nice if Cora lived closer.

One Saturday toward the end of January, Mattie and David awoke to the sound of dripping water.

The sun was shining through the window in the peak of the roof and the air inside the room was warmer.

"It's the January thaw!" exclaimed David jumping out of bed and peering out through the window. "I wonder how long it'll last."

"'Til April, I hope," said Mattie. "I'm that sick of snow." She rolled over as far as her belly would allow and buried her face in the pillow. It was not a comfortable position, so she rolled back. The sunlight seeped into her body and she began to feel better than she had for a long time. She clambered out of bed and put on her clothes without warming them first, then followed David downstairs.

Bright sunshine lighted the kitchen. Mattie stirred up the embers of last night's fire, and added a stick to it. She filled the kettle from the bucket and pushed it over the fire where it soon began to sing.

David shrugged into his coat. "I'm going to the barn, I'll be back in a few minutes." Since Pansy's milk had dried up, chores did not take as long. In a few minutes he was back with an armload of wood.

"It's beautiful out today," he said, dropping the wood into the wood box with a noisy clatter. "It's just like spring. Already there are bare patches in the yard."

Mattie stirred the porridge. "I'll go out after breakfast."

"No, no, come now. Just for a minute. You'll only need your shawl."

Mattie relented, but put on her coat. Already the snow banks had sagged at the edges. Water dripped from the icicles hanging from the corners of the eaves. The largest one let go and speared into the snow bank beneath it.

"I'd better knock the rest of those down before they fall and hurt one of us," said David.

Mattie stared around herself. It seems so strange to have this warmth from the sun after such a long time in the cold, she thought.

The red mud peeked through in the yard in the places where the snow had been blown away. The sky overhead was a brilliant blue. The squirrels who lived in the row of spruces behind the barn, chattered and scolded the pair of resident crows which cawed and flapped in lazy black circles against the sky. Mattie took a deep breath. The air was as fresh as spring, but still crisp with the reminder of the winter still to come.

Mattie sighed. "If only this'd last."

"It may last for a few days at least," encouraged David. "At any rate, in about six weeks we should be seeing the last of the heavy weather." He put his arm around her shoulders and Mattie didn't pull away as had been her habit. "Has it been that hard?" he asked.

She shrugged. "It's very lonely. With the snow so deep and no way out." She sighed again, then laughed in embarrassment. "I find myself talking to myself a lot lately, just to break the silence."

David pulled her around in front of him and rested his chin on the top of her head. "It won't always be like this, you know."

"It won't?" Mattie's voice drooped.

"Once the summer comes and the baby's here, you'll have a lot more freedom. People'll come and visit and we'll be able to go and visit them, and go to church. There'll be the school picnic at the end of the term. You'll be able to go to your mother's for a visit. You haven't seen Ellie since last summer, you'll have a lot to talk about."

"I probably won't know her. Momma said at the *ceilidh* that Ellie's taller than she is now, and such a help around the house." Mattie's voice mimicked her mother's tone on New Year's Eve. "As if I never was!"

David laughed. "Maybe you don't want to see her."

"Oh, yes, I do! Even if it is just to see if she's as awful as Momma makes her out to be."

"Now Mattie, your mother used to do the same thing about you, you know. That's how I came to be curious about you in the first place."

"How? Just because Momma made me out to

be a little prig?"

"No. Because she said what a good girl you were, and what a wonderful help around the house and with the little ones. 'Just like a little mother, herself,' she said one day."

"She said that? To you? About me?"

"She said it to Mrs. John one day when I was in the store. John had gone to get me something in the back so I had nothing to occupy my attention with besides what they were saying."

"Humph!" said Mattie, "why'd she never tell me that?"

"Maybe she didn't know how. Maybe you weren't listening."

Mattie sprang back out of David's arms and glared at him. "And maybe she didn't want me to get above myself either." She turned on her heel. "I'm going in. That porridge must be cooked to lumps by now." She went into the house and slammed the door.

Momma'd never praise me to my face, she raged to herself, giving the porridge a vigorous stir, it might make me prideful! "Pride goeth before a fall, and a haughty spirit before destruction." Her mother's voice echoed in her head. It's more than once I've heard her say that.

"Drat! This stuff's like a brick." Mattie poured a generous portion of water into the porridge and stirred it again.

Why couldn't she just once have said that I was doing a good job, or that she even liked me? The only time she ever said that I was a good girl, was when Poppa died. Mattie shoved the porridge pot back over the fire with a clang.

I suppose I should be thankful that she even said that. Mattie slammed the dishes onto the table.

"Mattie! Mattie! Take it easy! Those are the only dishes we have, and it's a long walk to get any more." David hung his coat behind the door. "What's got you so upset?"

"Momma!" Mattie glared across the room at him.

"You mean that I got you upset by mentioning your mother."

"It would seem so." She returned to her task.

David crossed the kitchen and took the knives and spoons out of Mattie's hands and laid them on the table. "Tell me about it." He took her hands in his. Their gentle warmth eased some of Mattie's anger.

Mattie stared up at him. "D'you really want to know?"

"I really want to know."

She sighed. "All my life I've tried so hard to please my mother, and I never could quite make it. No matter what I did, or how well I did it, or what she may have said about it, there was always the feeling that I could have done better, and I am so ashamed." A tear ran down Mattie's cheek. David pulled her into his arms and rocked her silently, waiting for her to continue.

"And d'you know what the worst part is? She's having a baby too, and my baby won't be nearly as good as her baby, and there's not a thing I can do about it." Mattie sniffed hugely, and David handed her his handkerchief. "I can't even discuss it with her, she'd have no idea what I was talking about. I hardly know what I'm talking about." She blew her nose and sniffed again.

David cleared his throat, then cleared it again. "Now, Mattie, I think we need to look at this another way."

"How?" she sniffed.

"Well, first of all, your mother does love you, even though she doesn't quite know how to demonstrate it. I'm not sure about this baby thing, but it seems to me that a baby's a baby with no one any better than the other once they're here and healthy. Our baby'll be a handsome baby, and smart besides, and it'll compare favourably with anything that your mother can produce. And don't forget, this'll be your little brother that you're talking about."

"Half brother," corrected Mattie, "and besides it might be a girl."

"Ours might too." He continued to rock her in silence for a few minutes. "Mattie, d'you think that you don't measure up here?"

She shrugged. "I don't know. I'm just here."

David's shoulders sagged, then straightened. He sighed. "I can see you have a lot to learn."

"Don't I always!"

"Mattie, stop it! You're a good wife. Just the kind of wife I've always wanted. We've made a baby and it'll be a fine human being just like its parents, no matter what your mother may imply. I don't know what else I can say, except that I think the porridge is burning." He reached over and pulled the pot away from the fire, then blew on his fingers to cool them.

Mattie lifted the lid and the odour of scorched oatmeal wafted into the room. "I can't even make porridge! This stuff's not even fit for the hens."

"I think you may have made this pot once too often."

The January thaw lasted three days, then ended in another raging snow storm. Overnight the snow was up to the eaves again, and the windows were darkened with frost.

"Only six more weeks," muttered Mattie dragging her clothes into bed with her to warm them. She lay there for a few minutes enjoying the last of the warmth until she could get downstairs and stir up the fire. A soft plunk inside her belly startled her. Was that the baby? she thought. She lay still waiting for it to come again. After a few minutes the sensation of being touched from the inside came again. It is the baby! she thought. How could I have been so dumb? It feels so strange. The soft touching came again. Great love for this tiny being washed over her almost bringing her to tears. If only David could feel this, she thought. She lay in bed as long as she dared, waiting for the sensation to come again, but her belly was silent. It must have just been turning over, she thought as she rolled out of bed at last.

As the days passed, the internal touching became more frequent and more pronounced. The baby took on a reality for Mattie that it hadn't had before. She began talking to it as if it were already born, and her loneliness eased.

She looked forward to David's time at home when they sat before the fireplace, David reading, or mending tools, and she, knitting or sewing, her needles flashing busily in the light from the fire. She gave a lot of thought to their conversation about being his wife and her mother's daughter, and about having babies. She sighed, then grunted, as the baby poked a knee into her diaphragm.

David looked up from his reading. "What's the matter?"

"The baby just kicked me in the stomach," she said "It's been getting pretty active lately." She rubbed her stomach to soothe it. "I hope it doesn't do that very often!" She smiled across at David, then grunted again as another knee pushed outward raising a ridge of flesh across her belly which then subsided. She watched it in amazement. "Did you see that?"

"Indeed I did." David laughed softly. "That's a strong one in there, it must be a boy." He reached over and patted Mattie's belly which had nearly outgrown the third alteration of her dresses. The baby moved beneath his hand. A look of wonder crossed his face. "Is this what you've been feeling all along?"

She nodded. "These last few weeks it's become more and more active. I've gotten kicked more than once. Elbowed too, I expect."

David rested his hand on Mattie's belly waiting for the next one. "Can you tell the difference?"

"No, not really. A knee or an elbow's all the same right now."

"Does it hurt?"

"Sometimes it's a little uncomfortable, but so far it hasn't actually hurt. At first it was just little touches, and I didn't know what it was. I thought there was something wrong."

The baby shifted beneath David's hand.

"It's so strong!"

"It's getting heavy too. My back aches with it sometimes. I get so tired."

"I'm sorry that you're so uncomfortable. And

you still have awhile to go." He sat back in his chair.

"I mind most not being able to bend these days. Up until a few weeks ago I could still do what I've always done without too much trouble. Now if I drop something, it's hard to pick it up." She chuckled. "I've had to devise a way of reaching down sideways for things on the floor."

"You could always leave it until I come home."

"And fail as a housewife?"

"You're not still worrying about that, are you?"

"No, not really, though I expect I'll always have a little of that on my mind. It's hard to get rid of once it's there. I just hope I don't pass it on to my daughters."

"Daughters, is it now?"

The weather continued cold. The snowstorms were no longer the raging blizzards of December and January. They dropped less snow, and did not last as long. David was able to be at school almost every day.

Toward the end of February just as Mattie thought she would slide into quiet madness from isolation and loneliness, a knock came at the door. Her heart soared. A visitor! She hurried to open it. It was Cora.

Mattie threw the door wide and smiled happily. "Come in, Cora, you must be half frozen." She hustled her friend into the warmth of the kitchen and shut the door against the coldness of the day. "It looks like we're in for some more snow."

Cora stood in the middle of the kitchen shivering and beginning to drip snow water all over the floor.

"Give me your coat, and I'll hang it by the fire." Mattie assisted Cora out of her coat and shawl. "What brings you out here in this weather?"

"W-we had an awful fight." Cora collapsed into the nearest rocker and burst into tears. "I ran away."

"We who?" asked Mattie. I have never seen Cora in such distress, she thought.

"M-Momma and me. We said the awfullest things!" Cora's sobbing increased.

"And you ran away from home?"

"I g-guess so. I sure don't want to g-go back." She rubbed at her face with the sleeve of her dress.

Mattie rooted in her pocket, handed Cora a clean handkerchief, and waited until the storm of weeping had passed.

"I'll make us some tea." She pushed the kettle over the fire.

Cora sniffed and blew her nose.

"So you ran away?" Mattie sat down in the other rocker.

"I guess so. If coming here is running away, I guess I did." She sniffed again.

"What did you fight about?" I can hardly

imagine Cora's mother angry enough to fight about anything, she thought.

"Those two old gossips from Pinette came visiting the other day, and told Momma about me kissing Charlie in the church barn, plus a lot of other stuff that wasn't true."

"D'you mean Mrs. Neil and and Mrs. Angus?"

"Yes, those two." Cora sniffed again and searched for a dry place on the crumpled handkerchief. "They think they know so much. Self-righteous old biddies! They probably did a lot worse when they were young."

"Cora! Even if they did, maybe they were trying to keep you from making the mistake of your life."

"They were just interfering."

"I don't think so," replied Mattie. "I heard the ladies talking about you at the *ceilidh* at the Gillis'. D'you want to end up married to the likes of Charlie?"

Cora shuddered. "No, of course not. Nor Robert West either."

"What's he got to do with it? He's practically an old man."

"Well, Momma heard about the barn before and gave me a talking to. Then those two arrived from Pinette with another load of gossip, most of which wasn't true, by the way."

"Gossip usually isn't."

"Anyway, Momma was just savage. She said that

if I couldn't behave myself I'd have to get married, and then she went and made arrangements with Robert West. He came calling last night. Ever since your Momma married Norman, Robert's been thinking that he should get married too, though why he picked on me, I don't know."

"What else were you doing that wasn't true?" asked Mattie.

"They said that I had been seen with George in the graveyard, sitting on a tombstone after dark, though how they could see in the dark, I don't know." Cora sniffed and scrubbed at her nose with the sodden handkerchief. "Have you got another of these? This one's awful wet."

Mattie rose to get Cora another handkerchief, and to set the tea. "And were you in the grave yard with George?"

"Well, sort of."

"Sort of? You either were or you weren't."

"Well, there were other people there, and it wasn't after dark. At least it wasn't that dark. Besides, that was months ago."

"What other people? No one we know would be traipsing around after dark with the boys."

"Colleen was there." Cora sniffed again. "And Tommy, too."

"Our Tommy?"

"Yes, your Tommy," said Cora with a note of triumph in her voice. "He's been seeing Colleen since the summer."

"I don't believe you." Maybe the stories are true, thought Mattie. After all, he didn't quite deny that he was seeing Colleen the other evening.

Cora shrugged. "Believe it or not, every time I've been there, he's been there too, and she's been right beside him."

"How many times have you been there, anyway?"

"A few."

"How'd you get out of the house?"

"I'd just say that I was tired and go upstairs to bed. Then when Colleen and her brothers came for me, I'd climb out on the porch roof and jump down onto the shed roof and then to the ground."

"How'd you get back?"

"Up the rose trellis."

"And you never got caught?"

"Poppa almost caught me once, but I lay down flat on the roof until he went inside again. He didn't see me."

"Cora! How could you? That's just plain deceitful. You'll go to hell!"

Cora began to cry again. "That's what Momma said, before she had the bright idea to marry me off to Robert West. Maybe that's what hell will be." She blew her nose and sniffed hard again. "Oh, Mattie, d'you really think I will?"

"I don't know. According to what Minister Mac-Donald said last fall, you're liable to, never mind the trouble you'll get into here in this world. The wages of sin is death." Mattie shook her head. "Whatever were you thinking to go off like that, and with that bunch?"

"You're talking about your own brother when you say that bunch."

"Yes, well, he should stay home too!" Mattie kept silent for a few moments while she poured the tea.

She handed a mug to Cora. "So what are your plans?"

"I don't have any. I don't even have any money."

"Well, you'll just have to go home and behave yourself."

"Can't I just stay here for a few days? At least until things cool off."

"Does your mother know you're here?"

"N-no, I didn't know when I left where I'd go. I thought first I'd walk to Charlottetown and stay with Sarah, but I got cold just walking to the end of our lane, so I thought of you."

"I see," said Mattie. "I'll have to send David back with news when he comes home from school, then."

"They'll come and take me back. They'll force me to marry Robert." Tears threatened in Cora's voice again.

"You can't leave them worrying about where you are! And even if they do, maybe you should get married. It'll keep you out of the other kind of trouble, at least."

"Oh, you're just like Momma." Cora burst into tears again. "Girls can never have any fun."

"Fun? Fun! Is this what you call fun? Fighting with your mother and running away from home and taking up with the likes of George and Charlie and making a name for yourself all the way to Pinette and maybe farther? The next thing you know you'll be in the family way and have to get married and not even Robert West'll have you then. And what about me? I've been your friend since we were children. How's it going to look for me if I take you in. I'm a respectable woman with a good husband and a baby of my own on the way. I don't want to spoil what I've got."

Cora sobbed harder. "Oh, Mattie, please don't be angry with me. You've never been like this before." She mopped at her tears with the handkerchief. "I thought you were my friend."

"I am your friend. I just don't like to see my friend making a fool of herself all in the name of fun. Fun's not what it's all about anyway."

"It's not?" Cora's sobs quieted to the occasional sniff. "What is it all about then?"

"It's about responsibility. It's about being where you're supposed to be when you're supposed to be there, and doing what you're supposed to do, and not letting others down, and not betraying trust. It's just being grown up."

"And I suppose you know all about that."

"I know a lot more about it than you do." Mattie's voice softened. "C'mon Cora, d'you think this is easy for me? I don't want to read the riot act to my best and only friend. But even less do I want you to ruin your life for a few minutes of 'fun.'"

"You've always been so reliable." Cora sniffed and blew her nose. "Whenever I'd do something wrong, Momma'd always say that I should take a lesson from you. It used to make me so mad, I'd go and do something ten times worse and try to drag you into it, but you'd never come, and I'd be in worse trouble." She sniffed again.

Mattie thought back to all the scrapes that Cora had been in over the years, and the many times Cora had tried to entice her into doing things that she knew instinctively were wrong. I'm glad now that I didn't give in, she thought, remembering the number of times that she had almost crumbled and gone with Cora.

"Momma would've skinned me alive if I'd done some of the things that you got up to," said Mattie. "I wouldn't have lived to tell about it."

"No, I suppose you wouldn't have." Cora's smile was almost a smirk.

"Well, maybe if your Momma had been a little harder on you, you wouldn't be in this mess now." Mattie got up to pour more tea. "It's getting dark.

David'll be home soon. He'll be tired. The big boys this year are more than a handful, and the little ones are learning bad manners from them. It takes all he's got just to keep order sometimes. I hate to send him back out in the cold, but we can't let your Momma and Poppa worry any longer than necessary."

"You won't make me go back, will you?"

Mattie sighed. "I can't make you go back. It's your decision, but I think you should think it over carefully before you do anything else foolish." She handed a cup of tea to Cora. "Here, have a biscuit with that. I have to start supper in a minute or two." She sat down in the rocker and silently regarded her friend's face until Cora began to squirm.

"Don't stare at me like that. You're making me nervous. Poppa always looks at me like that when I've done wrong."

Mattie looked away. "I'm sorry, I was just thinking about us and our families, and David and me and our baby. I hope our little girl doesn't lead us the jig that you've led your people."

"Oh, Mattie, I never thought about it like that before. I'll have a daughter someday."

"Maybe sooner rather than later, if you don't behave yourself." Mattie got to her feet again.

She left Cora sitting in silence before the fire while she peeled vegetables for supper in the pantry. Maybe she'll see some sense if I let her sit and think about it for awhile, she thought. She can't stay here very long. We really don't have much room for guests overnight, just that other room in the loft where the baby'll sleep, and there's not even a bed in there. I suppose we could bring in some straw from the barn and make a bed on the floor. It won't be very comfortable, but at least she'll be warm and we'll know where she is.

Mattie's mind worked busily over the mechanics of having a guest in such a small house. Her hands were just as busy on the potatoes. I'm glad I parboiled the salt hake this morning. I wasn't going to use it until tomorrow but there's just enough there for three, and it won't be too salty. I don't have enough meat left over from yesterday except for David. She finished chopping the vegetables into the pot and after putting some water on them, she put the lid on the pot with a clang, and carried it to the kitchen and hung it over the fire.

"There now, that won't take long." Mattie stirred up the fire with the poker and adding another two sticks. The fire caught on the dry wood and was soon popping cheerily, bringing warmth and brightness to the gathering dusk. She sat down in the rocker with a sigh. "I get so tired these days."

"Is it hard to be in the family way?" asked Cora.

"Tiresome, more than anything. I could sleep and sleep sometimes. Of course, I don't really have enough to do to keep me busy, and it's so quiet here that I may be tired from just that. I long for the time of day when David comes home."

Cora looked at Mattie. "You really care about him, don't you?"

The observation surprised Mattie. She thought about it seriously for a few minutes. "Yes, I guess I do. He's turned into a real friend."

Chapter Fifteen

Mattie and Cora sat staring silently into the fire as the evening shadows gathered and the room darkened. A thump on the outside wall announced David's return from the schoolhouse. Mattie rose stiffly and went into the pantry, returning in a moment with the fish. She placed it on top of the vegetables and covered the pot again, then went out to the porch to greet David.

"Cora's here."

"I thought she might be. Half the community's out looking for her. There's some say she drowned herself."

"Well she didn't, though that might have been the least of her worries." Mattie pulled her shawl more closely around her shoulders and shivered. "What made them think she'd drowned herself?"

"There was a hole in the ice over on Johnson's pond, and they said she was distraught over the fact that her parents wanted her to marry Robert West when she wanted to marry George O'Brien."

"Whew!" Mattie shook her head in disbelief. "Half of that would have been enough."

"So what's the real story?" David kicked off his

boots and stood in his stockinged feet.

"She and her momma had a fight over some gossip that those two old hens from Pinette saw fit to bring all the way up there. According to Cora, half of it wasn't true, but I think there was more true than not true, if I know Cora." Mattie shivered again. "It is true that her mother arranged for her to marry Robert West, and that's why Cora ran away, but it's not true that she wants to marry George, although she was out with him and his brothers and his sister, Colleen, when they thought she was home in bed. That's what started all of this."

David shook his head in wonderment. "So now she's here and we have to sort it out. Aye, well!" He squared his broad shoulders and went into the kitchen.

"So, Cora, you're here and not drowned."

A look of alarm flashed across Cora's face. "Why would I be drowned?"

"They say that you drowned yourself for the love of George O'Brien, and they're out dragging Johnson's pond for your body."

"Oh, for heaven's sake, how stupid can they be? I wouldn't drown myself over George O'Brien!"

"Robert West, then?"

"Nor him, either!"

"Well, no one knows where you are, and your mother's just frantic with worry."

Cora looked ashamed. "Let her worry," she muttered, "it's her own fault."

"I don't think so!" David towered above Cora as she sat in the rocking chair, his tone of voice not gentle. "As I understand it, it is your fault, and it's about high time you took some responsibility for your behaviour. You're not a child any longer, and have no right to be deliberately worrying your parents and everyone else and putting the blame on other people." David's dark blue eyes were snapping. "Now, I want to know the truth of the story before I turn you out in the snow. My wife's a decent woman and I'll not have her subjected to the gossip that's following you."

Cora swallowed hard and stared up at him, unable to say a word.

"Well? I'm waiting!"

"C-could you possibly sit down, sir?"

David sat abruptly and waited for Cora's response. Mattie sat on the edge of the lounge, away from the fire, and wrapped her shawl tightly around herself.

Cora's silly story came out in bits and pieces, accompanied by sobs, and promises never to do such things again.

"Alright, then. See that you don't. And now we'll have some supper and then I suppose I'll have to take you home. You can't walk all that distance in the dark by yourself."

A look of horror passed over Cora's tear-streaked face. "Home? I can't go home! Momma'll skin me." She looked as if she were about to cry again. "Please let me stay with you and Mattie for awhile. At least until Momma simmers down."

"I'll think about it," agreed David. "Now, I'm hungry and I want my supper. Then I have to see to the animals before I go back and put your family out of their worry."

"I-I'll do chores," she offered.

"Only if I decide to let you stay for a few days."

Cora and Mattie did the chores that evening while David trudged the five long miles to Cora's home, and another five miles back.

"How was Momma?" asked Cora when David arrived back home white-faced with weariness.

"Relieved." He pulled off his boots by the fire leaving a puddle of melting snow on the hearth. "She said you could stay until next week, but she wants you to come home after that." He looked at Cora. "She really does want you to come home, you know."

"Does she?" Cora looked over at David who was relaxing in the other rocker with his stock-inged feet stretched out toward the warmth of the fire. "What about Poppa?"

"Him even more than her. He was that worried

about you, he was almost sick with it." David fell silent and stared into the fire.

Mattie sliced bread and set out butter and molasses and cheese on the table for him. "Here, sit in and have a bite to eat. You must be half starved."

David looked up at her and smiled. "Thank you, Mattie, I am that." He settled in at the table and ate in silence for some minutes. "They've called another election for the first of March."

"There'll be some rare old doings at that. It was bad enough the first time, what with all the intimidation of the voters that went on," said Mattie. "I wouldn't want to be around the polls that day."

"They're going to try to keep it quiet if they can."

"If they can." She sniffed.

"Reverend MacDonald preached a sermon last Sunday on loving your enemies and doing good to them that curse you," offered Cora. "I heard that the priest did the same."

"Well, it's you that would know," said David.

Cora ducked her head and fell silent.

"Much good preaching about it is going to do," said Mattie. "They'll do well to keep them from killing each other after ruining the last election and having to do it all over again."

"I just hope no one gets hurt," said David.

"Yes, well, see to it that you do your voting early and get out of there before there's any fighting or drinking takes place," said Mattie.

"And what if I want to have a little nip myself? It's free you know," he teased. "The candidates'll be bringing it in by the keg."

"David, there's going to be trouble. I can feel it in my bones." Alarm made Mattie's voice sharp. "If they weren't afraid of trouble, Father Doyle and Minister MacDonald wouldn't have preached against it."

David laughed. "So you've got the second sight now, have you?"

"Indeed not!"

"Alright, Mattie, alright. I was just teasing. I won't do anything except vote and come home. In fact, I may even let school out early so that the children'll be home before anything starts, if it does start. Anyway, if there's any fighting, it won't be until after they've all had a skinful of the free stuff, so that won't be until after dark."

Cora and Mattie visited together for the next few days. Their talk was of marriage and babies and husbands. Cora learned a lot from Mattie's example. Mattie learned a lot about how others in the community saw her.

"I'll miss you when you go," said Mattie, the last afternoon of Cora's visit.

"We have had a lovely visit," agreed Cora. "You'll invite me back when the baby's born?"

"Of course. I hope you'll be the first one to come."

"Well, that'll all depend on Momma. I may not be allowed out of the house 'til I'm ninety." Cora made a face.

"Surely by that time!"

Cora sighed. "She was pretty cross. I'm not looking forward to going home."

"Maybe you'll be like the prodigal son, and they'll be so glad to see you that they'll kill the fatted calf." Mattie chuckled.

"More like the prodigal daughter, and we don't have a calf, fatted or otherwise."

"Well, if I know your mother, she'll be so glad to see you all in one piece that she'll give you anything you want just to keep you home."

"Maybe. Ever since James died she's sort of been like that. I think she's afraid of losing any more of us."

"D'you suppose that's why she let you do what you wanted to all this time?"

Cora shook her head. "No, I don't think so. She was a little like that anyway. The only difference was that when James died, any fight she might've had went out of her. She said one time that her own mother was as cross as two sticks, and she vowed that she'd never be like that with her own children."

"Maybe she went too far the other way." Mattie got up to stir the fire. She sat back down and picked up her sewing again, and looked inquiringly in Cora's direction.

Cora's dark head was bent over the nightgown she was making for the baby. "M-m, maybe. If I'm the example. Ouch! I stabbed myself." She stuck her thumb in her mouth and looked up from her work. "It's getting so dark in here it's a wonder I could see the nightgown, never mind my thumb."

"It is getting late. I wonder where David is?" Mattie got up again and went to peer out the window. "It's election day and he promised he wouldn't stay late this evening." She wandered restlessly around the room.

"Pacing's not going to hurry him along," said Cora, "so you might as well sit down and be comfortable."

Mattie sat down with a thump. "You're right. I get so restless when he's not home when he says he will be. My imagination goes wild. I really should start supper." She got up again and went into the pantry.

By eight o'clock that evening David still hadn't returned. Mattie's anxiety made her temper sharp. She lifted the cover to the pot and gave the vegetables a vigorous stir sending droplets of juice flying into the fire where they hissed and died in the heat.

"These vegetables'll be cooked to a mush." She returned the cover with a loud clang startling Cora who had been sitting in the rocker with her eyes closed and her head back.

Mattie made another trip to the window and peered out into the night blackness of the yard. "I hope he didn't get into any trouble. It's as black as ink out there." She roamed around the kitchen, picking things up and setting them down, then picking them up once more to stare at them without seeing them. Finally she forced herself to sit down again.

"He'll be home soon. He's not a rabble rouser."

"I'm not worried about what he'll do to others," replied Mattie. "It's what others might do to him."

A faint thump sounded in the porch. Mattie was on her feet again in an instant. The kitchen door opened.

"Tommy! What're you doing here? Where's David? You're hurt! Where's David?"

"He's coming." Tommy almost fell into the rocker by the fire. He leaned forward and put his head in his hands, winced and sat up again. "He'll be here any minute." Mattie's face set and she began scurrying about collecting things to tend to her brother's injuries.

"Is he hurt too?" Cora asked the question that Mattie was afraid to ask.

A strange look came over Tommy's face when

he saw Cora. "You're still here."

"Yes, I'm still here. Is David hurt?"

Tommy sighed. "No, he's not hurt, no thanks to you."

"What did I have to do with anything? I've been out here for days."

Tommy's smile did not quite reach his eyes. "Indeed you have." His smile faded. "I heard tonight that you're to marry Robert West." Mattie applied soap and water to Tommy's wounds. "Ouch, Mattie, take it easy!"

"Momma wants me to," said Cora. She says she'd rather see me have to get married that way, than to have to get married the other way."

"She's probably right, too." Tommy winced as Mattie applied soap and water to another part of his face which was rapidly swelling, now that he was in out of the cold.

"And what do you know about it?" asked Cora.

"Lots." Tommy caught his breath as Mattie applied liniment to his cuts and bruises.

The porch door squealed on its hinges and Mattie shoved the liniment into Cora's hands and hurried out to David.

Cora took over tending Tommy's wounds with vigour.

"Ow! Cora, you're worse than Mattie."

"So, just what do you know?" Cora applied a liberal dose of liniment.

"I know you're to marry Robert in the spring as soon as the banns are read."

"Is that so? Who says so?"

"The news is all over." Tommy winced again under Cora's less than gentle hand.

"Not if I can help it." Cora tipped the liniment bottle one more time.

Tommy pushed her hand away. "No more, Cora. Those cuts must be clean by now." He leaned forward on his elbows again, this time careful not to touch his battered face. "So what is the story?"

"What's it to you?" She sat down in the other rocker. "I just wish people would leave me alone and mind their own business."

"What's it to me? I got this face tonight because of you. I think I deserve to know." He glared across at her.

"You did?"

"Yes, I did." Tommy probed his face with gentle fingers and winced again.

"What happened?"

"I heard about your escapade from last week just yesterday. Nobody knows where you are except your mother and father, and they're not saying. They let it be known that you're to marry Robert in the spring and everyone's suspecting that you're at his place hiding out."

Cora gasped. "Momma and Poppa would never

let that story circulate if they knew."

"Well, that's the problem with gossip, isn't it? The ones that can set the story straight are always the last to find out. I figured you were out at O'Brien's, you and Colleen and the rest being so tight all summer."

"Now why would I go out there?"

"My goodness, you are dim, aren't you! George has been panting after you all summer long, and you didn't even realize it."

"I'm surprised you even noticed, you were so busy making sheep's eyes at Colleen!"

"I was not! I was only pretending that to keep you out of trouble."

"Keep me out of trouble! I wasn't in any trouble!"

"Well, it wouldn't have been long. All George could talk about was how he couldn't wait to get you alone and what he'd like to do to you. It wasn't pretty. He almost managed it, too. If I hadn't come along, you'd have more than this little bit of gossip to deal with!"

I was so mad at Tommy last summer, Cora thought. He was always in the way. George was paying attention to me and it was fun. At least until that one evening when he managed to get me away from the others. He'd been trying for awhile, but he frightened me. I was glad to see Tommy that night. He walked me the rest of the way home. George was never so attentive to me again.

"You seemed to always be there last summer," she said at last.

"You bet I was. George had no good intentions toward you, and he certainly wouldn't have married you, you being a Protestant and well on the way to making a name for yourself." Tommy sat silently for a few minutes staring into the fire. "And now you're going to marry old Robert West. He was a rival for my mother's affections, you know."

"I am not going to marry Robert, even if I have to be an old maid."

"Your mother and father may have something to say about that. And after all your shenanigans this past year, you won't have much to say about it. Your reputation is none too savoury right now, you're lucky people are still talking to you. The only reason they are is because I was able to put in a good word for you."

Cora was speechless. She sat in the rocker staring across at Tommy, her mouth opening and closing as if she were talking, but no sound came forth.

"Close your mouth Cora, you look like a fish."

She found her voice at last. "Tommy Cameron, how dare you!"

"How dare I what?" He smirked at Cora. His smile changed to a grimace as he disturbed his aching face. "Call you a fish?"

"That, and, and …"

"And follow you around all last summer to keep you out of trouble, and pretend I was interested in Colleen so I'd get invited on all the little evening outings, so that I could keep an eye on George."

"And, and …"

"And go and get beat up tonight just to protect your honour. I owe George for this one." He winced again as his fingers brushed across his face. "I think he loosened my tooth." He tried working the tooth with his tongue. "Well, maybe not."

"What did happen this evening?" asked Mattie. She came in from the porch with David close behind.

Tommy shrugged. "Just a little scuffle at the polls."

"A little scuffle! David just told me that one of them got killed."

"Yes, well, they were probably fighting over politics," replied Tommy with a twinkle in the eye that could still open. "I was just fighting over Cora."

"Fighting over Cora? Tommy, will you please tell me what happened this evening. What were you doing down there anyway? You aren't even old enough to vote yet."

Tommy's grin disappeared. "I heard that she'd been seen with George earlier today. I figured it would be just like her to be out traipsing around with that bunch to see what was going on, so I went to find her. It turned out that it was only Colleen, and George hadn't even seen Cora. He thought, like everyone else, that she was out at Robert's. Well, I knew she wasn't there, because I was over there this afternoon. Anyway, one thing led to another, and things got out of hand and if you think this is bad, you should see George."

"That's when I came along," said David. "I got detained at the store, and when I came out, there was an awful riot going on. It was pretty dark by this time, and I knew you'd be worrying, and all I wanted to do was go home. I'd already voted earlier. I couldn't tell what the whole thing was about, but I did see Tommy here laying a frightful beating on George. I managed to drag him off before he killed him, and brought him home here, since this is where he said he wanted to go."

Mattie shook her head. "You're all crazy! Why would you be fighting George?"

"I was trying to protect what's left of Cora's honour. Much good it did me."

"Momma's going to be wild when she hears about Tommy," whispered Mattie that night when she and David were settled in bed. The partition in the loft was thin and Cora was lying just a few feet away from them.

"That's why he didn't go home." David's voice was a soft growl in the darkness.

"I can't understand what's gotten into him lately, he's been so secretive. Ever since Poppa died."

"Your mother's partly to blame for that. He said she nagged him terribly about his activities until he finally wouldn't tell her anything."

"I can see Momma being like that. She never did it to me because I didn't have anything to tell, and now she won't because I'm your wife."

"I wonder what Cora is going to do now?" whispered David. "She and Tommy looked like they were scrapping when we came in this evening. I was rather hoping that this little go round would teach her a lesson."

"I know," sighed Mattie, "I was too, and I think maybe it has taught her something, at least about gossip. The thing of it is, she's really a good person. I don't know why she behaves like this. She was always up to something, even when we were children, and always trying to drag me into it, too."

"How'd you manage to escape?" David's soft chuckle rumbled in the darkness.

"Oh, my fear of Momma and her wrath kept me pretty much in line. Besides, the Smiths were our nearest neighbours with a child my age to play with, and if I got into trouble with Cora, I wouldn't have been allowed to see her at all, and then who would I have played with?"

"I see."

David was silent for so long after that, that Mattie thought he had fallen asleep. She was just about to turn over and do the same when his voice rumbled out of the darkness once more.

"Y'know, Mattie, I don't want to have to do this ever, but if Cora doesn't mend her ways, I'll have to forbid her our house. I can't have her coming here every time she gets into trouble of her own making. That kind of thing tends to stick, and I can't have your good name ruined too, it could cost me the school."

Mattie drew in her breath sharply. "I hadn't thought of that." She swallowed hard against the lump in her throat. "She's been my friend for always. She's not a bad girl."

"I know that, and you know that, but the rest of the world doesn't, and unfortunately it's appearances that count, and her behaviour is showing the world that she's a bad girl. At the moment they're still calling her misguided, and holding her mother responsible. But it won't be long before it'll be worse than that and she'll be branded a bad girl for the rest of her days."

Mattie drew a long wavering breath. The lump in her throat was making it hard to breathe. "I'll speak to her in the morning."

David's arm came around her. "I'm sorry,

Mattie, but that's the way it is. If it were just me, it wouldn't matter."

"I know," said Mattie. "There's three of us now."

Chapter Sixteen

Mattie opened her eyes the next morning to the low rumble of male voices from downstairs. The sound puzzled her for a moment, then the events of last night came back to her.

Cora. Tomm   y. It's such a mess, she thought. Her heart felt so heavy that her chest hurt with the weight of it.

She groaned and rolled onto her back and lay there for a moment thinking about what she had to say to Cora. Oh, Cora, I don't want to hurt you. Why couldn't you have behaved?

Tears gathered in her eyes and one rolled down her cheek. She sniffed. When we were children I told you that you'd get into some real trouble some day, and now you have. A second tear followed the first, and soon there were two more. She lay still and tried to stop them, but they followed fast on one another. She scrubbed at them with the edge of the sheet. Finally she just let them spill.

The tears didn't last long, and when they were over she lay thinking about all the good times they'd had together. We built grand playhouses in the woods, she thought. That birch tree that fell the winter before we turned nine made a wonderful house, especially when we filled the spaces between the branches with ferns to make walls. The dolls we made from bits and pieces from Momma's sewing projects. Momma was wild the day we took one of the scraps she was saving for the quilt she was piecing. Amy and Lyn were the best babies. Poor Amy had a squint because I couldn't find two buttons alike and the little one got sewed on crooked. We spoon-fed them from broken bits of china Cora brought over from the Smiths' rubbish heap. I still have Amy, I wonder if Cora still has Lyn?

The straw rustled on the other side of the partition as Cora stirred. Mattie's thoughts returned to the present. "Oh, Cora, I hope you've learned your lesson," she whispered. The baby moved inside her, a brief touching, like a stroke of comfort. Joy filled Mattie's heart. "Whatever happens to Cora, baby, I can't let you down."

"I'll walk with you as far as I can," said Mattie as Cora prepared to leave. "David shovelled the path almost to the gate over the winter, so it's easier now, and I won't need snowshoes." She put on her coat and buttoned it as far down as she could over her swollen belly.

She had said little during breakfast, mulling over the problem of what to say to Cora. David had watched her covertly as she served the meal and tidied up afterwards. Her face was softly serious, a vertical worry line, very like her mother's, etched between her eyebrows. Cora was to walk with him as far as the school, but he let the girls go ahead to say their goodbyes.

Mattie followed Cora up the path, still uncertain how to bring up the subject of their future friendship. She made several false starts.

"What's the matter, Mattie?" asked Cora. "You've had something on your mind all morning."

"Oh, Cora, d'you think you can behave like a good girl now?" Tears were floating in Mattie's voice.

"It'll be hard," she replied. "I'll miss a lot of fun."

"Oh, fun! Is that all you ever think about? You still don't even realize what's at stake here, do you?"

Cora looked at Mattie. "I guess not. What is at stake?"

"Our friendship, that's what! David and I had a long talk last night after we went to bed. You won't be able to come here anymore if you continue in your present activities," she recited. I'm thankful that David said that so precisely last night, she thought.

"Why ever not?" Laughter still lurked in Cora's voice.

"Because if you ruin your reputation for good

and all, and we still welcome you to our house,
it's liable to rub off on me. If that happens David
could lose the school, and then what would we
do?"

"That's not likely to happen. Why would they
blame you for something that I did?"

"You know that they do. They do it all the time.
Just think about poor Christy, and that didn't even
take very long either."

"Well, that won't happen to me. I'm not stupid
enough to do something like that, especially now
that I know how things work. I'm glad you told
me that. Momma never would have, nor Sarah
either."

"Nevertheless," said Mattie, "if there's any
more talk about you, I'll have to stop seeing you.
I cannot do anything to harm David or our baby.
Good-bye, Cora, safe home." She gave Cora a brief,
hard hug, then turned and walked swiftly back to
the sanctuary of her little house where she sat in
the rocking chair staring blankly into the dying
fire, not even bothering to take off her coat. David
found her there a few minutes later when he came
in to say good-bye.

"Where's Cora?"

"Waiting for you at the top of the path." Her
voice was stiff with the tears she was determined
not to shed.

"No, she's not. I was just up there."

"Well, I don't know, then. That's where she was."

"Drat that girl, where has she gotten to now?"

"Home, I hope." A tear fought its way past Mattie's determination and rolled down her cheek. "I can't worry about her anymore."

David knelt beside the rocker and took Mattie's cold hands in his. "You told her then?"

Mattie nodded and turned her face away as more tears forced their way past her slipping control. "S-She was my friend."

The days seemed very long after Cora's departure. Mattie's heart ached whenever she thought about her, so she tried not to think about her very much. David brought news that she had, in fact, gone home and that she had agreed to marry Robert West.

Maybe she's taken what I said to heart, thought Mattie. I hope she'll be happy with him. At least he'll be good to her, and she won't want for anything. He'll treat her like a queen. She thought of Robert's merry face with its tobacco stained grin and shuddered. I don't think I'd like to be the one having to kiss him.

The wedding's to take place in June, she thought. I suppose I'd better make her something for a gift. She rummaged in her sewing basket. I guess

I could make her a small quilt for the foot of her bed. I don't know if Robert has cold feet, but if he has, this'll be a welcome thing on a cold night in January. I wish I could see her before she gets married, but I guess I won't be able to. David says that the only place she's seen these days is in church and I can't go there looking like this. She regarded her belly with regret. It seems to be getting larger by the day, she thought.

I really miss church. I didn't think I would. David brings me news of everyone, but he doesn't know to ask the right questions so I really only hear half of it. She tried to imagine David listening to the gossip, then shook her head. I guess I'm lucky to get the news that I do. Not every woman has such an obliging husband. She thought back to the day Cora left. He was so gentle and kind that day, that I cried for the sweetness of it almost as much as for Cora.

The end of March brought cold slanting rain that left the snowbanks wilted and dirty. The yard was a red muddy field surrounded by collapsing drifts of old snow. Pansy's calf arrived, courtesy of a visit to Robert's bull last fall, and they would soon have milk again.

Thank goodness, thought Mattie, we were

down to our last bite of cheese. At least now we can have some curds and butter and buttermilk. Her mouth watered and the baby kicked. "I see you want some too," she said. The baby kicked again. "It's almost as if you can hear me." She stroked her belly.

The rain washed them well into April, and a watery sun began appearing more and more frequently. The air held that certain freshness that was only apparent in springtime. Mattie went to the door and breathed deeply, feeling the salt-fresh air penetrate her lungs, making her light-headed for a moment. It's finally spring, she thought. If the yard weren't so muddy I'd go for a walk. Why, there's David! He's home early. I wonder why? She waved and watched him as he waved back and quickened his pace down the path toward her. How much I've grown to enjoy his company!

"You're home early," she said as they stood together on the block of sandstone that formed the doorstep, enjoying the softness of the day.

"Spring's in the air, and I couldn't get the children to settle, nor myself either, so I let us all go early. We'll make it up the next rainy day."

"It'll soon be time for the potatoes anyway," she observed, "then you won't be able to hold them down for sure."

"I'll be losing a few then, too, and I'm heartily

thankful. That oldest Johnson boy's a handful. I could hardly keep ahead of him and his mischief! I thought for sure I would have to expel him from school last month after he loosened the stove pipe and it fell and nearly set fire to the schoolhouse. I still haven't found out who helped him."

"Someone'll give it away sometime," said Mattie as she led the way into the house. "I haven't started supper yet." She hung her shawl on the hook behind the door.

"I'll just relax a bit, then do the chores. That calf of Pansy's is a nice one. She'll be a good cow herself someday. I'll be able to get a good price for her."

Mattie stirred up the fire and added another stick. It caught fire and soon filled the kitchen with its smoky warmth. The rays of the late afternoon sun glinted off the candlestick holders on the mantel piece. Mattie's heart filled with joy. She smiled at David. "I'm glad you came home early," she said shyly.

He reached out and took her hand. "I'm glad too," he replied, and smiled up at her.

She blushed and pulled away. "I have to start supper."

David sighed, dropping his hand back into his lap. "I'll get at the chores, then."

§

Later that week, Mattie was sitting on the sandstone step with just her shawl wrapped around her shoulders, for the day finally had some warmth in it. In the corner that caught the sun, where the porch joined the house, the grass was looking distinctly greener, and an early dandelion shone. Mattie revelled in its sunny brightness.

"I don't feel like working today," she said to the crows which were flapping in lazy black circles above the spruces. I have that great stack of baby things that I've been working on all winter, and I don't feel like doing any more, she thought. She glanced up the path to the road. Why here comes Mrs. Gillis! What a nice surprise. Mattie stood up and waved to her neighbour.

Mrs. Gillis waved back, her auburn hair copper bright in the spring sunshine. Mattie waited for her by the door.

"G'day, Mrs. Gillis, come in. What brings you here?" Mattie opened the door and stood aside to let her visitor enter. The tiny lines in Anna's creamy skin seemed deeper today. She looks tired, thought Mattie. I hope there's nothing wrong.

"It's your mother, Mattie. She's had her baby."

Mattie paled and sat down with a thump in the rocker. "When?"

"I was with her all last night. I've just now gotten out of my own bed."

"Is she all right?"

"Aye, she'll do." Anna sighed tiredly and settled herself more comfortably in the rocker. "It was a hard birth. The baby came early and she was feet first. Those kind are always harder to come."

"And the baby?"

"It's tiny, of course. Barely four pounds. Ellie's tending it in the warming oven."

"Ellie is?" Mattie could not conceal her surprise.

"Oh, yes, she's very capable these days. Your mother's still resting in bed."

"Have they a name for it yet?"

"Mary Elizabeth, for your mother and for me. My second name's Elizabeth, you know."

"So it's a girl."

Anna nodded. "Poor Norman's so pleased and worried and proud all at the same time, it's a treat to watch him. If his chest sticks out much farther he'll not be able to see where his feet are going. He keeps running back and forth between your mother and the warming oven."

"He must have gotten her a stove then."

"Yes, just last month. She's that proud of it."

Mattie pursed her lips disapprovingly. "That Ellie'll be spoilt for a husband of her own." She sat in silence for a moment mulling over the whole business, then sighed. She got there ahead of me anyway, she thought. "I have a fresh 'bonnick' cooling in the pantry, will you have a bite and some jam?"

"Yes, thanks. You have jam left?"

"A bottle of raspberry that I saved in the back of the cupboard for spring. David didn't know it was there, and I forgot about it until today. He'll be pleased to see it. It's his favourite."

"That will be a nice treat, indeed."

"Have you seen Cora lately?" Mattie bustled about slicing the *bannoch* and setting out jam and new butter.

"I have and she's real thin and poor looking. Her mother's terrible worried about her."

"Is she sick?"

"She's mourning for something. There's some say she's breaking her heart over George, but she denies that." Anna sighed. "I don't know what'll happen to her, indeed I don't."

"I wish I could see her, but David thinks it's better if I don't right now."

"No, you want to keep your mind clear, or you're liable to mark your own baby."

"Maybe after the baby comes, then."

"It won't be long now, just a few more weeks."

"Thank goodness!" Mattie exclaimed, "I haven't seen my shoes for months."

Mattie walked to the top of the path with Mrs. Gillis. In the distance she could see David returning from school and waited for him. He dropped a kiss on her rosy cheek, making her blush even rosier.

"Oh, David, don't. Mrs. Gillis will see you."

"No she won't, she's going in the other direction." He kissed the other cheek, then took her by the hand.

"Momma's had her baby."

"I heard. The older girls were talking about it at noon." He opened the gate for Mattie. "You'll soon be having ours."

"Thank goodness! I'm getting awful tired of looking like this." She preceded him down the path.

"Your mother's was early, wasn't it?"

"Yes, by almost six weeks. She wasn't due until after me, and it came feet first." Mattie frowned. "I didn't know that babies could come feet first." She thought about what she knew about babies. "I guess I didn't know that they came head first either."

David shrugged. "Animals sometimes come feet first, so I suppose human babies can, too."

"D'you suppose it'd be alright if I go and see her?"

"You mean now?"

"Well, not today, but soon."

"Not until after our baby's born, I think."

"But that won't be for another month."

"Nevertheless," said David, "it's a long way, and you never know what you might see on the road. You don't want to mark our child, do you?"

"N-no. But in a month I might be dead." Mattie clamped her lips firmly shut.

"Are you still worrying about that?"

She nodded. "The closer the day gets, the more frightened I get."

He drew her into his arms and held her securely against him. For once she didn't fight it. "I'm sorry, Mattie. This is a lot harder for you than I thought. Didn't Mrs. Gillis tell you what to expect?"

Mattie slipped her arms inside the warmth of his coat, and she laid her head on his chest. She could hear his heart beating through the wool of his sweater. Her voice was muffled when she replied. "She said that it would take a long time and that it would hurt a lot."

David stroked her hair. "Poor Mattie, you have a hard job ahead of you."

They stood together in the middle of the yard for some time not saying anything. David absorbed the rare treat of holding Mattie in his arms somewhere besides in bed in the dark. Mattie absorbed the warmth and comfort of being held.

A new closeness developed between them in the weeks preceding the birth of their child. Mattie allowed David to put his arms around her more often now, and was surprised at the sense of flowering and gentleness within her. It's not the same feeling I have at night when we're together, she thought, trying to puzzle it out.

Her body seemed quieter to her now in these last weeks. The baby was moving less and was still for hours at a time, almost as if it were resting up for the ordeal to come. Her back ached more than ever, and sometimes she felt rhythmic tightenings and pullings in her back and thighs. She worried about this, but such was her altered state of mind that these thoughts didn't seem to last long. She wondered idly if she should be worried about her lack of worry but the thought soon faded.

A thump in the porch that evening brought her out of her reverie and she went to see what it was.

"Oh, David! A cradle!" She helped him carry it into the kitchen. "It's beautiful! Now I'll be able to have the baby down here by the fire during the day and not have to keep climbing up those steep stairs. Thank you!" She set down her end of the cradle and reached up and kissed his cheek.

"Oh!" she said, startled by her own boldness.

David laughed. "It's alright to kiss your husband, Mattie." He carried the cradle over to the fireplace. "Where do you want it?"

"Right there under the stairs," she replied, still blushing. "That'll be its own corner, and it'll be near the warmth of the fire too."

David set the cradle in its appointed place, then stood back and surveyed it. He reached for Mattie's hand. "That's just the right place for it," he said, smiling down at her.

Chapter Seventeen

Mattie's time was very near. David closed the school at noon on Friday so that he could stay with her.

"Potatoes, carrots, and neeps." He sat at the table making a list for their garden to help pass the time after their mid-day meal. "After that what do you want?"

Mattie didn't answer. She sat staring into space.

"Aren't you feeling well?" he asked. "You seem very edgy, not yourself."

"I don't know. I've been feeling anxious all morning. My back's aching more than usual. I wish Mrs. Gillis would come and visit." Suddenly she gasped and jumped to her feet. A flood of water gushed to the floor. "Go get Mrs. Gillis. Something's happened to the baby!"

David ran all the way to Anna's house. She deciphered his incoherent explanation, gathered her things together and hurried after him. They found Mattie, with pale face and tight lips, on her hands and knees scrubbing the floor.

Anna took the rag and bucket from her hands

and handed them to David. "You shouldn't be doing that."

Mattie sat back on her heels. "I had to, I made an awful mess." She grimaced and rubbed her back.

"How often are the pains, dear?" Anna assisted Mattie to her feet.

"Not very often." Mattie gasped and began rubbing her thighs.

"Just relax into them, it'll make them easier to bear. Sit down and rest yourself, it's going to take a long time. First babies are always slow."

But Mattie couldn't relax. Hours later she was still pacing. Her pains were more frequent now. She wished with all her heart that this agony would be over with.

It's true, she thought, Cora's sister was right, it does feel like I'm being ripped apart from the inside.

She retreated farther and farther into herself with every passing hour. She was no longer afraid of dying, she only wanted it to happen soon. Late that evening the bite of dinner she had managed to consume so many hours ago rebelled and she fled to the outdoors with Anna close behind her.

"That's good, dear," Anna said, as she led the white and shaking Mattie back indoors. "That means that the end is nearly in sight. Your pushing pains should begin any time now. Come and let me help you get ready for them."

The pains were coming faster now. Mattie could hardly bear them without crying out. David hovered nearby.

"David, I want you to begin tearing the sheet I brought with me into strips. I want two long narrow ones, and a long wide one. Then I want you to draw some water and set it to heating. I'm going to get Mattie ready, the baby should be here in the next hour or so." Anna started up the steep stairs after Mattie. "Oh, and hang a set of those baby clothes by the fire to warm, and don't forget a blanket." She disappeared into the sleeping loft.

David did as he was told. When he had finished he climbed the stairs to their bedroom, where Mattie lay, pale and sweating, on the rumpled bed. He hastened to her side. She looked up at him hardly seeing him. He took her clammy hand in his. Another pain began. Mattie couldn't contain her cry. She gripped David's hand with all her might, willing this ordeal to be over with.

"David, you shouldn't be here now," said Anna. "This is no place for a man."

"Indeed it is my place! I'm her husband and I'm staying. She needs me now. I'll not desert her."

Anna had no time to insist, for as she attended to Mattie she saw that the baby's head was right down, the little tufts of black hair already making their appearance. "Now Mattie, when the next pain comes I want you to bear down as hard as you can. The baby's almost here. Another good push or two should do it."

Mattie heard her dimly as if from a distance. She held tightly to David's hand. It was the life-line that connected her to the real world. Another pain came and she pushed with all her might. David's hand bore the marks of her fingernails for some time after.

She rested a few moments, then raised herself on her elbows as another contraction bore down on her. David supported her shoulders as she put almost the last of her strength into the effort.

"Not too much more," encouraged Anna, as she cleared the mouth and eyes of the emerging infant. "Another push will see the worst over with."

Mattie gathered the very last of her strength for the final effort. It was not long in coming. With great relief she could feel the slippery little body slide from her. She lay back exhausted against the sodden pillows.

"It's a girl." Anna placed the mewling infant on Mattie's belly. "I'll cut the cord in a moment and then you can hold her."

Anna waited until the cord had stopped pulsing and then tied it with one of the thin strips of cloth that David had prepared. Then she severed the baby's cord. She wrapped the baby securely in her belly band and then in the warmed blankets before giving her to Mattie. The baby continued to cry.

"You need to put her to breast now," she said. "It will do you both a lot of good. She's very hungry after all her exertions, and it will help you to deliver the after-birth. Your womb will come back into shape more quickly, too." She finished the delivery and tidied Mattie, and then went down to the kitchen to prepare the baby's first bath.

Mattie gazed in wonder at this tiny human being nursing at her breast. Her black curly hair was so like David's. Her tiny hand had the shape of Mattie's own.

David gazed in wonder at them both.

The next day Mattie sat in the kitchen rocking her baby. I didn't die, she thought, and David was a rock through it all. I'm glad that Mrs. Gillis let him stay. I was so afraid.

David came hurrying in to see them again, as he had been doing about every fifteen minutes all day. She looked up as he entered. Joy welled up from her heart at the sight of him. She smiled up at him.

"You're going to have her spoiled in no time if you keep holding her all the time."

"Oh, do you think so?" Mattie's face took on

a serious cast. "I'd better put her down then." She rose awkwardly from the rocker.

"Mattie, I was only teasing. You rock her as much as you want." David reached over and stirred up the fire, and added another stick. "What're we going to call her?"

"I've been thinking and thinking on that," she replied, "and I can't make up my mind. Momma's baby's called after her and Mrs. Gillis, so I can't call her that." She paused and thought some more. "Your mother's name was Helen, wasn't it?"

"Yes, she was Helen Margaret." He thought back to his mother who had died so young. He had only been eight when she had died, but he remembered so many things about her, the way she walked, the sound of her voice, the gentle-firm touch of her hands, especially when he hadn't wanted to obey her. And her smell. She had a sweet faint odour of … He couldn't quite place the scent, then with a flash he realized, she had smelled like Mattie! His smile stretched wide as he looked across at Mattie, so newly a mother herself. "That's what we'll call her. Helen Margaret."

Mattie looked down at her sleeping child and marvelled at her perfection. Her skin was softly pink with a faint blush of rose on her cheeks. She has hair like Himself, she thought, dark and wavy. I wonder if it'll stay dark like that? They say baby's first hair falls out, and you don't know what colour it'll be when they grow up. "D'you suppose her eyes'll stay blue?" she asked him.

"I don't know. Are they like kittens? Kittens' eyes change colour after they're born, I know."

Mattie giggled. "Oh, David, she's not a kitten!"

"Then I don't know."

"I suppose we'll just have to wait and see." Mattie looked down at her daughter and watched the steady rise and fall of her tiny chest beneath the blankets. "It's wonderful to watch them, isn't it?" She tucked a tiny mottled hand into the blanket, and cooed softly at her. "Your little handies are getting cold. Mustn't let that happen." She touched the baby's soft hair, and Helen Margaret opened her eyes and looked straight at her mother as if she recognized her. Mattie nearly cried for the joy of it. Her face grew serious. "David?"

David took his mind away from the contemplation of his daughter. "Yes, Mattie?"

"I promised Cora that she could come and see the baby before, before …"

"Before I told you she couldn't visit?"

Mattie nodded. "D'you suppose she could come for the afternoon in a few days? There hasn't been any new gossip about her, and she's promised to Robert now, and that's pretty respectable, isn't it?"

David pursed his lips. "I don't see why not, but only for the afternoon. I'll send word home to her mother tomorrow."

§

Two days later Cora arrived at Mattie's back door.

"Whatever is wrong with you?" asked Mattie. "You're that thin I can almost see through you." She took Cora's shawl and hung it on the hook behind the door.

Cora shivered. "I'm so cold." She rose and got her shawl and wrapped herself in it.

"You're so thin! You haven't enough meat on your bones to keep a flea warm."

"I have lost a little weight, I guess." Cora pulled her chair closer to the fire.

"A little! You look like you're about to starve. Are you sick?"

Cora lowered her eyes. "Sick at heart, I think. I'm to marry Robert in three weeks time, and I don't know how I'm going to do it. I can't talk to Momma about it, she's that anxious to get me off her hands so I won't cause any more trouble." Cora burst into tears. "Oh, Mattie, I just don't know what to do, and it's all my own fault."

"I'm sorry, Cora, I don't know what you can do either. After all, you have promised to marry him."

"But I didn't. Momma promised for me."

"Same thing." Mattie thrust her handkerchief into Cora's thin hands.

"Oh, Mattie, what am I going to do? The more

I think about marrying Robert, the more frightened I get." Cora blew her nose and sniffed. "All I can think of is doing that awful thing with him."

"I shouldn't have told you," said Mattie. A vivid picture of Robert's face looming over her own self flashed into the darkened bedroom of her mind. She shuddered.

"See, you know what I mean. If only he didn't chew tobacco, it might be easier." She swabbed at her nose again.

"Maybe he'll stop once you're married."

"I don't think so. I heard him and Poppa cackling over it the other night. They sounded just like two old bachelors comparing women, except they were comparing tobacco."

"Well, he is practically an old bachelor," said Mattie. "His wife died almost twenty years ago and they never had any children."

Cora looked at her and burst into a fresh bout of tears. "He's old enough to be my father's friend. Oh, I wish I was dead!"

"They say he's well off. You'll never have to worry about money, and before many years go by, you'll probably be a rich widow."

"They say he's tight too." Cora sniffed and searched for a dry spot on the handkerchief.

"I suppose he's had to be in order to become rich."

"I guess I could make long visits to Sarah. Then I'd only have to live with him occasionally."

"Cora! That's no way to be married. What about your children? What're you going to do with them?"

"Children? Babies?" Cora seemed to be on the edge of another outburst of weeping, but began to giggle. "They'll probably be born with grey whiskers and tobacco stains on their chins." Her laughter had an hysterical note to it. "They'll all play the fiddle and grin when they're pleased. And-and they'll snort when they laugh, and-and…"

"… kiss cows?" suggested Mattie.

"Kiss cows?" The hysteria left Cora's voice.

"Haven't you heard that one?"

"No, tell me."

"Well, I heard Poppa telling Momma about it a long time ago, so I may not get it quite right, but Robert used to raise milk cows for sale. That's how he made his money, you know."

"Go on." Cora settled herself more comfortably in the rocker.

"He didn't have much those times, so when he bought his first cow he had to put all the money he had on it, and when she calved the next spring, she delivered heifer twins. Robert was so excited that he threw his arms around her neck and kissed her right on the snout, and called her 'darlin'!"

"Oh, Mattie! That's awful! That's what he calls me all the time." Cora's laughter held real merriment this time. "I wish you hadn't told me that, now I'll never be able to kiss him."

"Well, you're going to have to sooner or later."

"I'll run away!" The hysterical note was back in Cora's voice again.

Mattie shook her head. "That didn't work so well the last time, did it? That's why you're in this mess. Besides, you've promised, and you can't break your promise. It's as good as being married to him right now. And anyway, if you do that, you'll never be able to come back here. Your name'll be mud."

"Cora Mudd! I think I like that better than Cora West."

"Cora, look, being married to Robert won't be so bad. You've made a commitment to him that's almost as good as being married to him, and you can't break that." Mattie banished the picture of Robert's cheerful tobacco-stained face from her mind. "Marriage isn't the easiest thing you'll ever do, I don't think anyone has an easy time of it. Look at old Sadie Shaw and her husband. He did something she didn't like soon after the wedding and they didn't speak to one another for twenty years. It put a terrible warp on their children."

"It's a wonder they even had children."

"She did what she had to do, and so will you." Mattie set her lips and began rocking. "Besides, who else would you marry around here? The boys we know are just that, and you can always visit here if things get too hard at home."

"I met Cora on the way home." David leaned over the cradle and admired Helen. "Did you two have a good visit?"

"I guess so. She's all upset about having to marry Robert, but I think I've managed to convince her to stick to her promise. She was threatening to run away."

David's expression hardened. "Well, she's not to run here this time."

"I told her that."

"She won't be welcome in the community either, if she does something like that."

"I told her that, too."

"It seems you've covered most of the points. Was she in any better frame of mind when she left?"

Mattie shrugged. "I think she's finally resigned herself to the situation, although she's not very happy about it."

Helen Margaret grew plump and rosy. She lay in the cradle looking up at the world with accepting blue eyes. Her world was Mattie, and for the moment, she was Mattie's. She rarely cried. It wasn't necessary. At the first sound of stirring in the cradle Mattie picked her up and rocked her and nursed her, then rocked her again until she fell asleep. Her first smile was for her mother, probably only because she was there and David wasn't. She bestowed one on David that same evening.

"I can almost see your crown," Mattie teased him.

David put his free arm around Mattie and drew her close. "I feel like a king," he said. "I am, indeed, a rich man!"

Mattie blushed and looked away. And I am a rich woman, she thought.

Mattie and Helen waited for David to appear at the top of the slight rise in the road on his return from school. Helen lay waving her plump arms and legs, and staring unfocusedly into the soft day. Mattie sat beside her and talked to her just as she had done before her birth.

"It's hard to believe that you weren't here six weeks ago," said Mattie. "It seems like you've always been here." She watched her daughter fondly, then glanced up. David had just appeared on the road. She waved at him and he waved back and hastened his steps. Her heart filled with gladness at the sight of him.

"He's looking worried today, Helen. I wonder what news he has?" Mattie scrambled to her feet and stood waiting for him to join her.

"Is it Momma?"

David shook his head. "No, it's Cora. She's run away."

"Oh, no! Her wedding was to be tomorrow."

"Well, she's gone, and they're all frantic for her. Her mother's taken to her bed and her father's just beside himself with worry. He keeps saying that he shouldn't have allowed her mother to force her to marry Robert. Everyone's out looking for her."

"They'll not find her," said Mattie with certainty in her voice.

David looked at her sharply. "You don't know where she is, do you?"

"Of course not. I didn't even know she was missing until now. It's just that she told me she'd like to run away. I persuaded her out of it, I thought, but I guess everything became too much for her." Mattie stooped to pick up the now sleeping Helen. "I hope she's alright."

They walked in silence down the path to the house. Why did you do this? she raged silently after Cora. Where are you?

"D'you suppose she'll ever come back?" Mattie stood aside for David to open the door.

"She won't if she has any sense," he said. "Not even Robert'll have her now."

"How is he?"

"Angry. If you can imagine him angry."

Mattie tried and failed. The only picture she could conjure up of Robert was his merry face that always seemed to be on the verge of smiling even in the worst of circumstances, and the perpetual streak of tobacco juice on his chin. "Poor Robert!" Mattie lay Helen down in her cradle and gave it a push to start it rocking. "He didn't deserve that."

They sat for a long time in front of the fire that evening, each absorbed in his own thoughts. At last David broke the silence.

"What're you going to do if she comes here?"

Mattie's reply was prompt and decisive. "What can I do? She's my friend. I can't see her hungry and cold with no place to go."

David sighed. "You're a loyal little thing aren't you."

"Yes, and it's a good thing, too. Besides, you wouldn't really want me to turn her away would you?"

David reached over and patted her hand that, for once, was lying idle in her lap. "No, of course I wouldn't. I was just hoping that the threat of separation would bring her to her senses."

"Well, it hasn't, and now she probably won't come here either." A thin thread of accusation wound itself through Mattie's voice.

"I know. I'm sorry about that." David rose and took a turn around the room. "She may be back home already. It was just this morning that they couldn't find her."

Hope flared in Mattie's heart. "I'll send word tomorrow and ask her how she is."

Chapter Eighteen

Mattie sent word with David the next morning, but Cora had not returned. A week went by with no word from her. Mattie was very worried, and her worry made Helen fretful.

"Hush, Helen," Mattie crooned as she walked back and forth jiggling the screaming Helen in her arms. "Poppa has to sleep so he can teach school tomorrow." Helen gulped into a momentary silence. Mattie stopped jiggling, and Helen began screaming again. "Oh, Helen, what can I do for you?"

"D'you want me to take her for awhile?" David appeared suddenly from the darkness of the sleeping loft. "This is the third night in a row you haven't gotten any sleep."

"Oh, yes, please, I'd be so glad to just get off my feet for a few minutes."

David climbed down the steep stairs in his night shirt and socks, his bare legs, darkly furred with curly hair, looking thin and vulnerable below the hem of his gown. He took the screaming infant from Mattie's arms. "You look exhausted."

"I'm fine. I sleep a little during the day."

"And worry the rest of the time, I would guess." David began pacing where Mattie had left off. Helen quieted and lay in his arms staring up at him with her near-sighted infant gaze. Presently an enormous belch erupted from her tummy. She sighed once, then closed her eyes and slept. David took a few more turns around the kitchen just to make sure, then laid her in her cradle. She stirred for a moment then settled into deeper sleep.

"Thank goodness," said Mattie. "I thought I was going to go crazy."

"You know, Mattie, she wouldn't be like this if you could stop worrying about Cora. She's gone now and no amount of worrying is going to bring her back." David sat down in the other rocker beside Mattie.

"I know. She's done a foolish thing. I only hope that she's not lying dead somewhere."

"She's probably not, you know. If she's smart, she'll have gone to the mainland and found herself a job as a house maid in a hotel or something. She could buy herself a wedding ring and portray herself as a poor widow."

"She could that." Mattie pursed her lips. "But you know, David, Cora's not smart. I've been over and over this in my mind ever since she disappeared, and I can't imagine where she could have gotten to, unless …" Mattie shuddered.

"Unless, what?"

"She said when she was here to visit Helen, that she wished she could die."

"Is this what you've been torturing yourself with all these days?"

Mattie nodded. "I've been trying to convince myself that she wouldn't do such a thing, but all I can see in my mind is Cora lying dead in some woods with the crows picking out her eyes."

"Good grief! It's no wonder the baby's colicky. I want you to stop thinking about this right now. It's all nonsense. Cora may not be smart but she's not going to do something that drastic. Anyway, if she does, there's nothing you can do about it." David rose from his seat. "That girl needs the switch if ever they find her. Now come up to bed and get some sleep."

Mattie made an effort not to think about Cora anymore. Every time she found herself thinking about her she pushed her firmly from her mind. David's right, Mattie thought, there's nothing I can do about it. Oh, but it's a heartache, all the same.

Mattie drowsed in the rocker by the cold hearth keeping half a sleepy eye on Helen who was lying on her back on a blanket on the floor trying to investigate her ever elusive toes. Her fingers had already been thoroughly explored and one plump fist was thrust up to the knuckles into her mouth.

A faint noise in the porch brought Mattie instantly alert. She reached for the broom and went to see what had made the noise. She opened the porch door a crack and peered into the gloom.

"Cora?" She blinked and looked again. "Cora!" She threw the door open wide and grabbed her friend by the arm and almost dragged her into the kitchen.

"What do you mean by scaring us all to death like this? How dare you! Your mother and father are heartbroken!" Mattie gave Cora a fierce hug, then continued to rage at her. "Where have you been? I've been worried sick, and making Helen sick because of it! How dare you worry us all like that? I thought you were dead; killed or drowned!" She stopped to draw breath.

Cora saw her opportunity and took it. "I'm sorry, Mattie. I'm truly sorry. I just couldn't marry Robert. I suppose he's very angry."

"I don't know any more. I suppose he is, and so he should be. You've made him the laughingstock of the whole Island."

"The poor man! He's not a bad fellow and he deserves a better wife than me."

"That's certain." Mattie's anger and distress began to seep away. "So where were you?"

"I hid out at Norman's old house for a few days. I didn't dare light a fire or a candle or someone would have found me."

"It must've been cool at night."

"Not too bad. It's still furnished, so there were blankets and things there. I was more hungry than cold."

"You're looking thinner than ever. Are you hungry now?"

"I could eat. Tommy brought me some food, but by that time I was so hungry that it didn't last long."

"Tommy knew where you were?"

Cora nodded. "He found me about the third day I was there. Norman sent him over to pick up something from the barn and he saw me through the window."

Mattie sniffed. "I suppose if you'd known he'd be coming, you would've hid."

Cora sighed. "I don't know. I think by that time I was too scared and tired of my own company to not want to be found."

"Well, sit in to the table and I'll make us a bite." Mattie bustled off to the pantry. "Does your mother know you're all right?" She returned in a moment with plates and cutlery.

"Yes, we sent word last night."

Mattie frowned. "We?"

Cora blushed and looked away. "Me'n Tommy. We're married, you know."

Mattie set the dishes on the table with great care and dropped with a thump into the nearest

chair. "You are?" She sat staring at Cora in disbelief. "When? Who? Where?"

"Two days ago, at the manse in Murray River.
Mr. MacDonald wasn't available and probably
wouldn't have done it anyway after all the trouble
I've caused, so we didn't ask him."

"Well!" exclaimed Mattie. "Well!" Her mind
flitted here and there. "Does Momma know? She'll
be livid."

"She knows." Cora made a face. "Livid wasn't
the word for it. I thought she'd have apoplexy!
Her last words were to Tommy. She said, 'It's
your bed, and you made it. I hope for your sake
it's not too uncomfortable.' We left then and went
back to Norman's old place. He wasn't so upset
and said that we could live there as long as we
wanted to. Your Momma's a lucky woman."

"She's luckier than she knows." Mattie rose and
finished setting the table. "Where's Tommy now?"

"Out talking to Pansy, I guess. He's waiting for
me to call him after I'd told you. He was afraid
that you'd take it like your mother."

"I'm not my mother!" snapped Mattie. "Go and
call him!"

In a few minutes they were all sitting around
the table. Mattie's wrath had subsided and she
was full of questions. "So how did you come to
get married?" She passed Tommy the bread and
butter.

"I've wanted to marry Cora all along, but first I was too young, and too poor. Then she started running with the wrong crowd, and I had to make sure she didn't get into trouble."

"So that's why you were hanging around with Colleen."

Tommy nodded and continued his story. "Then she was engaged to Robert and I thought I'd lost her for good and all. Then she ran away and no one could find her. I was sure she was dead. I walked the banks of all the ponds and brooks around here and looked into every thicket that was big enough to hide a body. I was that frantic! I even went down to the shore one day and walked along the beach looking for her. Norman couldn't figure out what had come over me.

"I was just trying to reconcile myself to the idea that I'd probably never see her again when Norman sent me over to the old house to get the extra scythe and I saw her through the window asleep on the lounge. I figured I'd better take my chance then and marry her before she disappeared again. And here we are."

"Yes, well, she's caused us plenty of grief. I hope she doesn't cause you the same."

Tommy laughed. "You know, you sound just like Momma."

Mattie glared at him. "I'm not Momma, but I am a woman and I know about these things.

How is Momma?"

"She's fine. Not as energetic as she used to be. Having the baby kind of took it out of her. She leaves a lot of the housework to Ellie these days." He passed the cheese to Cora.

"Well, as she tells it, Ellie's the best little house-keeper that ever walked the Island," said Mattie.

"I suppose that could be said about her," agreed Tommy, "but I wouldn't say it. Momma doesn't see half of what goes on when her back is turned."

"Ellie never would try when I was home," said Mattie. "I guess it's no wonder that she can't do things now. How's the baby?"

Tommy shrugged. "Fine, I guess. She's still real tiny and fragile. I never touch her, she looks like she'd break." He looked down at his calloused hands so like his father's, but even larger. "They were afraid for a long time she wouldn't live."

"I know. Poor Momma. It must have been hard for her."

"Norman too. He set such a store by having one of his own, and then for it to arrive and be sick and weak and likely to die. I think he may have kept it alive by the sheer force of his wanting it."

"I wish I could go and see them all," said Mattie. "It's almost a year since I left."

"Momma'd like that. She said to tell you to come before fall."

§

Tommy and Cora left before David returned home that evening. Mattie felt lonely for her family for the first time since before Helen was born.

I can hardly believe that it's almost a year since David came to get me, she thought as she tidied up the kitchen and started preparations for supper. So much has happened. She looked across at Helen asleep in the cradle under the stairs, her cheeks sleep-rosy, and her little hands curled into fists. She stirred, her mouth making small sucking noises, then she lay still. Mattie's heart filled with the joy of watching her daughter sleep.

Poor Momma, she might have missed all this, she thought. I hope Mary Elizabeth will be alright.

Mattie was sitting in the rocker contemplating the past year when David returned from school.

"You didn't come to meet me." David leaned over to kiss her cheek. "There's nothing wrong, is there?"

She shook her head and smiled at him. "No, there's nothing wrong. Helen was sleeping so soundly I didn't want to wake her."

He lifted the lid of the stew pot and sniffed. "Rabbit stew. Smells good. Where'd you get the rabbits?"

"Tommy brought them when he was here today."

"Tommy was here?"

"And Cora."

"Cora, too! So she wasn't drowned after all."

"No. They got married instead."

"Well, now!" David sat down across from Mattie. "How have the parents taken that bit of news?"

Mattie shrugged. "Good, I guess. There's not much they can do about it. Momma wasn't pleased. She said that Tommy'd made his bed, and he'd have to lie in it, and she hoped that it wouldn't be too uncomfortable."

David chuckled. "I can just hear her! It'll be awhile before Tommy'll hear the last of this."

"Or Cora either, for that matter. Momma will be just waiting to say 'I told you so.' I wouldn't want to be in Cora's shoes."

"Nor me, either. Your mother can be quite fierce when she takes a notion to be."

Mattie sat watching the stew pot send little bubbles of broth popping and hissing into the fire. "David?"

"Yes?"

"Am I very like my mother?"

"Sometimes you sound like her, but no, you're not very much like her otherwise. Why?"

"Just something that Tommy said today. I was getting on about how much grief Cora'd caused and he said that I sounded just like Momma, that's all."

"Well, you can't really help that, you know. Who else would you be like if your mother's the only woman you've had contact with all these years? I think you're remarkably unlike her for all that."

"It must have been Poppa's good influence."

"C'mon now, your Momma's not so bad really, and if I thought I was marrying a twin of your mother's, I wouldn't have done it, you know."

"How would you have known? I was just a child when you brought me here."

"I knew. You were a gentle, innocent child then, and you've grown into a lovely, shy young woman and I'm glad and proud to have you for my wife. I've seen how you managed to steer Cora onto a right path. It was as if she were your own sister."

"Well," replied Mattie hardly able to speak for the joy and confusion brought on by David's words, "she's Tommy's problem now." She rose to stir the stew.

"Mattie, I've been thinking. Would you like to go and visit your mother soon?"

"Oh, David, could we? I haven't seen the boys and Ellie since last fall, and Momma sent word with Tommy today that she'd like me to come."

"School lets out at noon on Saturday. We'll go then."

CHAPTER NINETEEN

Mattie waited impatiently for Saturday to come. She hurried through breakfast and tried to hurry Helen into her clothes. "C'mon Helen, co-operate, please. Your fists are everywhere but where they're supposed to be."

Mattie put on her own shoes, threw her shawl around her shoulders, and picked up Helen. "We're ready." Her blue eyes were bright with excitement.

"So I see." David pulled on his jacket. "We're not anxious or anything, are we?"

The day was fresh and bright and still damp with dew. As they walked up the path and out of sight, Mattie fancied that the pair of crows that lived in the spruces called good-bye to them. I haven't been out of the yard since before Helen was born, she thought.

She spent the morning with Mrs. Gillis. They talked of babies and David and Cora and Tommy and then babies again. The morning flew by, and after a bite of dinner, Mattie and David were on their way again.

The narrow red road, not much more than a track, had a distant familiarity to it. It seems more overgrown than it used to be, she thought, savouring the sweet scent of spruce and the sight of the bright yellow black-eyed Susans that grew in the shallow ditches. Daisies and buttercups made their contrast with the encroaching forest. A squirrel, high in the branches of a maple tree, chirred at them as they passed. The sharp cheBEK, cheBEK of a least flycatcher, and the clear fluting of a nearby hermit thrush were silenced by the harsh warning cry of a bluejay.

I'm glad I have shoes on. These pebbles are much larger than I remember them, she thought. As they passed Cora's gate she thought of Cora and the worry she had caused everyone. So much trouble, and all because Cora had to have fun.

"I wonder if Mrs. Smith's recovered from Cora's antics yet?" she said.

"I heard she was out of bed. I guess the whole business aged her terribly. I haven't seen her, but Mrs. John said that her hair has gone stark white, and she's only forty."

"Well, at least Cora's settled with Tommy now, so she should be happy."

They walked on in silence for awhile, enjoying the warmth and softness of the day. A fresh salt breeze blew from the Northumberland Strait lifting the wisps of hair around Mattie's face. A yellow butterfly fluttered past and rested momentarily on the bright orange blossom of a devil's paintbrush, then fluttered onward.

The sweet scent of wild roses filled the air as they passed an empty homestead, the occupants long ago returned to Scotland. "This place always made me uneasy when I was little," said Mattie. "It looked so forsaken."

"It's too bad they were so homesick for the old country they couldn't bring themselves to remain here for more than one winter. It's a shame they didn't have any family to give it to. With the roof caved in like that it won't last many more winters. It'll be gone to waste and ruin."

They continued their walk in silence. Helen slept in Mattie's arms.

Presently Mattie asked, "Shall we take the path across the fields?"

"I don't think so. Robert's bull has turned cross. Robert was at the school the other day warning the children to stay away from it."

"That's too bad, I always liked to walk by the brook, and the only way to get there is across his pasture."

"D'you want me to carry Helen for awhile?"

Mattie handed the baby over to him and flexed her arms. "She's getting so heavy. It's hard to believe she's already two months old."

"And such a bonny child, too!" David's eyes

twinkled down at his daughter. "Perfect in every way."

"That's because she's your own. You'll have her spoilt before she's seen her first birthday."

The last mile seemed the longest. Mattie's feet could not go fast enough. At last the end of the lane came into view, and she stopped. It seems strange coming to the house from this direction, she thought. I wonder if the boys will know me? A strange wave of uneasiness rippled in her stomach. It won't be the same anymore.

This realization caught her off-balance, and she stood stalk still in the middle of the track. The feelings of her childhood tried to reassert themselves and she fought against them. The struggle showed on her face.

"Are you alright, Mattie?"

"I'm afraid," she whispered. "Everything's changed. Momma'll be mad at me."

David put his free arm around Mattie's narrow shoulders. "Nothing's changed except yourself. You're a woman now, with a home and a husband and a child of your own. Your mother has no right to be mad at you."

She relaxed against him. "You're right. For a moment I felt like I used to when I was a child, and that I'd somehow done wrong."

"How can anything as perfect as Helen be wrong?"

Mattie straightened her shoulders and walked on. "She can't, and anyway Momma hasn't seen her yet."

The lane seems longer than I remember it. "Oh, there's the boys. My goodness, how much they've grown." She watched William and Johnny chasing a hen around the yard, their voices faint on the air.

"Don't chase her so much, Johnny, she'll be tough as shoe leather, and Momma'll be mad."

"You mean Ellie'll be mad."

"Then why doesn't she come out and kill it herself?"

The wind changed direction, and the rest of the exchange was lost. Mattie smiled at the image of Ellie doing anything as messy as killing a chicken.

Ellie would never feed them, never mind catch one and kill it, thought Mattie as they walked toward the house. The lane seems narrower than it used to be.

"There's the spruce tree I was up in when you came to get me last year."

"I didn't know that's where you were." David laughed. "I've always wondered why your hands were so sticky."

At that moment William and Johnny saw them and came running, Johnny dangling the flapping, squawking chicken by its feet. "Mattie! You're home!" They skidded to a stop in front of her and fell silent.

"Hello, William, hello, Johnny." Mattie bent over to give them each a hug and a kiss on the cheek.

The boys stared at the ground and scuffed their feet in the red sand.

"What's the matter," she asked, "aren't you glad to see me?"

"Sure, Mattie," replied William. A dull red crept up his cheeks. "But you're different now."

"How'm I different?" She swallowed hard against the pain of loss and change in her heart.

"I don't know." He shrugged one shoulder. "Just different."

"You don't look the same," said Johnny. He swung the hen by its feet. "C'mon, William, we got to kill this hen for supper." The two boys ran off.

"Well," said Mattie, "I didn't think I'd changed that much. It's only been November since I saw them last. I wonder how Ellie'll be?"

Ellie had grown too, and was not glad to see Mattie. She accepted her embrace with reserve and said little.

Mattie observed Ellie from across the room. She's so cold! She's taller than I am. Mattie looked around the kitchen. If Ellie's doing the housekeeping, she's doing a pretty good job.

"Where's Momma?" Mattie arranged Helen on a blanket on the floor.

"Lying down," replied Ellie.

"But she never rests in the middle of the day. Is she sick?"

"No, she just rests a lot since the baby came."

"I'll just go down and see her." Mattie rose and went to her mother's bedroom off the kitchen. I can't think about this being Norman's room, too, she thought. She opened the door and peered the darkened room. That thin little hump in the bed can't possibly be Momma!

"Hello, Mattie, come in." Her mother's voice sounded tired and old. "Let me look at you."

"Hello, Momma." Mattie opened the curtains, shocked at the streak of white that had come in her mother's brown hair since she had last seen her. "I don't know how you can see anything in this darkness." She kept the astonishment out of her voice with an effort. "How are you?"

"I'm fine, although I don't seem to have gotten my strength back since the baby was born." Mary Cameron Martin threw back the blanket and swung her legs over the side of the bed. "She'll be my last one, I think. Six is enough for any woman to have." She began folding the blanket. "I don't know how these women do it that have fifteen of them, all barely a year apart." She sniffed. "It's just lack of self control, that's all."

"Where is she?"

"In the cradle there. She hardly makes any noise, and almost never cries. She's so different from the rest of you."

Mattie leaned over the cradle to see her new sister. "She's a pretty little thing." The baby stirred and opened her eyes. Mattie could hardly suppress her gasp. The baby has a cast in her eye! She's blind in her left eye! she thought in dismay. Poor Momma! Poor Norman! Poor Mary Elizabeth! "She's very tiny," Mattie croaked.

"It's taking her a long time to catch up from being born too early, and my milk isn't what it used to be. We're giving her gruel now with her breakfast and she seems to be gaining a little weight."

Mattie reached into the cradle and picked her up trying not to stare too hard at her eyes, yet, at the same time, trying to see. She feels so much lighter than Helen, and she's a month older, she thought as she sat on the side of the bed and rocked Mary Elizabeth. "Who's giving her gruel?"

"It was Ellie's idea, and it seems to be working." Her mother fluffed the pillows. "I couldn't get by without Ellie anymore."

"It's good that you have her." Mattie suppressed a twinge of jealousy. "She's certainly grown up in the last year."

"Yes, and that nice MacPherson boy has been coming to see her these last few weeks. I wouldn't like to call it courting and her so young, but I expect I'll be losing her before very long. He's just turned twenty-one, and he's already his father's right hand man and a hard worker, too. They own that big farm in Flat River."

"She'll be a long way from home if she marries him."

Her mother sighed. "I know. Then I'll just have the boys and Mary Elizabeth, if she lives."

"And Norman," said Mattie.

"And Himself." Mary sat down on the other end of the bed.

"Where is he today?"

"He and Tommy are cutting the back field. He'll be in after awhile."

"How's Tommy?"

"I wouldn't know. I haven't seen him since he married that Cora." Mary's voice was resentful.

She sounds more like herself, thought Mattie. "D'you mean he never comes here?"

"That's what I mean. Norman sent him off to Murray River the other day to pick up that plough blade off the boat, and he came home with her and said they'd gotten married. After her being gone almost a week. I told him what I thought of it all. He's probably mad at me, but I don't care. The dance that girl led her parents and all, and now she's my daughter. She'll lead him a merry waltz, or I'll miss my guess!"

"Well, they've only been married a week. They're not past the honeymoon yet."

"And how do you know so much about it?"

"They came to visit me just after they came home. He said they're living in Norman's old house."

"I suppose he told you how it all came about."

"Yes," said Mattie, "he did."

"Well, it's more than he told me. I still don't understand how he could have taken up with her after all the trouble she's created."

"She's better than Colleen O'Brien."

Her mother sniffed. "Not much, but at least she's not an R. C." She gave the pillow another vigorous thumping. "It's time to go see what those two imps are up to with that chicken."

Mattie laughed. "The last I saw of them and the chicken, they were chasing it around the yard after Johnny dropped it on the way to the woodshed."

"Och, it'll be like shoe leather before they're done with it. I should have done it myself."

"Momma said that John Angus has been coming to see you lately." Mattie was sitting in the rocker by the stove after supper, nursing Helen.

Ellie blushed. "Momma thinks so. He's a friend of Tommy's, so it's likely him he's coming to see." She gathered up the stack of dishes from the table and carried them into the pantry. "Anyway, what would he want with me? I'm still a child." She returned with the dishcloth and began wiping the table.

"You're old enough. You're almost as old as I was when David came for me." Mattie lifted Helen and patted her rhythmically on the back. Helen obliged with a tiny belch. Mattie shifted her to the other breast. "I thought that I was still a child too, and look at me now, and it's less than a year."

"Well, he does go out of his way to speak to me and be pleasant," she agreed.

"There! You see? He is interested."

Ellie blushed again. "I hope so! I want to have a house like yours, and a baby too. Momma said you had a nice place for just starting out."

"She did?"

"Yes, she did. She's always bragging about you. My Mattie this and my Mattie that. I get quite sick of it. You'd think to hear her talk that I couldn't do anything right."

Mattie savoured Ellie's words for a few moments before responding. "Well, you know she does the same thing to me. Her latest was, 'I can't get by without Ellie anymore.' She said that just this afternoon."

Ellie sighed. "I wish, for once, she'd tell me. I always feel so worthless." She picked up the broom and began sweeping the hearth.

"It's awful, isn't it." Mattie laughed. "Let's make a bargain. I'll tell you when she says something nice about you, and you can do the same for me."

Ellie began to laugh, too. "Oh, Mattie, it's so good to see you again. I didn't think I wanted you to come back, but now I'm glad you did."

"Well, it's only for a visit, so whatever you were thinking, I'll be gone tomorrow. You'll have to come over and visit me before the snow flies."

"Oh, I couldn't do that. What would Momma do without me?"

They burst into peals of laughter.

"What's the joke?" asked Mary, coming in with a basket of eggs.

"Nothing, Momma," they said in chorus, wiping the tears from their eyes.

"That's a nice stove you've got there, Momma," said Mattie. "When did you get that?"

"In January. Norman and Tommy went to the River for it, and dragged it back on the sled. It was the only way they could get it here."

"Well, it's a nice one. Does it give the heat of a fireplace?"

"Oh, yes, and more, and it's easier to cook on, too. I can set the pots up and not be burning myself trying to drag them off the fire when I need to tend them. It'll be great for doing jelly this summer."

"You're happy, then?" Mattie looked down at the sleeping Helen and smiled.

"Oh, yes, if that's what it's all about, I am."

"Norman's good to you?"

"He's kind, and he's good to the boys. That's what's important. He and Tommy have decided to continue to run the both farms as one. That way they figure to make a better profit."

"I think David and I are going to run over to visit with Tommy and Cora after chores this evening." Mattie buttoned her dress and got up to lay the sleeping Helen in the cradle with Mary Elizabeth. "Can you mind Helen, too?" she asked Ellie.

"Oh, I think I can manage that."

Later that evening Mattie and David walked over in the gathering dusk to visit with Tommy and Cora. The evening air was soft and sweet with the smell of the new mown hay. The winding clay path stretched darkly red before them. Behind them the last rays of the summer sun stained the water of the Strait translucent gold. From the east, the darkness was already encroaching, its velvety blackness pricked with early stars.

"What a lovely night!" exclaimed Mattie. "I just love nights like these. When we were little we always used to stay out as long as we could on these kinds of nights."

"It is wonderful weather. Tommy says they have most of their hay in now, and the grain's ripening fast. They didn't think they'd be able to keep up for awhile."

"Tommy seems happy working with Norman?"

"Oh, I think so. At least he's not unhappy. And they have great plans to farm both places between the two of them. When William and Johnny get old enough, they can come in too, if they want to."

"It sounds as if Norman was a good thing to have happen here."

"Tommy has Cora now, too, don't forget."

"That he has." She trudged on in silence for a few minutes. Soon the white blur of Norman's tiny house appeared against the nighttime darkness of the spruce woods. The row of yellow birches that Norman's mother had planted so many years ago stood like ghostly sentinels between the house and the barn. Presently they were knocking on Tommy's door.

Cora answered almost before they had made it.

"I heard you coming." She gave Mattie a bear hug. "I'm that glad to see you! Come inside and sit down." She grabbed Mattie's hand and almost dragged her into the kitchen so similar to Mattie's own. "Where's Helen?"

"I left her with Ellie. It's the first time we've been out by ourselves since she was born."

"It's the first time that you've been out yourself since she was born," reminded David. "I've been out plenty. Where's Tommy?"

"He's just finishing our chores. He usually helps Norman first, then comes home and does ours."

"I'll go and give him a hand, so you ladies can visit to your heart's content."

"Well, you're certainly looking radiant," said Mattie when the back door had closed behind David. "Marriage must be agreeing with you."

Cora glowed. "I just love being married. It's such fun, and Tommy's so good to me. Yesterday he brought me a bouquet of wild flowers. It was an awful mess and they died overnight, but I trimmed them up and set them in water and they were fine for the day and so pretty." She dragged a couple of chairs over by the fireplace, and lighted a candle from the dying embers. "Sit down, then, Mattie. I'll just stir up the fire a little and we'll have a cup of tea in awhile."

"So you've found your fun, have you?" Mattie settled herself in the nearest chair.

"It seems so, but I never in the world thought it would be here." She gave a little skip in the middle of the kitchen floor. "Oh, Mattie, I can hardly believe I'm so happy. This time last week I thought I'd never be happy again. I'm such a lucky woman."

"Luckier than you realize, I think. How's Momma been taking it all, these last few days?"

Cora frowned. "She's not pleased, but I think she'll come around. Was she always this cross?" Cora sank into the chair across from Mattie.

Mattie nodded. "Her bark's mostly worse

than her bite, but she does bite once in awhile, and she's definitely not happy to have you for a daughter-in-law."

"I can tell." Cora made a face. "She tore strips off Tommy when he brought me home, and she didn't care that I was right there to hear it all, either."

"She must have been really cross, she usually has some consideration for people's feelings. You'll have to learn when she's just letting off steam and when she's really angry. I always ignored her when she was just growling. How's your mother?"

"Better. I went to visit her one afternoon a few days ago. We had a long talk about everything. She's pleased that I married Tommy, but she doesn't see yet why I had to run away to do it."

"I'm not sure that I do either. Couldn't you have just told Robert that you couldn't marry him and let Tommy come courting in a normal fashion?"

Cora sighed. "Not by that time. Nobody was listening to me anymore. They were just telling me to do things that I couldn't do."

"Can I ask you something, Cora?"

Cora nodded. "What?"

"I heard that your mother's hair has turned stark white. Is that true?"

"It's true. It's almost completely white. And oh, Mattie, I was the one that did it to her."

"Good-bye, Mattie," said her mother the next morning as Mattie and David were leaving. "Don't be so long coming to see us the next time."

"I won't." Mattie kissed her mother's cheek. "You can come and see us, too, you know."

"Good-bye, Mattie." Ellie gave Mattie a hard hug. "Maybe I'll see you this fall."

"Good-bye, good-bye everyone." David and Mattie started down the lane. David carried Helen. Mattie tucked her hand into his elbow. When they were out of sight of the house, Mattie gave a little skip. "Oh, it's so good to be going home!"

*Learn more about Margaret Westlie, her books
and her life, at www.margaretwestlie.com*

www.ingramcontent.com/pod-product-compliance
Lightning Source LLC
Chambersburg PA
CBHW071158020726
47502CB00002B/457